Praise for the Callie Parrish Mysteries

"What a wonderfully realized set of characters in an authentic and welcoming sense of place. Callie is wonderful! It's such fun following her and very moving as well."
—David Dean, Author of *The Thirteenth Child*.

"Callie Parrish is a hoot! I laughed so hard I dropped my book in the bathtub."
—Gwen Hunter, Author of the Rhea Lynch, M.D. Suspense Mysteries, the Delande Saga, and more.

"Fran Rizer's Callie Parrish and St. Mary, S.C., are as Southern as fried chicken and sweet tea—and just as delightful."
—Walter Edgar, *Walter Edgar's Journal*, SCETV Radio.

"A lively sleuth who manages to make funeral homes funny."
—Maggie Sefton, Author of the Molly Mallone Suspense Mysteries and the Kelly Flinn Knitting Mystery Series.

The Callie Parrish Mysteries by Fran Rizer

A Tisket, a Tasket, a **Fancy Stolen Casket**

Hey Diddle, Diddle, the **Corpse and the Fiddle**

Rub-a-Dub, Dub, There's a **Dead Man in the Tub**
(published as **Casket Case**)

Twinkle, Twinkle, Little Star, **There's a Body in the Car**

Mother Hubbard Has **A Corpse in the Cupboard**

Mother Hubbard Has

A Corpse
in the
Cupboard

A Callie Parrish Mystery

Fran Rizer

Mother Hubbard Has A Corpse In The Cupboard
ISBN 978-1-62268-032-0

First Print Edition May 2013

Library of Congress Control Number: 2013934748

Also available in e-book form: ISBN 978-1-62268-033-7

BellaRosaBooks and logo are trademarks of Bella Rosa Books.

10   9   8   7   6   5   4   3   2

Dedicated to my biggest fan,

my mother

Frances Willene Baker Gates.

December 8, 1926 – April 25, 2012

Song Lyrics Partially Quoted in Text

"One of These Days," BMI Work 1124477
Written by Earl Montgomery.
Publishing by Songs of Universal, Inc.

"Sweeter than the Flowers," BMI Work 1441926
Written by Ervin T. Rouse (ASCAP), Morry Burns, Lois
Mann, Aubrey W. Mullican.
Publishing by Fort Knox Music, Inc. and Trio Music
Company.

"Will the Circle Be Unbroken?" BMI Work 1675255
Written by A.P Carter, based on traditional hymn.
Publishing by APRS.

A Corpse
in the
Cupboard

Chapter One

James Brown burst from my bra just as I took a sip of Coors from my red Solo cup, the kind Toby Keith likes to sing about. Ex—scuse me. I didn't mean James Brown, the man. First, he's dead and buried somewhere—I think in Georgia. Second, my bra was fully inflated, but there would be no way to put even an action figure in there. What I meant to say is that since I tend to lose my cell phone so often, I sometimes carry it in my cleavage, and since I love James Brown's old songs, I'd loaded his voice singing "I Feel Good" for my ringtone and turned it up loud that afternoon.

"What's that?" my friend Jane asked as she plucked a long swatch of blue cotton candy off her paper cone, crammed it in her mouth, and then drank from her Dr Pepper can. She swears that pink cotton candy doesn't taste like the blue. I'd never noticed any difference, but Jane is blind, so her taste buds are probably more sensitive than mine. School teachers, even ex-ones like I am, should be politically correct, so I'll say Jane is visually impaired—extremely so since she was born with no optic nerves. She wasn't drinking beer though we were in Mother Hubbard's Beer Garden because we weren't sure yet if she was pregnant. I had strong feelings about that, but I wasn't ready to share.

"It's the new ringtone on my cell phone," I told her.

Rizzie Profit, the third person at our rickety table beneath the canvas tent, is Gullah and gorgeous. Her scoop-necked black leotard top showed off voluptuous ta tas. The ankle-length skirt of red and gold African print cloth wrapped around her tiny waist with a split to the top of her thigh that revealed her long legs my brother would describe as going from the ground to heaven. Skin like Lady Godiva chocolate and eyes as black as obsidian contrasted sharply with Rizzie's wide smile and bright white teeth. She had recently stopped wearing a cloth wrapped turban style around her head and had her black hair buzz-cut to a natural about half an inch long all over. The cut set off her marvelous bone structure.

The only woman I know who can chug Budweiser straight from a long-neck bottle and still look like a lady, Rizzie owns Gastric Gullah Grill in our hometown, St. Mary, on the coast of South Carolina. I'd had a hard time convincing her to come to the Jade County Fair for a "ladies' day out" and leave her grandmother Maum and her fourteen-year-old brother Tyrone to close the restaurant for the night.

I removed the cell phone from its safe haven and pressed the warm plastic to my ear as I said, "Hello."

Noise blared all around us from other customers, some of whom were well on the way to being hammered. Besides that, the canvas tent did little to block out the sounds of calliope music from the merry-go-round or the strident rock'n'roll from the adult rides. I could hear cooking sounds coming from behind Jane where a canvas wall separated the dining area of the tent from the kitchen/prep space. Servers dashed back and forth through an opening beside Jane, carrying beers, sodas, and fair food.

"I can't hear you," I yelled into the receiver.

"It's Tyrone," the young voice shouted. "Rizzie's not answering her phone and I need her."

"She's right here," I said. "I'll put her on." No surprise Rizzie didn't hear her ringtone. It's soft, classical music.

"No!" Tyrone shouted. "Don't put Rizzie on. Just tell her Maum fell, and I couldn't get her up. We're at the Jade County Hospital. Tell Rizzie to come *now*." At times, Tyrone seems like a full-grown man. On the telephone, he sounded like a scared little boy.

I passed the phone over to Rizzie. She said, "Hello. Hello. Hello?" and handed it back to me. "Who was it?"

"Tyrone," I replied. "Maum fell and he wants us to meet him at Jade County Hospital."

Rizzie and Jane jumped up, but Jane stumbled and fell. I moved around the table to help her as she explained, "My sandal came off."

When I bent over Jane, I saw that the canvas behind her had flipped up and lay draped over her leg.

"Go!" I yelled to Rizzie and handed her the keys to my Mustang.

"Aren't we going with her?" Jane asked.

"No!" I waved Rizzie away and told her, "We'll get a ride there later. If the doctors move Maum to another hospital, call me." Where they'd taken Maum is small—more like a clinic or infirmary. Most major cases are transferred to larger facilities.

Rizzie flashed a puzzled expression, grabbed my car keys, and ran out of Mother Hubbard's. I hoped she remembered to toss that beer bottle in a trash container before she drove the car. She wasn't risking a DUI. It was our only beer of the day, and we'd only planned on one each, but an open container is a jail offense whether a driver is drinking from it or not. Just ask my brother Mike about that. He spent a night in jail for having a beer keg seat-belted into the front seat of his truck.

"Why aren't we going with her?" Jane asked. She did that flipping thing she does with her long red hair. I have actually sat in front of a mirror and practiced that move, but it never looks as fetching when I do it, regardless of what my hair color *du jour* is at the time.

"We've got to call the sheriff," I said. "There's something on the ground near you."

"OMG, Callie!" she squealed. "Is it a snake? If there's something behind me, why didn't you see it when I sat down?"

"Because it was covered by the canvas behind you, but when you stumbled, you kicked the cloth up."

"What is it?"

"What do you think it is? We need the sheriff, and I didn't want Rizzie to see it and have to hang around answering questions when she should be with Tyrone finding out about Maum."

Jane stepped around the table and felt for Rizzie's chair.

"What are you doing?" I asked.

"Getting away from whatever corpse you've found now." She flipped her hair again, and then continued, "I swear, Callie, I'm going to stop hanging out with you. You'll mark my baby with dead people." She rubbed her middle, which was as concave as ever. "That cotton candy didn't do anything for my stomach. I'm still hungry, and I smell good things like chocolate and bacon, French fries with vinegar, and those Polish sausage dogs piled high with fried onions and peppers."

I hit 911 on my cell phone and reported a body in Mother Hubbard's Beer Garden—the one closest to the main gate of the fairgrounds.

A shaggy-haired young man wearing jeans, a denim shirt, and a short burgundy apron with "Mother Hubbard's" embroidered on it came from the back. I beckoned to him. He scurried over and asked, "May I help you?" with a smile.

"Yes," I said, "I want to speak to your manager."

His expression changed to a cross between despair and anger. "Lady, don't complain about me," he whined. "I didn't know you wanted anything else or I'd have come before."

"What I want to tell management has nothing to do with you, but since you're here, please bring my friend a sausage dog."

"With extra peppers." Jane added.

"If you want added peppers, you must not be having much nausea," I commented to Jane as the young man went back through the canvas opening beside her. I totally expected to hear a scream when he saw the body, but he popped right back out.

"The manager is at another food service, but I sent for

him, and I'll get the lady's order now."

"Wait!" I confess I almost shouted though I've been taught calmness in my profession. "Didn't you see the corpse in there?"

His turn to scream.

"Come look," I said and motioned behind where Jane had been seated.

The young man leaned over and peered at the body. He gagged. His eyes rolled up in his head. He keeled over, flat on the dirt floor, right beside the dead man.

Several of his co-workers ran to us. When they saw the body beside him, they stepped away.

"What's going on?" No mistaking the voice of authority. A tall, handsome man wearing jeans and a white shirt with "Mother Hubbard's Concessions" on the chest pocket. He looked Indian—not Native American, but East Indian. "I'm Jetendre Patel, J. T. Patel, owner of Mother Hubbard Concessions."

"There's a body behind this table. I'm surprised your workers didn't see it inside the prep area." I couldn't stop looking at him. He was possibly the best looking man I'd ever seen.

Patel bent over the corpse, felt the carotid artery, and looked up at me. "You're right. He's dead. My people wouldn't have seen him because he's actually lying in a space we have curtained off in the back for pantry and storage." He called another server over, motioned toward the shaggy-haired guy on the ground, and instructed, "Get a wet cloth and pat his face and hands."

Jane gasped.

Patel glanced at her and asked, "What's wrong with her?"

"She's upset because she's terrified by dead people and she can't see where he is."

"Tell her to take off those crazy purple sunglasses so she can see."

"That wouldn't make any difference." I turned my attention to Jane and touched her hand. "It's okay. You're not very close to him, and the sheriff is on his way."

Patel understood then. "Sorry. I didn't realize . . ." His last word faded as though he was embarrassed to state what he hadn't known.

"Why are they going to wash off a dead person's hands and face before the cops arrive?" Jane interrupted.

"The fellow who was getting your sausage dog fainted. The wet cloth is for him, not the dead man."

"Is the body anyone we know?"

"No. He must work at the fair because he's wearing a Middleton's Midway denim windbreaker." Didn't tell her that the bloody hole went right through the "e" in "Middleton's."

"A Middleton's jacket? A mortuary coat? Did Otis and Odell order funeral home T-shirts, too? When?" Her voice took on a shrill pitch.

I couldn't help it. I cannot tell a lie. Well, I can, but I try not to. I burst out laughing just about as loud as James Brown sings out of my cell phone. Not the best thing to do under the circumstances, but the mental image of the Middletons advertising the funeral home on T-shirts was funny. "My bosses don't have printed shirts. You know our uniforms are black or midnight blue suits for male employees and black dresses for females," I answered, still trying to calm her by patting her hand. That's one of the first rules in Mortuary 101—appropriate touch is calming. When working with the bereaved, pat them on the shoulder and say, "Now, now," in a comforting tone.

"Middleton's Midway is the name of the company that runs the midway, the people who work running the games and rides," I explained.

The wet cloth had roused the shaggy-haired fellow, and other employees helped him back through the opening to the kitchen area.

"Did you say you've called the police?" Patel asked me.

"Yes, they should be here any minute."

"Will you help me move him out of the tent?" He reached

down and grasped one of the corpse's hands. I slapped Patel's arm away without even considering that hitting a stranger could be considered assault. I was raised with five older brothers and never thought twice about popping them when I disagreed with whatever they said or did, which resulted in lots of swats when we were kids. I grew up, but I'm not so sure my brothers will ever behave like adults, which is why I refer to them as The Boys with a capital T and a capital B.

"You can't move the body," I scolded in a tone that, even to me, sounded like a stern teacher voice. I probably shot him a severe look, too.

"That's tampering with evidence." Same tone. Then it occurred to me that Patel's cultural heritage was probably less understanding of a woman swatting a man than the cultural upbringing of my redneck brothers.

"All your customers know he's here, and what if the sheriff arrives while you're moving him? You could be arrested." I added, trying to convince him that his welfare was my concern.

"What customers?" Patel asked.

Sure enough, the clientele had rushed out, carrying their food trays, cups, bottles, and cans with them, apparently unaware that the law allows drinking alcohol at the Jade County Fair, but only inside establishments with alcohol licenses. It's illegal to walk around drinking a beer, and Sheriff Harmon's deputies won't hesitate to haul anyone guilty off to the pokey.

"I just wanted to move the victim away from the tent. As you can see, it's not good for business," Patel defended himself.

"The victim?" Jane yelled. "Did he say 'victim'? You mean it's not some old man or woman who had a heart attack? Is this another murder?" She burst into tears.

"Not unless a heart attack leaves a bloody hole in a man's back." Sarcasm dripped from Patel's lips.

Jane sobbed even harder and began touching the calves of her legs. "Do I have blood on me?" she demanded.

I saw a reddish brown spot on her jeans near her knee, but I wasn't about to say so. If I did, she'd really go ballistic. Just then, a server placed a paper food tray with a sausage dog and vinegar raw fries in front of Jane. I picked up the bill and pulled my wallet from my jeans. Jane carries her own money and amazes me by always knowing exactly how much she has, but she was busy crying. I thought it could be her hormones, but the truth is she always cries around dead people, while it doesn't bother me as much because of my job.

"No, no" Patel said and snatched the slip of paper, brushing my hand as he did. *Well,* I thought, *that was almost as strong as my hitting his hand. He just assaulted me right back.*

"Let me treat the blind girl," he said as he scribbled something on the bill and handed it to the server.

That did it. Jane exploded. "Blind girl? Blind girl? You think I can't handle my own money because I can't see?" She jumped up, tears streaming down her face. "How much is it?"

The server read the bill to her. Jane reached into her pocket, pulled out a modest roll of paper money with a rubber band around it, and counted out the correct amount before shoving the bills back into her pocket and pulling a handful of change from the pocket on her other side. She counted out exact change, then said to the server. "He comp'ed the charges. This is your tip. When's the last time someone tipped you a hundred percent?"

"How'd she do that?" Patel watched with amazement.

"She can distinguish the coins by feel," I answered. "She keeps her paper money in an exact order and has a system of folding it that lets her know the value of any bill she has in her pocket."

"Amazing," he said, then jumped when "I Feel Good . . ." shouted from my chest.

"Just my phone," I explained and then answered it, "Middleton's Mortuary. Callie Parrish speaking. How may I help you?"

"Callie, you're not at work," Rizzie said. "What's going on? Why didn't you and Jane come with me?"

"Think hard and you can guess. What keeps showing up in

my life?"

"Men?"

I chuckled, "I wish, but first, tell me about Maum. Is she all right?"

"No, her hip is broken. We got Dr. Redmond, the same cardiologist that treated your dad. Tests show that Maum's heartbeat is irregular and that's probably what caused her to fall, but Tyrone is convinced he should have done something to prevent it." I heard a catch in Rizzie's voice before she continued. "The heart doctor is moving her to Healing Heart Medical Center and calling in Dr. Midlands. He's supposed to be the best orthopedic surgeon for elderly hip replacement. Come when you can. I've gotta go. Maum is being put in the ambulance now, and I'm going to follow."

"Did Tyrone drive to the hospital?" He was only fourteen, and Rizzie normally wouldn't let him drive in town although he's been driving on Surcie Island since he was ten years old.

"The ambulance driver wouldn't let him ride with them, so he came in the Gastric Gullah Econoline. Don't worry. I won't let him drive your Mustang." I heard Rizzie sniffle and knew she'd been crying. "I have to go now."

Patel stared as I tucked my cell phone back into my bra before returning to the topic of the dead man. "I wish you hadn't called anyone about this body. We're like old-fashioned carnies and gypsies. We take care of our own problems."

"Buh-leeve me. That won't fly in Jade County."

"What won't fly in Jade County?" a familiar voice asked from behind me as a comforting hand patted my shoulder.

Chapter Two

"Okay, Callie, where's the corpse this time?" Sheriff Wayne Harmon asked as I turned around.

Dalmation! The word exploded in my mind. When I used to teach five-year-olds, I'd cleaned up the language I'd learned from my brothers and created kindergarten cussing. *Dalmation* for mildly cussable situations, followed by *One Hundred and One Dalmations,* and for the cussedest word of all—*Shih tzu!*

Though I'd called the Jade County Sheriff's Department, I hadn't expected the sheriff himself to report to the scene. Only six weeks before, all five of the fingers on his right hand had been shattered by a crazy murderer with a hammer. Wayne had undergone extensive surgery and still wore casts.

Seeing his arm supported by a sling brought unpleasant images to my brain. I claim to never give nor take guilt trips, but my conscience sometimes nags me about the man I shot, and I don't like to remember that day. The killer deserved to die for at least two murders he'd committed or maybe even for what he did to Wayne Harmon's hand, and it was self-defense, but I fired the bullet that killed him, so what does that make me? I don't like to think about it.

"Over there." I pointed.

"Callie," Jane said, "will you guide me to the table farthest away from the body?"

I helped her to the opposite side of the tent and then returned to the sheriff. Same old. Same old. I had to answer questions. Like I knew anything this time. The man was a stranger and even though Patel had been part of the fair for years, he claimed he'd never seen the dead man before. Or if he'd seen him working the midway, he'd never noticed him.

The forensics team worked while Jed Amick, Jade County's coroner, who is our very own Ichabod Crane—tall, skinny, and dorky, but a smart man—watched. I moved away from the vicinity of the corpse and sat with Jane. She'd finished her sausage dog and Dr Pepper. Now she twisted her head from side to side.

"What are you looking for?" I asked.

Ex—scuse me. Jane can't actually "look" for anything, but we've been friends since high school, and I've picked up her habit of using sight words though she can't see anything.

"I smell something," she said and sniffed.

"Don't start that," I scolded. "It's your imagination. That body isn't smelling yet."

"I don't mean that. It's something delicious to eat."

I inhaled hard then, but I couldn't identify any new odors beyond the usual fair foods. Thank heaven we weren't near the farm exhibits. Even clean, hog pens and other animal enclosures have odors that I never learned to love growing up on Daddy's farm.

Sheriff Wayne Harmon walked over to our table. Well, actually, he strutted. He's got great abs and a cocky walk, but I've never considered him date material. The sheriff is twelve years older than I, but that's not why I've never thought of him romantically. He was my older brother John's best friend when I was a little girl, and he was over at our house so much that he seems like my sixth brother. Dating Wayne would feel like incest.

"You two look like geese straining your heads around."

Just then "I Feel Good . . ." sounded loud and clear from my chest. "It's my cell phone," I explained as I pulled it from my bra and said, "Hello."

"What's going on?" Rizzie asked. "Why aren't you and Jane here yet?"

"First, is Maum all right?"

"They've got her here at Healing Heart, but she's not handling this well. She doesn't understand about breaking her hip. She's crying to go home. She has to have surgery, but the doctors need to regulate her heart before they can fix the hip. Tyrone is all upset that he didn't catch her when she fell, but the cardiologist said her heartbeat is really irregular and a sudden drop in the rhythm is probably what caused her the accident." Rizzie's words piled out right on top of each other.

"She's already been admitted?

"Yes, but what I called to tell you is we've got your Mustang and my van here at Healing Heart. Dr. Midlands has been by and says he'll operate as soon as Dr. Redmond okays it, but that may be several days."

"As soon as we can, Jane and I will meet you at the medical center."

"I still want to know why you didn't come with me."

"I found something and knew I'd have to talk to law enforcement. I shooed you out of here so you could get to Maum and Tyrone without being delayed."

"I'm not asking anything more. You can tell me when I see you." Her heavy, exaggerated sigh told me she'd probably guessed what I'd found.

Wayne had been listening. "Who's at the hospital?" he asked.

When I explained about Maum, he said, "I already know you found the body, and Jane didn't see anything, so you can go meet Rizzie if you want. I'll get a more formal statement from you later."

"I can't," I explained. "Rizzie has my car."

"Call one of your brothers to come get you. Otis or Odell will be here to pick up the body, but we don't know how long that will be. Gotta wait for forensics to finish and then no telling how much time Amick will take."

Patel politely looked away when I reached back into my bosom for my phone. Sheriff Harmon didn't give it a second glance. He's used to me and never seems too surprised at anything I do.

I called my brother Frankie. He's the youngest next to me, only two years older, and we're closer than I am to my other brothers except John, the oldest. Besides, Frankie is engaged to Jane, so he should be the one to come get us. When I explained the situation, he got ticked off at me.

"Why do you drag Jane into these things?" he demanded. "If you keep getting her into situations like this, I'm going to make her stop hanging out with you as well as quit that job of hers."

That was unreasonable since Jane and I have been BFFs since she moved to St. Mary when we were both in ninth grade, which is quite a few years back because we're both in our early thirties. We even live next door to one another in a duplex over on Oak Street. Yes, it's true, I do seem to have the misfortune of sometimes finding corpses in strange places, but Jane has been known to do much worse things intentionally—like shoplifting lingerie from Victoria's Secret—though not lately.

Frankie knew what Jane did for a living before they began dating. She calls herself a "fantasy actress," but to call a spade a flippin' shovel, Jane is a 900 telephone sex operator who goes by the name Roxanne. She's done other work, but the pay is better for this and she doesn't have to arrange transportation because she works from a separate phone line at her home.

Buh-leeve me. I tried to hold back my words, but I couldn't. "Until you get a regular job and can support Jane, I don't think you have the right to criticize her or try to make her quit. Now, are you coming or do I need to call someone else?"

"You know I'll come get you."

"Do you want us to wait outside the gate?"

"Of course. You don't think I want to pay to get into the fair and have to turn right around and leave, do you?" He chuckled and added, "Will you bring me a candied apple?"

I laughed and agreed. I love Frankie. In fact, I love all my brothers even when they aggravate the dickens out of me. I tucked my telephone back into its safe place, told Wayne we were meeting Frankie at the gate, and led Jane away from Mother Hubbard's. What had started out to be a girls' fun time at the fair had turned ugly. Poor Maum had a heart condition and a broken hip, and I'd found another dead body. I had no idea who he was or what had happened to him, but working at Middleton's Mortuary has taught me that there's someone who hurts and grieves over every death, and I felt sorry for the people who loved the dead man lying in Mother Hubbard's Beer Garden.

When Jane learned I was buying a candied apple for Frankie, she wanted one, too. I don't see how that woman eats the way she does and doesn't gain weight. I passed on the apple. I had a fresh box of MoonPies at my apartment, and a chocolate MoonPie is my favorite comfort food. I understand that chocolate is the original flavor, but now they have others including banana and strawberry. I looked up MoonPies on the Internet. They're made in Tennessee and are basically two round graham crackers filled with marshmallow cream and then dipped in chocolate or another flavor covering. Not only do I love them, my dog, Big Boy eats MoonPies whenever I let him. I try not to share mine with him because I understand that chocolate is bad for dogs, so I buy the banana ones for him.

Standing outside the fairground gates, Jane couldn't resist opening her candied apple. By the time Frankie pulled up in his old Ford 150, she'd eaten it to the core and tucked the remains into her pocket. Jane has some bad habits, but littering isn't one of them.

"Hop in, girls," Frankie said. He leaned over and opened the passenger door. Heaven forbid he should walk around and open the door for us. Frankie's truck is a regular bench seat model. Jane climbed in the middle, and I sat on the far passenger side. I reached across Jane and handed Frankie his candied apple.

"What's that?" Jane asked.

"A candied apple," Frankie answered.

"Are you going to eat it?" Jane persisted.

"That's why I told Callie to buy me one—so I could eat it," Frankie answered as he pulled back onto the road while peeling the cellophane wrapping from the apple. "Why?"

"Could I have a bite?" Jane said.

"Don't you dare give her your apple," I snapped at Frankie. "She's already had an elephant ear, a corndog, and bacon dipped in chocolate before we went to Mother Hubbard's. Since then, she's eaten cotton candy, a sausage dog, potatoes, and her own candied apple."

"Well, if she's hungry, I'm not depriving my girlfriend of whatever she wants," Frankie said, took one tiny taste of the apple, and handed it to Jane. Frankie is convinced Jane's pregnant. She's had some of the signs, including morning sickness, but every time one of us makes her a doctor's appointment, Jane cancels it. I'm especially concerned because her "morning" sickness seems to happen at any time of the day or night.

We were almost to Healing Heart Medical Center when Jane retched. Frankie pulled the truck over off the side of the road, and I jumped out immediately. Between her BFF and her fiancée, I figured Jane would choose to throw up on me instead of him. Barfing, puking, upchucking, tossing your cookies— whatever you want to call it, isn't pleasant under any conditions. I'm not too proud to admit that I vomit myself sometimes— mainly whenever I get scared—but that doesn't mean I like being around it.

After several minutes of awful noises accompanied by a very unpleasant smell, Jane wiped her mouth with the back of her arm and climbed back in. Frankie cleaned her arm off with a cloth he'd pulled from behind the seat. There was probably a little oil on the rag, but better for Jane to have that on her arm than throw up.

"I think it might be best to let me off at the medical center and you take Jane home" I said.

"Oh, I'll be okay. I should be there to support Rizzie," Jane protested.

"No, you need to go home and rest. Rizzie has enough to worry about without you there throwing up all over."

For a wonder, I won because when Frankie drove into the ER entrance, he put his arm around Jane and slid her closer to him. I jumped out and slammed the door. He pulled off.

I found Rizzie and Tyrone in the waiting room outside the coronary tests unit after calling her cell phone. They have all these privacy rules at hospitals, and I figured it would take forever to track down Maum through the information desk, so I just called Rizzie. When I walked in, Rizzie and Tyrone hugged me.

Rizzie's tears didn't surprise me even though I'd never seen her weep before. Tyrone wasn't crying, but his eyes were red, and he looked like a terrified little kid.

"Callie, oh, Callie. The doctors don't know yet if they can fix her hip. What happens if her heart isn't strong enough for the surgery? She was in horrible pain until they gave her a shot of morphine." The words tumbled from Rizzie without a pause for breath. I swear, if Rizzie kept talking so fast, she was gonna turn into a Yankee.

"Now she's drunk off the medicine," Tyrone said. "I don't like seeing Maum like that."

"It's better than seeing her suffer," I said.

"Yes," Rizzie agreed.

The three of us sat on a fake leather couch and drank coffee for what seemed forever before a doctor came to us and extended his hand for hearty shakes. "Hello, I'm Dr. Dean Redmond. I've started Mrs. Profit on some medicine to regulate her heart rhythm, and we're moving her to the coronary care unit."

"What about her hip?" Rizzie asked.

"Right now we're going to get the heart condition under control, but Dr. Midlands will operate as soon as possible. He'll be by her room to talk to you in the morning. I suggest you stop by to see Mrs. Profit in cardiac, then go home and rest so you can be back about dawn tomorrow. Dr. Midlands makes early rounds."

"Is Maum in danger of dying?" Tyrone asked in a serious, worried tone.

"Anyone in her nineties is in danger of dying, especially with this heart arrhythmia and the trauma of the break, but we need to remain optimistic, and she's responding to stabilization. I'll see you again soon."

He shook our hands again and left the room.

A kind, friendly nurse wearing a name tag identifying her as Kathleen told us that Maum would be in Room 407 and gave us directions. When we got there, we had to wait outside the room while the staff moved Maum from a gurney onto her bed. When they allowed us in to see her, Maum looked smaller than ever. I'd been struck by her tiny stature since I met her on Surcie Island several years ago, and I thought of her as dynamite in a small package. Her green print hospital gown swallowed her, and the red fingernail polish I used every week or so when I gave her a manicure seemed brighter against the skin of her fingers sticking out of the splint brace on her left wrist. I can't say Maum looked pale because her skin was naturally dark. Perhaps "dull" as compared to its usual richness is the best word to describe her complexion as she lay there so horribly injured.

I stroked Maum's hand while Rizzie and Tyrone each kissed her goodnight—Rizzie on the cheek, Tyrone on her forehead. We all tried to say encouraging and loving words to her, but the meds that had made Tyrone describe her as "drunk" now made her sleep. Kathleen, the nurse from downstairs, stopped by at the end of her shift to check on Maum. All medical personnel should be as compassionate as that nurse. When she left, a different attendant assured Rizzie that the hospital would call if there were any change in Maum's condition. We just stood there by the bedside watching Maum sleep until the nurse finally said, "You need to leave now."

Since Tyrone had not been allowed to ride in the ambulance from Gastric Gullah to the Jade County Hospital, he had driven their Econoline behind the first ambulance. When Maum moved to Healing Heart Medical Center, Tyrone drove the van while Rizzie drove my Mustang. After much discussion about whether they wanted to go home with me to my apartment, which was closer to the hospital than their house on Surcie Island was, I waved goodbye and watched two of the saddest people I'd ever seen ride away in the Gastric Gullah van.

Chapter Three

Dreadful. My day off had become horrific. A fun day at the fair with my friends had ended with a lady that I'd grown to love lying in the hospital waiting to be "well" enough for major surgery and me finding another dead person.

I didn't have to, but I decided to go by Middleton's and see if they needed me for anything.

"What are you doing here on your day off?" Otis asked when I let myself in through the employee door in back. "Odell's gone to take that man from the fairgrounds to Charleston for a post-mortem. Nothing going on here that I can't handle. Gonna lock up soon and transfer the phone lines to my cell."

"I just wasn't ready to go home."

"Yes, I feel that way sometimes. Let me get you some coffee. Or would you rather have tea? I just made myself a cup of 'Constant Comment' and cut a fresh lemon." He gestured toward his cup. "They should call this 'Constant Comfort.' It's delicious."

"That would be nice." My work covers lots of areas, and some people would describe me as a 'girl Friday,' who also makes up corpses, but unlike some 'girls Friday,' my chores don't include making coffee or waiting on my bosses, brothers Otis and Odell Middleton. Oh sure, I carry the silver coffee service tray out to customers with our genuine Wedgwood china cups, but the Middletons treat me with professionalism and gentlemanly charm, and I'm not expected to step and fetch for them.

Otis and I sat in his office and talked over our tea. He beamed at me. "You made quite an impression on that man at the fair."

I confess I looked at him in bewilderment. "Which one— the dead one or the fellow who passed out when I showed him the body?"

"Neither. The owner of the Mother Hubbard concessions. The Indian man."

"Oh, J. T. Patel. What makes you say I made an impression on him?"

"He asked your name and made very sure I knew he wasn't talking about the red haired woman or the tall one. He was asking about the blonde. You're the blonde." He chuckled. "At least you're blonde this week." I'm known to change my hair color with my moods.

"What did he want to know?"

"Your name and if you're married."

"What did you tell him?"

"That your name is Calamine Lotion Parrish."

"You didn't!"

"No, even though that's your real name, I told him Callie." Calamine Lotion Parrish *is* my name. I'm the youngest of six children and the only female. My mother died when I was born, and my daddy got drunk—really drunk. He'd never named a girl baby before, and he couldn't think of anything girly except the color pink. The only pink he could think of was calamine lotion; hence, my name. Thank heaven nobody calls me Calamine except Daddy, who insists he thinks it sounds pretty and that he'll change it to Pepto Bismol if I don't like the name he chose for me.

"What else did you tell Patel?" Since Dr. Donald Walters, my most recent boyfriend, had abruptly stopped calling, I was kind of pleased to learn someone had noticed me.

"Told him you work here." Otis smiled.

"You better hope he's not some stalker kind of guy and

waiting for me when I head home."

Speak of the devil—well, not really the devil. I hardly knew the man and couldn't honestly call him that, but sometimes my mouth gets in front of my brain. Anyway, the phone rang and Otis answered it.

"Middleton's Mortuary. Otis Middleton speaking. How may I help you?" A significant pause during which he grinned like that cat in *Alice in Wonderland*. "Yes, as a matter of fact, she's here right now." He handed the receiver to me.

"Hello." I expected the caller to be Daddy or Jane, hopefully not Rizzie with bad news.

"Hello, is this Miss Parrish?" Low male voice.

"Yes, how may I help you?"

"Are you the young lady who discovered the corpse at Mother Hubbard's Beer Garden this afternoon?"

"Yes, I am." I recognized the voice then, just before he identified himself.

"This is J. T. Patel, and I know it will sound strange, like I'm tracking you down, but I decided to be daring and call you."

"Is something wrong?" I asked. Otis sat there sipping tea and smirking.

"No, I just wanted to talk to you. I told Mr. Middleton that I would telephone you tomorrow because he said you were off work today, but I decided to call and leave my number for you instead. I'm glad I reached you. Are you busy?"

"No, I'm about to go home now. What do you need?"

Otis laughed silently so hard that he almost fell out of his chair.

"I'm only in town for two weeks, and I want to take you to dinner. I understand that you don't know me, so I would never expect you to let me pick you up to go out, but I thought we might meet at a restaurant."

"Are you inviting me to come back to the fair and eat corndogs with you?"

His turn to laugh. "No, I'd like to take you to the nicest

restaurant in town. All you have to do is name it?"

Didn't have to think twice.

"Andre's."

I'd only been there one time. My first date with Dr. Donald. Not my ex-husband Dr. Donnie, but the Dr. Donald Walters who was now my ex-boyfriend. We'd dated off and on a few years, but never got past disagreements and his woman-izing nature until a while back when we'd become intimate for the first time. We'd gone home together from my brother Bill's wedding to Molly. From then on, we'd been together every time we were both off until a few weeks ago when his calls came to a sudden, crashing end. He didn't answer his cell or respond to my texts, so I'd finally broke down and called him at work. The receptionist took my message, but he never returned my call.

"Then Andre's it shall be." Patel's voice brought me back to the present.

"I was kidding. Andre's is very expensive."

"I asked you to name the best, and the best always costs more. Have you eaten? I know this is short notice, but I'd like to go tonight if possible. If not, how about tomorrow?"

"It *is* sudden, but, yes, I think I'd like to have dinner with you tonight."

Otis raised his eyebrows.

"Just give me directions or an address to key into my GPS and tell me what time to be there."

I did, and we agreed to meet in an hour.

"Don't you let that man know where you live, Callie," Otis cautioned when I was off the telephone.

"I know that." I was a little offended. Did my boss think I was stupid? "I'm not a little girl. I'm a grown woman."

"I know. That's what scares me."

Anything but black. Lots of women choose a little black dress with pearls when going somewhere swanky, but since black clothing is required at work, I never wear it out socially. I'd had a quick shower and put on my newest dress, a dark purple with a gold thread through the fabric. Not having time to really do my hair, I pulled it into a sleek knot at the nape of my neck. I'd been thinking of having it cut, but the longer length worked well for a quick up-sweep. A dash of lip gloss and I was ready to go.

Andre's is located between St. Mary and Beaufort, right off of Highway 21, almost exactly half way between my apartment and the fairgrounds. I spotted the British racing green Mini Cooper parked beneath the Spanish moss draping off the live oak trees when I pulled into Andre's parking lot, but I didn't expect it to be Patel's car. He was watching for me because he was out of the Mini Cooper and standing by my Mustang by the time I parked. He held the door for me, and I liked that. Other women can have all the liberation they want. I expect equal pay for equal work, but I love having men hold doors for me, and there's no question that if I'm dining somewhere like Andre's, I won't ever go Dutch treat.

"You look beautiful." His dark eyes sparkled. I don't know what I'd expected. Surely not the jeans he'd worn earlier that day and not traditional Indian garb. He wore a brown suit with a cream shirt, open at the neck. Maybe it was the moonlight, but I found him even more handsome than he'd been at the beer garden.

"Should I put on a tie? I have one in the car," he said as he took my hand, not my elbow, and we walked up to the portico covered by a forest green canvas awning discreetly labeled "Andre's" in white cursive over the door of the stucco building.

"Wait and see if it's a requirement," I answered.

A doorman welcomed us in with separate polite bows to each of us. Patel didn't go into any details about reservations. He simply said, "J. T. Patel." We were then met by the maître d' who led us through a long hall with several closed doors on each side. Massive gold-framed impressionistic oil paintings hung on the pale peach walls. Slate floors edged around plush area rugs in shades of green and peach. From my previous visit, I expected a private dining room, and I wasn't disappointed.

Smaller oil paintings adorned the dark green silk-covered walls, and a round table covered with a floor-length peach linen cloth centered the area. Patel held one of the two ornate French chairs with peach and green needlepoint cushions for me. As I was seated, I noticed that the peach roses on the table were fresh, not silk, and the vase and candleholders appeared to be lead crystal.

When we were seated, the maître d' touched a switch by the door, and the tiny recessed spotlights shining on the paintings dimmed so that most of the remaining brightness came from the candles on the table.

No sooner had the maître d' bowed out of the room than a server entered and presented a wine list to Patel. He looked at me. "Do you prefer a specific wine?" he asked.

"Actually, I don't want wine tonight," I said.

Patel smiled. "I do not care for wine either," he said. "I find this lady's beauty to be intoxicating enough for me."

Oh, my heavens! I'd done it again. Here I was with another smooth-talker. Put ten men in a line-up, and I'll be attracted to the one who turns out to be a womanizer, and usually they're the smooth-talkers. Know why? Because they've had so much practice.

On my previous evening at Andre's, Donald had ordered everything, including escargots for the appetizer, without asking me for any of my preferences. I don't know why a woman who chows down on catfish and crawdads would feel queasy thinking about eating snails or slugs, but I had. This time was different.

"What would you like for an hors d'oeuvre?" Patel handed the starter menu to me. I'd had Burgundy Mushrooms before, and they were good, so I suggested those. He requested them and added an order of Basil Calamari. I sipped mineral water from a glass that was definitely fine crystal while we waited. The server brought the appetizers in small oval dishes with two delicate china plates. Though we each had a full setting of flatware he gave us each a sterling silver appetizer fork.

Donald had fed me appetizers off his plate. Patel graciously served the mushrooms and calamari from the dishes onto our plates and engaged me in polite conversation.

"Are you from here?" he asked.

"Born less than twenty miles from where we sit. I grew up here but went to school in Columbia."

"Colombia? Why so far away?"

That led to a discussion of my education in Columbia, South Carolina, only three hours' drive from St. Mary. Before I knew it, I was telling him about my divorce and changing professions from teaching kindergarten to working in a mortuary. "I was tired of dealing with five-year-olds who wouldn't take their naps or be quiet. Now I work on people who lie still, never make noise, and don't have to tee tee every minute." Oops! I realized his culture was different from mine and he might not approve of a female talking about "tee tee" to a man she'd just met.

He laughed. "I grew tired of running a restaurant where all the customers thought everything should be curry. A lot of Indian food does have curry seasoning, but we eat many dishes that do not. I also had a bit of wanderlust, wanted to travel. The circus always fascinated me, but it was easier to get into food services at carnivals and fairs, so here I am."

"Where are you from?" I'd wanted to ask that question earlier, but I'd hesitated for some silly reason.

"Born in Nepal, but I was brought here as an infant. I grew up in Florida, which is where I live during the off season. I still have an Indian restaurant there, specializing in the food my mother learned to cook before coming to America. Nepal is not part of India, but much of the diet is the same. My brother takes care of it when I'm on the circuit. "

The server cleared our places and brought in the entrees. Once more, Patel allowed me to choose for myself instead of ordering for me. I liked that. A different waiter came in with a wheeled cart full of different kinds of breads. Patel asked which I would prefer, but I left that up to him. He selected crusty rolls baked with rosemary in them.

Several times he told me I could call him J. T. or Jetendre, but he was set in my mind as Patel. He assured me that would be all right, too. It was nice to be treated so well, to be eating such first-class food in such an elaborate setting. I could almost forget how horrible the day had been.

Then he said, "I noticed you when you and your friends came into Mother Hubbard's. The red-haired one and the tall one are both attractive, but you stood out."

Uh-oh! I hadn't known he was there. I'd understood the bushy-haired guy to say he'd called for Patel after I reported the body. Was Patel in that canvas cupboard, perhaps shooting a man?

"You were there when we sat down?" I questioned.

"I was in the kitchen area, but I could see the three of you. I don't miss three good-looking women when they come in. I had to go to another one of the tents on business or I would have simply stayed there and enjoyed the pleasure of watching you."

"You didn't know the man who was killed?"

"No, and that's strange. He was wearing a Middleton's Midway jacket, but I'd never seen him. I have several different food stands, so I circulate all over the fairgrounds, but when the authorities turned him over, they had me look at him to see if I could ID him. I didn't recognize him. Of course, he could be a roustabout that I'd never noticed, but I try to be aware of the people around me."

My expression must have indicated that "roustabout" was not a familiar term to me.

"Do you know what I mean?" Patel asked, and I shook my head no.

"A roustabout is a person who assembles the rides and games when the fair arrives and takes everything down when we leave. I explained that to your sheriff when he asked if I knew the victim. That's when I spoke with him to ask who you were, but instead of him answering, the older man with the funeral home told me about you."

"That would have been one of my bosses. What did he say about me?"

"Your name and that you work for him." He looked sheepish. "And, yes, I asked if you are married. I'm not interested in married women."

That was nice to know. I'm not interested in married men.

"What about you? Are you married?" I asked.

"No, and I'm not divorced. My wife was killed in a car accident during the first year of our marriage. I have no children either."

That made me sad, but not so despondent that I turned down dessert when the server showed us a tray of sweets. Patel chose some kind of fancy concoction with mangos in it, while I chose—chocolate!

Too soon we'd finished eating, though in reality, we'd been there quite a while. I just like to sound literary once in a while, and saying "too soon" makes me feel smart.

"Is there anywhere around here where we might dance?" he asked.

"Kenny B's has a band and Georgio's is a piano bar. They both have dance floors, and they're both near here." I knew it was time to go home, but it felt good to be with someone who appreciated me so much. I was having such a wonderful time that I didn't want the evening to end, and I didn't want to think about Maum in the hospital.

Patel took care of the bill and left a generous tip. He walked me to the Mustang. "You choose the place." He smiled. I chose Georgio's. The dance floor there is small, but Kenny B's is a meat market kind of place, and I didn't want to go there.

Patel followed me to Georgio's and still made it out of his little Mini Cooper car and over to the Mustang to open my door for me. On the way inside, I asked, "Do you travel in such a small car?"

He laughed. "No, I tow that small car behind the motor home I travel and live in when I'm with the fair. Tonight I drove it out to meet a beautiful woman who found a dead man in my beer garden." I didn't tell him that I once found a dead man in my brother's motor home at a bluegrass festival. TMI. That would definitely have been TMI.

I was glad we'd come. Dimly lit and cozy, the piano music begged us to dance, and we did. Patel wasn't one of those men who talk while they dance. Until dinner, I'd had an unpleasant day. Now it was comforting just to let him hold me. If I'd wanted to say anything when we began dancing, it would have been, "Don't talk now," but I didn't need to say it. He held me close without squeezing too tight and without trying to cop a feel.

We moved slowly around the dance floor in perfect tune with each other. I could feel the strength in his muscles and his tenderness at the same time. I didn't want the night to end, but I knew I needed to go home before I was tempted to take him with me. I'm not saying I've been pure since my divorce, and I only recently ended my self-imposed abstinence before Dr. Donald, but I've never had a one-night stand either, and I had no intention of starting. I couldn't help it that parts of me flamed warmer and warmer.

By the time he walked me back to my car around midnight, I knew he was going to kiss me, and he did. Those warm places blazed scorching hot.

When he asked, "May I call you tomorrow?" I gave him my cell number. "And it's okay to call during the day when you're at work?" he continued.

I almost screamed my answer.

"Yes!"

Chapter Four

Big Boy greeted me as he always does—joyfully, with his big paws on my shoulders and his tongue lapping my face. When he was given to me as a puppy, I didn't realize at first that my cocker spaniel sized dog would be a *great* Dane in size as well as breed. He weighed more than I do before his first birthday.

I grabbed his leash off the door knob, and we went outside. He could hardly wait to squat. He gets bigger every day, but he still squats to tee tee like a girl dog. He also thinks he's smaller than the oak tree in my front yard and tries to play hide and seek with me by standing behind the tree. He hasn't realized that his head sticks out of one side and his tail out of the other.

As soon as Big Boy finished his business, he tugged his leash, dragging me to the sidewalk, and led me around the block a few times. St. Mary is a small town. I feel safe even after midnight, and who would bother me with Big Boy by my side? I don't know how I ever got along without Big Boy. I've been married—and divorced—once each and I grew up in a house with Daddy, five brothers, and whatever assorted friends were visiting, but I've never felt so welcomed and loved when I arrived home as I do since Big Boy became part of my life.

My sister-in-law Molly, who breeds dogs, keeps insisting I have him neutered. He's been to the vet for shots. He was also poisoned once, and he's had his ears cropped, so it's not that I'm too cheap to pay for it, but I haven't had him fixed yet. Molly keeps telling me if I don't have it done, I'm risking Big

Boy getting loose when I walk him if the circumstances prompt him to chase a female dog for a little loving. That's her word—loving—not mine. I call a spade a flippin' shovel, and she's not talking about loving; she's talking about dog boinking.

No point in thinking about that tonight. I just wanted to finish the walk. When we were back inside, I poured Kibbles'n Bits into Big Boy's food bowl and checked out my pantry to see if I had anything to give him as a treat besides MoonPies. Someday, I'm going to start buying groceries on a regular basis and get all kinds of special dog bones, but I never get around to food shopping. Not that my social life has been what's kept me busy since Dr. Donald dropped out of my life.

Jane is a much better cook than I am, and when we shared her apartment while mine was being remodeled, I never had to even consider food. She always had something good cooked, and if I didn't get home at meal time, I could microwave a plate. Nights when I knew Jane and Frankie were eating out, I'd stop by Gastric Gullah and pick up food to go. Maum's fall would put a stop to that. She and Rizzie were the only cooks at the restaurant, and I knew Rizzie would close the business until Maum was in better condition.

Big Boy gobbled down some of the Kibbles'n Bits in his bowl while I stood staring into my empty refrigerator. Oh, well, I didn't feel like going back out and trying to find something else to eat. I'd had a delicious gourmet dinner, but I still wanted something. What I really desired wouldn't be in the fridge anyway, but I thought food might take my mind off the warmth.

Finding nothing else to eat, I took the box of MoonPies into the bedroom and put them on the bedside table. I stripped and dropped my clothes on the floor by the bathtub. Big Boy lay down on the floor beside my bed and eyed the unopened box of MoonPies. After a brisk scrub with peach-scented body wash and shampoo, I wrapped myself in a towel and went to the kitchen for a banana MoonPie for Big Boy. He gobbled it down while I put on an old flannel nightgown. The weather outside wasn't cold, but that gown is as comforting to me as

MoonPies are. I slipped into bed and rummaged through the drawer of the nightstand until I found a book I'd been planning to read.

I went to the University of South Carolina in Columbia, which is where I married and taught kindergarten before I realized both of those were mistakes. Don't get me wrong. I loved the little children, but by the time I'd been through the divorce, I was tired of dealing with almost every aspect of my life, including five-year-olds who wouldn't be quiet or lie down to take their naps. I came home to St. Mary and lived with Daddy for a while. I had taken voc ed in high school and earned my state cosmetology license.

In South Carolina, people who cosmetize (Funeraleze for putting on makeup and doing hair and nails of dead people) must have either a funeral director's license or a cosmetology license. I got a job at Middleton's Mortuary where I cosmetize and work as a girl Friday for Otis and Odell Middleton. I like it. The people I work on lie still and quiet.

Anyway, while I lived in Columbia, I met this writer named David Lee Jones. I enjoyed his first book, *Dark Side Of The Planet*, which is a collection of short stories, some of them rather Stephen King-ish. I read on Facebook that David Lee has written a sci-fi trilogy, so I ordered them through Amazon. Now, I'm a mystery fanatic to the extent that my second bedroom is full of stacks of mysteries instead of a bed. I don't usually read sci-fi nor fantasy, but reading the first one of the three, *MoriaVaratu*, hooked me. Couldn't put it down. When my work is caught up at the funeral home and I'm just answering the phone, Otis and Odell have no objection to my reading, but I'd been saving David Lee's second in the trilogy, *The PyraMorians*, for a time to read without interruption. I settled in beneath the comforter and began consuming MoonPies and sci-fi.

I should have expected it. The phone rang. Two o'clock in the morning. I fantasized it was Patel, wanting to tell me that he was so infatuated with me that he couldn't sleep either. I jumped so fast that Big Boy stood and looked at me. If it wasn't Patel, I was afraid it was Rizzie with bad news.

"Callie?" The voice was Odell Middleton's. He and his brother Otis are twins, identical twins, but no one could tell it by looking at them. Otis is a vegetarian who works out, tans in the tanning bed he had installed in the prep area (Funeraleze for embalming room), and had hair plugs put in when he started balding. Odell eats barbecue buffets almost daily, weighs at least fifty pounds more than his twin, and began shaving his head when his hair thinned. Their temperaments are as different as their looks, but I get along with both of them.

"Yes, this is Callie," I answered.

"Gonna need you here at eight o'clock in the morning. I know you planned to come in late, after you saw Mrs. Profit, but we need you at eight sharp." He giggled. "I apologize for calling so late, but Otis bet me you weren't home yet, and I planned to leave you a message on the machine."

"Do we have someone?" I asked, which is a polite way of asking if we have a new corpse. Otis and Odell don't like for any of the workers to refer to dead bodies except by name or living terms.

"Yes, and you know her. Bill's wife Molly's Aunt Nina Gorman died earlier this evening, but I got tied up at the fairgrounds, and the sheriff told me you'd gone to the hospital because Rizzie's Maum fell. I wound up taking the man who was killed at the fairgrounds to Charleston for a post mortem, and I'm sorry but this is the first chance I've had to call you."

"Molly's aunt? We were at a bridal shower for Bill and Molly at the little old ladies' house not long before the wedding. They were precious and still looked alike, not like you and Otis."

"I know. I went to that shower."

"Is the sister coming in at eight to make arrangements?" Ten is about as early as anyone ever has a planning conference at Middleton's. "You won't prep tonight, will you?" I have filled a chair at a planning session, but making arrangements is usually a job for Otis or Odell, not me.

"I'll let Nila explain it to you. Just be there and be on time." He harrumphed, which he does often. "How is Mrs. Profit?"

"Not good at all. She has a broken hip and wrist as well as a heart condition they just discovered."

"Come in early, and as soon as you finish with the Gormans, you can go over and spend some time with Rizzie at the hospital."

"Thanks, Odell."

I disconnected the phone and returned to *The PyraMorians*. Big Boy settled back beside the bed. I'd just gotten into the book when the phone rang again.

This time I didn't jump. I just reached over and answered it.

"Hello."

"Calamine? This is your pa."

Like I don't know my own father's voice, and like anyone besides him calls me Calamine.

"Yes, Daddy, how are you?"

"I'm okay."

"Are you sticking to your diet and walking each day?"

"I am a grown man, and I can follow my doctor's orders without my six young'uns thinking they've got to check up on me. Even Jim called me from the Middle East to ask me what I ate for breakfast one day last week." Jim's my next to oldest brother, two years younger than John, and he's career Navy, so we don't see him often.

"Don't get upset, Daddy. It's not good for your heart."

"Then don't tell me what to do. I talked to Frankie, and he says Rizzie's gramma's in the hospital. How is she?"

I went through the whole thing again.

"I called you at midnight, and you weren't home. Where were you?"

"I'm grown, too, Daddy." Then I thought about his heart condition. No point in getting him riled up. "I may have been out with Big Boy for a bathroom break."

"It's not good for a girl to be out so late, not even in your own front yard. You should just move back in with Mike and me."

No point in arguing with Daddy. I faked a yawn and claimed to be sleepy. After mutual goodbyes, I settled back into the pillows with David Lee Jones's book and a fresh MoonPie. Only problem was that as good as MoonPies are, they're a treat that needs something to wet your whistle. I went back to the kitchen to look for something to drink—preferably a Diet Coke. Big Boy followed and parked himself smack in front of the cupboard that held the banana MoonPies. I really need to buy him some of those doggy snack bones or fake bacon, but he sure loves banana MoonPies. The empty refrigerator didn't yield Cokes nor anything else to drink, so I settled for instant hot chocolate with tiny little dried up marshmallows and treated Big Boy to just one more MoonPie.

As soon as I was settled back under the covers with my book and snacks, the phone rang again. I threw the book across the room like a two-year-old having a temper tantrum. "Hello!" I snapped.

"Callie?" I immediately took one of those guilt trips I swear I don't take. The caller was Rizzie. "Can you come get Tyrone and take him home? The head nurse called. Maum was unresponsive, but it wasn't a heart attack. It was reaction to the medicine. Tyrone and I came back to the hospital, and they'd done some kind of rapid response thing and had her awake. We've talked with her, and she's gone back to sleep." She sobbed, then continued, "I was going to take Tyrone home because he needs sleep so he won't miss school tomorrow." Her breath hitched. "Callie, I've wrecked the van."

"Where are you?" I asked as I pulled off the flannel gown and slipped into jeans and a T-shirt.

"Right here in the medical center parking lot. I accidentally hit the accelerator and rammed the Econoline against a light post. The whole front end is smashed."

"Are you or Tyrone hurt?"

"No, we both had our seat belts on, so we're just shook up, but I really want to get Tyrone away from here. He's even more upset."

"I'm on the way. Go back in and sit in the waiting room."

"I can't. I've got to wait for a wrecker to move the van out of the way. The officer who came suggested a service he says is cheap."

"I'll be there as fast as possible."

"Don't say that. Just drive carefully and don't have an accident."

Big Boy never potties during the night, but now that I was in a hurry, he had to go outside. I refused to walk him. Just let him squat like he always does, then put him back in the apartment. As a last thought, I grabbed the box with the rest of the MoonPies and took them with me.

I saw the flames and heard the sirens before I reached the parking lot. Even in the middle of the night, several people had gathered around, though at what they thought was a safe distance. Personally, I think the safe distance from a burning vehicle is in the next county. Rizzie and Tyrone were sitting on the curb by the ER door. Through the glass doors, I could see hospital personnel as well as patients waiting to be seen, and people kept stepping around Rizzie and Tyrone to go in and out. I parked way out at the edge of the lot and walked over to them. There wasn't any doubt that the blazing vehicle was Rizzie's. The magnetic "Gastric Gullah" sign was on the side.

"Dalmation!" I exclaimed. "What the dickens happened?"

"I don't know. The policeman said he didn't have to write a report because no other car was involved and we were in a parking lot. The pole wasn't damaged when we hit it, but I don't know if the flames will hurt it or not."

"The fire didn't start when you wrecked?"

"No. It began after the officer left. I was over here with Ty when we heard a boom and it ignited."

Tyrone tapped Rizzie on her arm, and said, "Somebody ran by the van just before the fire."

Rizzie nor I paid much attention to him.

"Just be glad neither you nor Tyrone were in there." I patted Rizzie on her shoulder, right above where Tyrone had touched her, using that casual contact thing we do at the funeral home. If I hadn't sworn off swearing when I taught kindergarten, I'd swear it really does work.

All of a sudden, Rizzie burst into laughter. "Guess what, Callie. Things have been slow at the restaurant, and my vehicle insurance lapsed last week."

The words that came out of my mouth weren't at all related to my usual silly exclamatory words which I call kindergarten cussing. I've been slipping lately and using words that don't fit into my self-imposed method of profanity. Gotta get back to *Dalmation!* and *Shih tzu!*

Rizzie continued laughing.

"What's so funny?" I asked. Was my Gullah friend having a meltdown?

"I'm laughing with joy. I renewed the insurance yesterday, and we got hospitalization for the restaurant employees last month, including Maum. Without that, I'd be up that well-known stream—the one you'd probably call 'Ca Ca Creek.'"

"See? It could be worse," I consoled.

"It sure could. They might not have been able to revive Maum when she was unresponsive. They have some special kind of medicine that reverses the effect of narcotics."

I went back to my Mustang and got the box of MoonPies. I sat on the curb beside Rizzie and Tyrone, eating MoonPies while we watched the firemen put out the flames. When they'd finished, one of them who went to high school with Jane and me walked over. A big man, well over six feet tall and full-bearded, he pulled a cigar from his pocket, cut the end of it off, and then fired it up.

"Callie Parrish, who do you think you are—Stephanie

Plum?" He said to me. "I've heard about your finding bodies all over. Are you gonna start blowing up and burning vehicles now?"

"I had nothing to do with this." I motioned toward Rizzie and asked the man. "Do you know Rizzie Profit here?" I was hoping I didn't have to do intros because I couldn't remember the guy's name.

"Sure do," he answered. "Gastric Gullah, best food in town."

"Thanks, Dixon," Rizzie mumbled, and then asked, "How do you know about Stephanie Plum? You don't strike me as someone who reads those books."

"My wife reads 'em when we travel, and she reads the funny parts out loud to me."

I promise, I tried not to say it, but I couldn't resist. "Are you telling us that cars and vans exploding and burning are funny to a fireman?"

"No, but Stephanie Plum's reaction to them and those two men of hers are hilarious. You should hear my wife read that stuff!"

The man, whose name was Dixon according to Rizzie, stood around talking until the other workers finished rolling up the hoses and getting everything ready to leave. A deputy that I didn't know filled out some papers with Rizzie.

"Do you want us to wait for you?" I asked.

"No, just take Tyrone home. When I finish dealing with this, I'm going back in and sit with Maum. Can you get him to school tomorrow morning?"

"He's not going to get much sleep."

"Maum would want him in school."

"What time and where?"

"Seven-thirty. St. Mary High School."

"You don't go to school on the island?" I asked Tyrone.

"No, ma'am. They closed the Surcie Island School. We ride buses into St. Mary."

"I guess we need to go to your house for his books," I told

Rizzie.

"Nope," Tyrone said, "they were in the van."

"What about your iPad?" Rizzie asked. St. Mary schools had issued iPads to every student, but most of the teachers still used books and paper work as well.

"I left it in my locker."

"Good," Rizzie breathed in relief. "I don't want to have to pay for it, but didn't we decide you wouldn't leave it at school? If someone breaks into your locker and steals your iPad, I'll have to reimburse the school for it."

"I forgot, but I think it's good I didn't remember it because it would have been in the fire with my book bag."

"We'll stay at my apartment tonight," I said to Rizzie before the iPad discussion could erupt into a real argument. They were both pretty uptight. "We'll call you in the morning and check on Maum. Then I'll drop Tyrone off, go do whatever Odell needs at eight in the morning, then scoot over here. Want me to bring you some breakfast?"

"Since when do you cook breakfast?"

"I don't, but McDonald's does. I'll need to stop to get breakfast for Tyrone and me anyway."

"Okay. Bring me a bacon, egg, and cheese biscuit."

"Will do."

"I don't think I can go to school tomorrow," Tyrone said. "I worked in the kitchen all afternoon in these clothes. I can't go to school like this."

"No problem," I answered. "When we get home, we'll wash them."

"I'm not taking my clothes off at your house with nothing to put on." If it's possible to be defensive and offensive at the same time, he was both.

Okay, I wanted to tell him I'd lend him a nightgown, but I didn't have the heart to tease him after the evening he'd had. "First off, I've got five brothers. I've seen teenaged boys in their underwear before. Second, all we have to do is let you get under the covers before you take your clothes off and hand them to me to wash for you."

"I want to stay with Maum," the teenager protested.

"Rizzie will call us if there's any change during the night, won't you, Rizzie?" I assured him.

"Of course."

"Are there any more of those MoonPies?" That boy ate as much as Jane did.

"Nope, but I have a few of the banana ones at my place."

Rizzie cut Tyrone a look—not a teacher stare, but a big-sister expression.

"Now, don't give Callie any trouble," she told him.

"I won't." He looked at Rizzie, then stepped over to her and hugged her. "I'm sorry I let Maum get hurt," he said.

"You heard the doctor. It wasn't your fault. Go on with Callie and get some rest, even if it's only a couple of hours. I want you in school tomorrow. There may be other days when it's more important for you to miss classes."

We all knew what Rizzie meant, but I tried to soften the thought. "Yes, when Maum has her surgery and when she comes home."

After we reached my apartment, I told Tyrone I'd walk Big Boy while he showered. When we got back, a small spark beside the small oak tree in the front yard caught my attention. I turned to walk over there, but the light went out. I'd thought it might be the glow from a cigarette, but it must have been my imagination or a lightning bug, so we went on inside.

Tyrone watched television while I showered, and then I made him take my room, and I slept on the couch listening for the washing machine to cut off so I could put his clothes in the dryer.

Rizzie didn't call during the night.

Chapter Five

T'was morning at McDonald's
And all over the place
Everyone was busy
Happily stuffing their face
Tyrone in his kerchief
And I in my cap...

Just kidding. Those few years I taught kindergarten sometimes shoot nursery rhymes and kiddie poems through my head. Tyrone had on his clothes I'd washed the night before, and I wore one of my standard black work dresses with sheer black stockings and black medium low leather pumps. I'd finished my sausage biscuit and was on my third cup of coffee while Tyrone was still working on his second McGriddle combo.

This time James Brown blasted from my purse instead of my bra. My cell phone was in there because I remembered that, at fourteen, boys were either embarrassed by boobs or would get excited if I pulled my phone from my bra. Too bad I hadn't thought to change the ringtone. Better remember to do that before going to the mortuary.

The caller was Rizzie. She asked for Tyrone. He took the phone, listened for a minute or so, then handed the telephone back to me.

"Maum slept most of the night and is resting comfortably." Rizzie sounded exhausted. "They changed her pain medicine and it's not knocking her out, but it does keep her a little groggy."

I explained that I would be there as soon as I finished whatever I had to do at work. "Good, and, Callie," she added, "please write a note explaining why Ty doesn't have his books. Tell the school I'll pay to replace them."

Good grief! I'm good at writing obituaries, but I'd never written a note to a high school before. *Get a grip, Callie*, I thought. *You used to be a teacher, and even kindergarten kids brought notes from home sometimes.*

After Tyrone and I both told Rizzie goodbye, I asked him, "Do you have a pen and paper?"

The kid looked at me like I was cuckoo for Cocoa Puffs.

"I need something to write a note to your teacher," I said.

"I'm in high school. I have an instructor for each subject."

"Okay, we'll make it to your homeroom teacher."

"Fine, but my notebook was in the van with my books."

"We'll stop at the drugstore and buy you a composition book, some pencils, and a pen." I felt like we were playing the "yeah-but" game, with Tyrone having a negative answer for every one of my suggestions. "What should I say on the note?"

"Don't worry about that. Maum has always let me write my own notes. She just signs them. I'll write it and you can sign it."

When we were in the Mustang headed toward the CVS, Tyrone asked, "Will you buy me some gum, too?"

"Do they let students chew gum at school?" I asked.

"Not if they catch you, but I want it for after school."

"Okay, and I'll stop at the ATM and get you some lunch money on the way."

Sure enough, the kid produced a beautifully written note to his homeroom teacher.

Dear Mr. Adams,
    Mrs. Profit, Tyrone Profit's grandmother, who usually signs Tyrone Profit's excuses, is in the hospital. I am signing this

*for his older sister who is at the hospital with Mrs. Profit.
Tyrone's books and school supplies were burned accidentally last
night. Please notify us how much we need to pay for them.*

He drew a signature line at the bottom then printed my
name and cell number beneath it.

I signed "Rizzie Profit by Callie Parrish."

To be honest, and I try to be, even after growing up with
all those brothers, a teenaged boy makes me nervous. I don't
understand them these days. I was happy to drop him off at the
school and promise to pick him up when it was over or before
then if his grandmother's condition changed.

I always get a comfortable feeling when I approach Middleton's Mortuary. This morning was especially touching. Sunshine glistened off the windows of the building, which is a
beautiful classic two-story white house with a wrap-around
verandah on the front and both sides. White rocking chairs like
at the Cracker Barrel and clay pots full of seasonal flowers
create a pleasant ambiance. When my bosses, Otis and Odell,
were little boys, they lived upstairs with their parents and played
hide and seek among the stored coffins.

My assigned parking spot is in the back, between the loading dock and the new storage building. We still kept caskets on
the second floor of the house until a few months ago. There's a
small forklift that would raise the casket from the downstairs
loading dock to the second floor. Once the casket was upstairs
and situated, matching carpet disguised the opening where
items were unloaded. The mechanism had developed some
kinks. My bosses, Otis and Odell, solved the problem with a
new storage building out back, but they'd saved most of the
huge live oaks dripping with Spanish moss around the lot, and I
like the pleasant plunking sound of acorns falling on the ragtop
of my Mustang.

I was barely through the back entrance when I heard an
instrumental version of "It Is No Secret" signal that the front
door was open. I caught up with Otis as we reached the front

door.

"This will be Miss Nila Gorman," Otis said. "Her twin sister, Miss Nina Gorman, is the deceased. Visitation is tonight, six 'til eight. Services tomorrow at the Lutheran church at one o'clock."

"Couldn't she have left clothing with you?" I grumbled. "I really wanted to go check on Maum and Rizzie."

Otis didn't answer because right then, Miss Gorman came through the door carrying a large garment bag, puffed out with what must have been a lot of clothes. He might not have answered anyway—Otis can't stand whining.

"Good morning, Miss Gorman," he said. "This is Miss Parrish, who dresses our ladies for us. She'll be taking care of your sister just as you requested."

"I remember you," Miss Gorman said to me in a sweet old-lady voice with a drawl. "You were at Molly's shower. Her husband Bill is your brother." The lady was the epitome of an elderly lady of the South with her sturdy lace-up shoes and crocheted shawl wrapped around a mint green sweater set that matched her wool slacks. I hadn't been even slightly cool outside, but Maum always says, "Old bones are cold bones," so I supposed Miss Gorman might have felt a chill in the air.

"Yes, ma'am," I answered. "I see you've brought more than one outfit. Let's go in here and take a look."

I guided her into the first consultation room.

Glad Otis had told me Nina was the one who died, I wondered what happened to the pastel shades of hair the twins had worn at the shower. One of them had a slight blue rinse on her hair; the other, a light lavender. Today, Miss Nila Gorman's hair was snow white, no way to tell which twin she was. I couldn't remember who had been lavender and who was blue anyway.

"I'm going to leave you ladies to discuss the details, but you call me if you need me," Otis said and left the room.

Miss Gorman sat in one of the burgundy velvet overstuffed chairs at the round mahogany table and opened the zippered bag. She laid two identical pink dresses and two identical beige skirt suits across the table, and then she set two pairs of low-heeled pink shoes and two pairs of taupe on the table beside the dresses.

My first thought was the woman wasn't quite sure which size her sister would need, but they all appeared to be the same size. Beside the shoes, she placed two ziplock bags.

"The tan is for Nina to wear tonight for the visitation," she said, "and the pink is her funeral dress for tomorrow."

I sat silent for a moment. Since I'd come to work for the Middletons, I'd never had anyone want me to change the body's clothes between the visitation and the service, but I could certainly do it for her. Our goal at Middleton's is to make the customer as happy as possible under the difficult circumstances of their loss.

"Yes, ma'am," I said. I touched one pair of the taupe shoes. "And she's to wear these shoes tonight?" I asked.

"Now what do you think?" I had obviously annoyed the woman. "Nina's to wear beige this evening with the pearl earrings and necklace. She wouldn't wear the pink shoes with that." She patted one of the ziplock bags. "Tomorrow, Nina's to wear pink with the diamond earrings and pendant." She lifted the plastic bag and held it toward me. "Do be very careful with these because they are real pearls and the diamonds aren't CZ. They're genuine, too. I've put a picture in here that shows how I want her hair done for each occasion."

"So, you're saying that her hair will be different tonight and tomorrow?"

"You can do that, can't you?"

"Certainly, but you might want to check with the Middletons. There may be an extra charge for a second hair style."

"That's between the men and me. This is lady-talk. Until a few years ago, Nina and I dressed alike and always looked the same. A while back, she got the idea we needed to express our individualism. That's when we started putting those ridiculous rinses on our hair and buying clothes of different colors. I want us to go out of this world the way we came in—identical."

"Yes, ma'am. I understand that."

"How can you understand? You don't have a twin. I understand you're the only girl in Bill's family." A sweet lady, but she seemed easy to irritate. But then, her sister had died. Not just a sister, but an identical twin.

"Yes, ma'am. I meant I understand your wishes, not that I have a twin."

"Now, here's the important part. I'm of an age where a lot of my friends are dying. Some of them have been buried by Middleton's and some by other funeral homes. It looks to me like some of those places just paint everyone's face to look the same. I haven't noticed that when I've been here. You seem to make bodies look nice and natural."

I beamed. "Thank you, Miss Gorman. I take my work very seriously and do the best I can for every family."

"I need to know if you're licensed to work on living people also or just dead ones."

"My South Carolina Cosmetology License authorizes me to perform services for both."

"Good! I'll be back here at four this afternoon. You're to have my sister ready for tonight, so that you'll have time to do my hair and makeup exactly like hers. I'll come in tomorrow morning between ten and eleven for you to do the same thing before the service."

She smiled. I sat, too stunned to speak.

"Do you understand?" she asked.

"Yes, ma'am."

"You look confused. Can you do this?"

"Yes, ma'am."

"And you understand that the duplicate clothes are for me to put on after you do my hair and makeup?"

"Yes, ma'am."

"Are you sure there's nothing wrong with you? You're not challenged, are you?"

"No, ma'am."

"Thank the Lord you can say something besides 'yes, ma'am.'" She stood. "Now, you take good care of those bags. The jewelry is valuable and so are the photographs." She paused. "I put Nina's undergarments in the bottom of the garment bag." She glanced at it. "I saw Mr. Odell Middleton yesterday and Mr. Otis Middleton this morning. I'd heard they're identical twins, but that must be some mistake. They don't look alike."

I explained about the differences in their habits.

"So the difference is because of their life styles," Miss Gorman said. "That's one reason it never bothered me that neither Nina nor I ever wed. If one of us had married, had children, or lived somewhere else, it would probably have changed one of us, but not both. I always liked that we lived together our whole lives and stayed together like the Good Lord intended."

"Yes, ma'am," I acknowledged.

After I walked Nila Gorman to the door and closed it behind her to the tune of "Rock of Ages," I called Otis to come up to the conference room. We carried everything down to my work room.

"Did you know what she wanted?" I asked.

"Yes, but I thought it best to let her explain to you."

"Is the body prepped?" I asked him.

"Odell stayed and took care of her last night. She's ready for you now or you can go to the hospital to see Mrs. Profit so long as you're back in time to finish with Miss Nina before Miss Nila comes back."

"Are there any more clients here today?"

"Not yet."

"Then I'll be back right after lunch to get started."

When I entered Maum's room, Dr. Redmond, the heart doctor, stood on one side of her bed and Rizzie on the other. "Her heart is responding to the treatment. If everything continues as it is, we'll know about the hip surgery within a day or two."

"But what happens if she doesn't get well enough for the surgery?" Rizzie looked calm, but her voice had a frantic edge.

The doctor reached across the bed and patted Rizzie's hand. "Now, let's not cross that bridge until we come to it. I'm hoping and expecting your grandmother's heart to respond well enough for Dr. Midlands to replace that hip soon." He smiled and withdrew his hand. "Any questions?"

"No, not right now," Rizzie answered. The doctor left the room, and Rizzie turned to me.

"Did you bring me anything to eat?"

"By the time I left Middleton's, the short order places had stopped serving biscuits. I brought you a chicken sandwich, a cup of carrot salad, and a Coke from Chick-fil-A." I held the bag out toward her. Rizzie opened it as she sat down in the bedside chair. I remained standing by Maum and began stroking her arm above where the IV was inserted.

"Did you get any rest?" I asked Rizzie.

"This chair opens out to a recliner, so I tried to lie down, but I couldn't sleep. Every time I closed my eyes, I opened them again to be sure Maum was breathing." She took a bite of the sandwich.

"Too bad she doesn't snore," I commented. We both laughed.

"Everything go okay with Ty?" Rizzie talked and chewed carrots at the same time.

"Fine. I gave him lunch money for the week."

"What?" Rizzie hit the ceiling. "Did he ask you for lunch money?"

"No, but I remembered when I was in school, we paid by the week."

"That boy's double-dipping. Your money went in his pocket. I'll make him give it back to you. I paid for his lunches for a month by check only last week. I have to do that to be sure he's got food available at school. Otherwise, if I give him cash, he'll spend the money on something else and go hungry."

She finished the salad. "I pay him well for the time he works at the restaurant, but teenagers have so many wants these days. He's a good kid, but I don't manage him as well as Maum does. Like the double-dipping, he tries to get things over on me, and since he started going to school in St. Mary, I think he resents having to live on the island."

"Boys his age are always a little nutty," I said.

Rizzie laughed, "That's exactly what's wrong with them."

Maum opened her eyes and moaned softly. Rizzie jumped up and pressed the call button. I leaned over Maum and spoke softly, "You're in the hospital. Rizzie and the nurses are taking care of you to get you well."

"Hurt," Maum whispered, and a tear slid down her cheek. "Cold," she added.

Rizzie tucked the blankets around Maum's chin and said, "She needs something for pain," to the nurse who came through the door at that moment.

"It's fifteen minutes before she gets anything," the new nurse said, making me wish we still had that nice Kathleen. "Maybe I can make her more comfortable until then." She leaned over, lifted Maum's head slightly, and fluffed the pillow. "I'll get her another blanket, too."

Rizzie's voice rose. "Another blanket and her pillow aren't going to make her feel any better. Her hip is broken and it hurts. Last night, you people gave her so much medicine that she almost died. Are you telling me that today you can't even keep her comfortable?"

"Mrs. Profit didn't almost die last night. It's hard to determine dosage with elderly patients. That's why we watch them so carefully. We were aware when she became unresponsive, and we took care of it."

Rizzie stepped toward the nurse, and for a moment, I thought she was going to hit her. Rizzie is long-legged and tall. The nurse was short and petite. I moved closer to my friend and put my hand on her arm. "Rizzie, the nurse can't decide how much medicine Maum gets or how often. Last night, it was too high. This morning, it's too low. All the nurse can do is call the doctor to see if they can adjust Maum's pain meds."

I'm sure the nurse had been startled by Rizzie's size and the threat in her voice, or she would have suggested something herself. She seemed relieved to hurry from the room while assuring us, "I'll call Mrs. Profit's doctor."

Rizzie burst into tears as Maum opened her eyes. "Don't cry, Teresa," the grandmother said. "What happened?"

"You don't remember? You fell late yesterday afternoon at the restaurant. Now you're at Healing Heart Medical Center.

Maum looked up at me and held up her left hand. She spread her fingers out as much as the wrist brace allowed. "I need my nails done, Callie."

"Yes, ma'am. I'll give you a manicure and a pedicure as soon as your hip is repaired, but before then, I'll trim and buff your nails." I knew the hospital wouldn't want her nails painted bright red during her surgery—something to do with anesthetic. Unlike Rizzie, I was confident the doctors wouldn't just leave Maum with a broken hip. I don't know what I thought they would do if her heart didn't respond to the treatment—maybe put in a pacemaker—but I didn't think they'd just let an elderly lady lie in bed with a broken hip.

Her dark brown, almost black, eyes widened, and Maum asked, "What do you mean 'repair' my hip? Is that why it hurts so bad?"

I left that for Rizzie to answer. It hadn't occurred to me that Maum wouldn't be aware of the break.

"Maum," Rizzie said, "the doctors think you fell because your heart wasn't beating regularly. They've started you on treatment to make it right, but the X-ray shows your hip and wrist are broken. The brace will be okay for your arm, but you need surgery for your hip."

"I've never been in a hospital before." I hadn't thought about that, but Maum had spent her whole life on Surcie Island until Rizzie needed her at Gastric Gullah. "I had my babies at the house," she continued, "and the home remedies helped me when I was sick. I don't think I want anyone cutting on me."

The few tears she'd been shedding multiplied into a waterfall, and I have no idea what Rizzie would have said if the nurse hadn't come in at that moment with a liquid-filled hypodermic.

"On a scale of one to ten," she asked, "how would you rate your pain?"

Maum looked at her like the question was outrageous. "It hurts," she said. "It hurts."

"Put eight or nine," Rizzie said. "Maum is a strong, staunch lady. She doesn't complain about anything minor.

The nurse injected the fluid into Maum's IV, and almost instantly, Maum's eyes closed. She seemed asleep.

Sometimes my mouth has a mind of its own, and I can't control it. Right then, I didn't know what to say. Maum was the matriarch of Rizzie's world. Maum made very few demands or requests, but we all followed her instructions. What if she refused the surgery? There I was, doing my exercise by jumping to conclusions like Magdalena in Tamar Myers's books. We would just have to convince Maum that the operation was unavoidable. Then again, there was always that magical syringe and needle.

A gentle knock on the door. I looked up, hoping to see a doctor. Instead, Sheriff Harmon walked in. He went to Rizzie and gave her a little shoulder hug. "How's your grandmother?" he asked and nodded at Maum, who'd begun snoring softly.

"The doctors say the heart treatment is working, but her hip is broken. She needs surgery, and she's scared."

Until then, I hadn't realized that "not wanting anyone to cut on me" was an expression of fear.

"I'm sorry about all this. Would you like me to put a sign on the restaurant door? Tell people when you might be re-opening? We've had a couple of calls from customers who were worried about you, Tyrone, and Mrs. Profit. They'd gone there to eat and found the place unlocked but unoccupied."

"Ty must have forgotten to lock up when the ambulance

left. He's pretty upset."

"Well, I locked the doors. It doesn't appear anyone has trashed the place or robbed you."

For the first time since this began, I saw Rizzie smile. "Our customers are our friends. They'd never do anything like that."

"But not everyone in town is part of your clientele. St. Mary is changing. I'm concerned about what's happening. People need to start locking the doors at their houses, too. That's why my deputies and I are attending so many conferences and classes, trying to learn to deal with things small towns like ours never had to before."

"Like what?" I interrupted. "I mean, after all, we've certainly had our share of crazies and murders the past few years."

"We can talk about it later," Wayne answered. "I came by to check on you girls and Mrs. Profit."

When I'm a hundred and three, Sheriff Wayne Harmon will still think of me as a "girl," not a woman. Maybe that's why we've never had any chemistry. Why on earth was my mind focusing on chemistry? Had my evening with Patel made me more conscious of being alone?

"I guess Maum is doing as well as can be expected," Rizzie said. "I thought the orthopedic surgeon would be here early, but I haven't seen him." She stroked Maum's forehead gently while continuing to talk to the sheriff. "If you want to put up a sign, it needs to say that I don't know when I'll reopen. I'm not leaving Maum until she's a whole lot better or until she . . ." Rizzie sobbed. Both Wayne and I hugged her. The gentle touch helps sometimes, but not always enough.

When she'd pulled herself together, Rizzie sat down in the bedside chair. I stood by the bed and took over patting Maum's arm.

Wayne told her, "I'll have a sign put on the door telling everyone the restaurant is temporarily closed and under the jurisdiction of the Jade County Sheriff's Department. We'll do regular ride-bys, also." He turned toward me. "Callie, I need a statement from you about the body you found yesterday. Do you want me to come by Middleton's or will you come to the station? I talked to Otis earlier. That's how I knew where to find you. I'm glad you're here with Rizzie, but he said you have a client today."

"Yes, I have to go back to work to take care of Miss Gorman, and then I promised to pick up Tyrone from school and bring him here to be with Rizzie and Maum. It's not going to be much of a statement anyway. Jane stumbled. I went to help her and saw a body. I didn't touch it or anything, just called it in."

"And sent Rizzie away." Wayne wasn't happy with me.

"She never saw the body and didn't know it was there." I paused. "Let's talk about this later."

The sheriff had the good grace to look embarrassed. Guess it hadn't occurred to him how inappropriate it was to be talking about a dead body in a hospital room or to appear angry because I hadn't kept Rizzie from getting to Tyrone and Maum as fast as possible.

I glanced at my watch. "I need to head back to Middleton's. I'll bring Tyrone when he gets out of school, but I won't come in. Miss Gorman's sister is scheduled to be there at four, so I'll need to get right back to work. Call me if you find out anything or if there's any change."

Don't know how I knew it, but as I headed down the hall, I saw a doctor that I guessed was the orthopedic surgeon. Sure enough, he went in Maum's door. I turned around and followed him.

An average-sized man with graying hair, he wore midnight blue dress pants and a powder blue shirt with a red and navy striped tie. He went directly to Rizzie and shook hands. I couldn't hear what she said, but his answer was reassuring.

"Just don't even think like that," the doctor was telling Rizzie. "Of course, your grandmother's hip will be repaired. Dr. Midlands corrects hip fractures in patients older than she is frequently. He did successful surgery on a ninety-five-year-old last week. I'll be checking in on Mrs. Profit. She'll have her surgery just as soon as possible. Meanwhile, we'll be keeping her comfortable until the cardiologists regulate her heart beat."

When he left, I asked Rizzie, "That wasn't Dr. Midlands?"

"No, he's one of Dr. Midlands's associates. Go on to work so you can pick Tyrone up on time. I don't like him hanging around after school."

Almost to my car, the sheriff met me. "Were you waiting for me?" I asked. Should have known he wouldn't leave without scheduling my statement.

"No, I had some other business in the hospital to take care of, but we do need to decide." He grinned. "Your place or mine?"

"My place. I'll put you on my work table," I teased.

Wayne sees gruesome scenes as part of his position as sheriff, but like many others, the technical aspects of what Jessica Mitford called *The American Way of Death* and scenes from *Six Feet Under* creep him out. He's not comfortable in my work room, and he flatly refuses to talk to Otis or Odell while they're embalming someone. He claims he's happy that autopsies for our area are performed in Charleston, so he doesn't have to sit in on them like the law enforcement officers in books and TV.

"No kidding. I do need a statement," he said.

"Well, I saw the body and called you. That's all I know. Do you have any information about him yet? I guess he's with the fair and not a local." I wasn't about to tell him that Patel had told me he didn't think the dead man worked on the midway.

"We don't have an ID. The man appears to be young, no more than early twenties, which would make sense if he's a midway operator."

"Why do you say, 'if'? He was wearing a Midlands Midway windbreaker."

"But nobody working at the fair can identify him. My men spent the morning over there showing his picture around, and no one recognizes him."

"A lot of people look very different after death. I know

because my job is to make them look like their relatives and friends think of them. Sometimes there doesn't seem to be much resemblance between the person when alive and the dead body." I looked at my watch again.

"I've got to get over to Middleton's. You can come and get the statement while I work if you like. Otherwise, I'm afraid that if I have to go to the station, it's probably going to be tomorrow."

"Okay," Wayne said, "I'll get back to you."

I watched him swagger away and wondered, not for the first time, why I'd never had a crush on him. Must have been that brother thing from having him hang around with John while I grew up. Good grief! There were a dozen more important things for me to be thinking about than who I did or did not have a crush on. Maybe it was because the man I'd been seeing had pulled that old business of getting me used to having him around and then stopped calling, but more likely it was because last night's dancing and hugging had stirred up my hormones.

Dalmation! A hundred and one dalmations!

Chapter Six

Miss Nina Gorman awaited me at Middleton's. Covered neatly with a clean, white sheet, she lay on the table in my work room. I knew that she wore pristine cotton underwear that I would replace with her own. Otis and Odell always put underwear on the decedents before they brought them to my work room. New white boxers, never skivvies, on the males, while the females get white bras and full panties, never thongs or bikinis. If relatives didn't bring underwear, the white cotton stayed on through cremation or burial. If the family supplied what they wanted, the mortuary underwear was discarded. The Middletons are always respectful to me and to the deceased. Actually, they are respectful to everyone except each other.

I pulled on my smock and gloves before removing the photograph from its plastic bag. In the picture of them wearing beige dresses, both ladies had their hair short and curly, not quite as long as Miss Nina's was. I'd just use some very tiny curlers. I sprayed setting lotion on her hair—no problem since she lay with her head slightly elevated on a wedge—and rolled it on the tiniest curlers I had. I don't have to shampoo hair as part of my job. Otis or Odell washes the head during the prep. Sometimes, the hair is still damp when the person is brought to me, but Miss Nina had been embalmed the night before, so her hair was totally dry until I sprayed it.

When I removed the sheet to manicure her nails and do makeup, I felt more emotional than I sometimes do when working with someone. I view my job as an opportunity to provide families with peaceful, pretty memories of their loved ones. After a few years on this job, the only cases that really upset me are when I have to work on children. This time, the elderly Miss Nina made me think of Maum. When the time came, would Rizzie want my services? I just hoped it wouldn't be soon.

By the time I had Miss Nina dressed in her beige outfit with her hair all curly, nails a pretty mauve, and her pearls on, I needed to go pick up Tyrone. I paged Otis. He came and helped me casket the body. "Casket" as a verb is Funeraleze meaning to put the deceased in the selected coffin. The head is turned slightly to the right though it looks like the person is lying flat on his or her back. We wheeled the bier into Slumber Room A and parked it in the usual place. Otis said he would take care of placing the floral arrangements while I was gone. I stepped back and took a good look at Miss Nina. She looked lovely lying there in her pink casket with its silver handles. I hoped I could do as well matching her sister's appearance to hers.

Though I'd usually ridden the school bus, Daddy or one of my brothers had picked me up from school occasionally, but I didn't remember it being the madhouse that confronted me in the parking lot at St. Mary High School. There were kids all over, and they didn't seem to fear walking right in front of a moving car. For a moment, I wished I'd driven the hearse. Bet that would have slowed them down.

Some of the teenagers still looked like little kids, but most of them could pass for grown. The girls had bigger ta ta's than I do unless I'm wearing one of my inflatable bras. I scanned the crowd of noisy kids, but I didn't see Tyrone. Finally, he sauntered out from behind the building, and I leaned over and opened the passenger door for him.

"Don't do that next time," he said. "It makes me look like a little kid being picked up by their mama." Oh, well, Wayne thought of me as a little girl while Tyrone thought of me as old enough to be his mother. Come to think of it, I *am* old enough to be his mom if I'd had him in my teens. I didn't bother to tell him that grammatically "kid" and "their" didn't go together.

"How's Maum?" he asked as I pulled off.

"She's not ready for the surgery yet, but she's responding to the heart medicine."

"Maum's not crying, is she?" he asked. "She had tears last night, and I don't think I can stand to see her do that anymore."

"The medicine is making her sleep a lot," I answered, not having the heart to tell him that I'd seen her weep that morning. Tyrone's lip quivered, but he managed to hold back the tears. I knew the kid was having a rough time and asked, "Are you hungry?"

"Yes, I could really go for a cheeseburger right now," he answered.

My brothers had always had room for cheeseburgers, too.

McDonald's drive-through. Three of those quarter-pounders with cheese. Doesn't matter what new burger they put on the menu, my favorite will always be quarter-pounders. I'd opened mine and taken the first bite as I sat at the end of the drive waiting for traffic to slow down and let me pull back onto the road. Four boys walked across, right in front of the Mustang. I wasn't paying much attention to them until one of them stopped, turned to face the car, and made humping movements at me.

Tyrone went ballistic. "What the (really bad word) do you think you're doing?" he screamed and threw open his door. I grabbed the back of his shirt and literally held him in the car. The humper ran while his friends laughed.

"Come on!" I yelled. "Maum and Rizzie need you. That jerk's not worth your time."

He slammed his door shut, shoved his burger back into the bag, and sat sulking all the way to the hospital. When I stopped at the entrance, he jumped out, banged the door closed, and left the bag on the seat.

I hit the horn and held it. He couldn't ignore the loud blaring behind him. When he opened the door to see what I wanted, I handed him the McDonald's bag.

"I don't want it now!" he snapped.

"I don't care," I snapped back. "That other burger is for your sister. You take it to her."

"She's not my sister; she's my cousin." Defiant and angry.

"Well, take it to your cousin before I ram it up your . . ." Oops, I was forgetting my kindergarten cussing and somehow I didn't think "tush" or "booty" would have the desired effect, so I didn't say anything more. He stalked off, and I thanked my lucky stars that when I taught school, my students had been five-year-olds, not teenagers.

Surprisingly, I hadn't spoken to Jane all day even though she's my BFF and we usually talk several times a day. I hit her number on my cell phone as I headed back to Middleton's.

"This is Roxanne," came that husky, slow drawl she uses on her business line. "I'm soooo glad you called. I . . ."

"Jane," I laughed, "you're not working. You're on your own telephone, and this is Callie."

"I know. I thought Frankie was on the phone, and I was trying to get a rise out of him." She paused. "I haven't seen you all day. How's Rizzie's grandmamma?"

When I first met Jane, I tried to avoid sight references, but she refers to seeing people and uses sight words all the time. With no comment about the fact that Roxanne wouldn't get Jane's usual rise out of Frankie since he hated her fantasy actress personality, I answered, "They're going to operate on her when her heart is beating more regularly. How are you today? Still puking?"

"You don't have to say it like that. It sounds so crude."

"Well, are you?"

"Yes, but not as bad as yesterday."

"How much have you eaten today?"

"Oh, I had breakfast and lunch. Haven't had dinner yet."

I laughed. "It's too early for dinner. Did you eat everything in sight this morning?"

Jane laughed louder than I had. "Now, what is ever in sight for me?" She paused, but not long enough for me to think of a come-back, and then added, "But don't ever think I have to see it, to eat it."

"Seriously," I answered, "I think some of the throwing up is because you're overeating."

"I'm hungry. I may be eating for two."

"Then it's time for you to see a doctor and get those vitamins and all that other stuff pregnant women need."

"I will. I'm just not ready."

"There's no ready to it. If you're getting a baby bump, you need to see a doctor."

She did what she always does when she doesn't like what I say. She changed the subject.

"When will you be home?"

"I'll be home before too late unless Rizzie needs me. Tyrone spent the night at my place last night, and I'll probably have him there tonight, too, if he stops acting like a jerk. I can't believe that sweet little boy we've known for two years has turned so yucky."

"Take it easy on him, Callie. He's worried that his grandmother will die. You don't remember losing your mom, and I don't remember my daddy leaving, but I do remember Mommy dying. I still cry about it sometimes, and I'd already finished high school when I lost her. Tyrone's a lot younger, and he's reacting to being afraid and to feeling guilty that she fell while he was there without Rizzie."

"Jane, you're right." It's not always easy for me to admit being wrong, but I knew Jane was dead-on about this. "I should have thought of all that myself. I'm afraid I was pretty rough with him."

"Did you forget to kindergarten cuss?"

"Afraid I did," I answered.

"He'll get over it. Have you heard from Dr. Donald?" she

asked.

"When he calls, I'll tell you," I answered, then corrected myself, "I should say *if*." He hadn't called for a couple of weeks after seeing me almost daily for a while. I'd begun telling her about dinner and dancing last night with Patel when call waiting beeped in.

I glanced at the phone and told Jane, "Gotta go."

"Hello, this is Callie Parrish," I answered without thinking. Kind of ridiculous to identify myself when someone calls me on my own cell phone.

"I'm glad. I'd hate to think the gorgeous lady I dined and danced with last night gave me a fake phone number."

"Not me. I never lie." *Liar, liar, pants on fire.*

"I've got to hang around the fairgrounds tonight. Could I talk you into that corndog you thought I was inviting you for last night?"

"I really wish I could, but I'll be baby-sitting." I explained about Maum and my being responsible for Tyrone.

"You can bring him with you. I'll give him passes to ride everything he wants, see all the shows, and eat everything offered at Mother Hubbard's. He can even have a friend meet him out here, if he doesn't want to hang with us. Most teenagers don't want to do the fair with two adults."

"I really don't think so. We'll probably stay at the hospital pretty late, hoping the heart doctors will okay Maum's surgery."

"If you change your mind, call and let me know. You've got my number on your cell now, right?"

"Yes." His invitation sounded like fun, and I liked the fact that he was willing to include Tyrone, but it didn't seem right to go have fun at the fair while Rizzie and Maum were at the hospital.

She was drunk. That's the only word for it. Miss Nila Gorman was drunk as a skunk. That's a ridiculous statement. I've never seen a skunk drink. Better would be, "Drunk as a punk." I've seen a few drunk punks in my time, especially back when I was in college. I don't see how the old lady didn't pass out before she got that inebriated. A hot mess with hair sticking out in all directions and makeup smeared on her face, she staggered through the front door of Middleton's to the recorded melody of "The Old Rugged Cross" and spotted the beautiful pink casket in Slumber Room A. Her slurred words rang out over the music.

"Oh, Nina," she sobbed, "why couldn't I have gone first? Why did you leave me? I can't go on. I just can't go on." She reached the casket before I caught up with her, and I barely managed to keep her from grabbing her sister.

"Come now, Miss Gorman," I said in Odell's Undertaker 101 tone. "Let's go back here and get you all fixed up."

"She looks so pretty," Miss Nila mumbled.

"Yes, she does, and you look just like her," I agreed as I led her back to my office. I'd decided I would have to do Miss Nila's hair and makeup there where I'd already put her clothes and the supplies I'd need. I'm not supposed to take anyone into my work room, but I wished I could lay her out on the table and let her sleep it off. I nudged Miss Nila to sit down in my office chair.

Now, I know as well as anyone else that coffee doesn't really sober people, but I hoped it would at least help. I left her sitting there while I went to the kitchen. Forget about the dainty Wedgwood china with silver coffee service on a tray. I poured a cup of black coffee into a mug and got out of the kitchen just in time to see Miss Nila Gorman staggering back toward Slumber Room A with a set of car keys dangling from her right hand.

"I'm taking you home, Nina. Gonna take you home with me," she cried.

I couldn't let her drive away in her condition, and I certainly couldn't let her take her deceased sister out of the casket in any condition.

"Miss Gorman," I said as I caught up with her, "don't you

want to come with me and let me do your hair and help you
dress up just like your sister?" I set the coffee mug on a table
and lifted the car keys from her hand. I gently took hold of the
elderly lady. It would be just my luck for her to fall and hurt
herself on my watch.

"No!" She was adamant. "I want to take Nina home and
forget all about this place."

"Now, you know Miss Nina's friends and relatives are
coming in a few hours to show their respect for Miss Nina. We
need to get you prettied up."

"Oh, that's right. Show respect for my sister. Where's the
beauty parlor? I've gotta get ready."

I led her back to my office and once more nudged her into
the chair. She sat still, closed her eyes, and soon began snoring
as I curled her hair on tiny rollers and misted it with super hold
hair spray. I let it set while I manicured her nails and then
tweezed the wiry white stray hairs from her eyebrows. Buh-
leeve me. If I can tweeze someone's brows and not wake that
person up, she's not sleeping. She's either passed out or dead. I
leaned over and listened. I could hear her breathing. Her
sleeping didn't bother me. I'm used to working on people who
stay quiet and still.

At a quarter 'til six, I awoke Miss Gorman (Nila, not Nina)
and coerced her into drinking two cups of coffee. I still didn't
believe it would sober her up, but I hoped the caffeine might
help her look more alive than her sister. I helped Miss Nila into
her dress and accessories and silently marveled at how clear-
headed she seemed. But then, I had an idea that Miss Nila had
lots of practice sobering up or at least pretending to since I now
remembered that she'd been tipsy at my brother's wedding
shower.

"Amazing Grace" announced the first arrivals at the visitation. Less than thirty minutes after it began, Otis came in.

"Good job, Callie," he said. "They look just alike."

I didn't know if that meant they both looked dead like Miss
Nina or they both looked alive like Miss Nila, so I just thanked

him for the compliment.

Otis smiled and added, "You can leave now, and I'll see you in the morning."

He didn't have to tell me twice. I called Jane and told her I was headed to the hospital to check on Maum. "Do you need anything?"

"Nope," she answered. "I'm thinking about cooking dinner, and I expect you and Tyrone to eat *here* when you leave the hospital, not at your dad's."

"Why would I eat at Daddy's?"

"I was supposed to tell you that John showed up this morning, so your daddy's cooking stew and playing music tonight. I told Frankie I'd rather stay home. I'm still not feeling good."

"Then just send Frankie to Daddy's. Why cook?"

"Because I want to, and that should be reason enough. I'm tired of people telling me what to do."

Jane's mention of food made me think Rizzie was probably hungry, so I decided to stop somewhere and pick up something for her.

Big black letters across the top of the *St. Mary News* in the newspaper dispenser at the Waffle House asked, "DO YOU KNOW THIS MAN?" I didn't recognize the face, but I'd seen him before.

I dropped the necessary quarters into the coin slot, took out a newspaper, and read it while the cook prepared a pecan waffle to go. Rizzie loves waffles, and the Waffle House serves them, hot and freshly cooked, any time day or night.

Folks look different when they're dead, but the man in the picture was deceased when I first saw him. The reason his face wasn't familiar to me was because he'd been lying face-down at Mother Hubbard's Beer Garden. The article told a lot that I already knew—when and where the body was found and that he'd been wearing a Middleton's Midway jacket.

Thank heaven the paper didn't say I was the one who found him. Sometimes I get more publicity than the Middletons or I want when I do something like finding a dead body or shooting someone. What I didn't already know was that the medical examiner who'd performed the autopsy in Charleston said the decedent was between eighteen and twenty-three and had died of a gunshot wound in his back. He'd had no identification on him, and so far, law enforcement hadn't located anyone who recognized him.

When the server gave me the bag with Rizzie's waffle in its Styrofoam tray, I wished I'd ordered one for me, too. I hadn't because I planned to either stop and eat after I picked up Tyrone or go to a drive-through on the way home. I put the bag on the back seat, hoping that would lessen the cake-like aroma and make me less tempted to go back and buy a waffle for myself before I reached Healing Heart Medical Center.

When James Brown started singing, I told myself aloud, "Change that *today!*" Though I expected the call to be from Rizzie, Jane, or Daddy, the voice on the line was Sheriff Wayne Harmon. I put my cell on speaker phone in case he asked me if I was driving while we talked.

"Callie, we have a problem that I need to tell Rizzie about, but I want to discuss it with you before I talk to her. How's her grandmother?"

"Still waiting to have the hip replacement surgery. What do you want to talk to Rizzie about?"

"Her van. It seems that it didn't catch fire because of damage to the engine. One of the firemen who put it out called and suggested I have it checked further. Said the more he thought about it, he figures it was arson."

"Arson? Rizzie said she and Tyrone were sitting on the curb waiting for a tow truck when flames shot out."

"I know, but when the fire marshall went to the garage and checked the van, he found evidence that someone threw a Molotov cocktail on the front seat."

"Molotov cocktail?"

"A homemade fire bomb."

"I know what it is. I just can't imagine why anyone would do that or how they would do it with Rizzie and Tyrone sitting across the lot."

"That's why I want to talk to Rizzie, but I'm hesitant to tell her when her grandmother's condition is so serious."

"But if someone did that on purpose, Rizzie could be in danger. I think you have to tell her, Wayne."

"I'd like you there when I talk to her."

"I'm headed there now."

"I'm right behind you."

I thought he'd been speaking figuratively, but when I glanced into my rearview mirror, I saw the sheriff's tan cruiser.

Chapter Seven

Maum looked awful, and Rizzie didn't look much better. Maum's eyes and cheeks had sunk into her face, and I wondered if she were dehydrating, but the IV solutions she was receiving should be taking care of that. The room felt like an oven, and sweat popped out on my forehead immediately, just like on Rizzie's. Maum was covered in several blankets pulled up to her chin and tucked around her neck.

"Where's Tyrone?" I asked. He wasn't in the room, and the bathroom door was partly open, so I could see he wasn't in there.

"Mad at me. I jumped him about the lunch money you gave him. He got all defensive, but he couldn't show me the money or a receipt for putting it on his lunch ticket. He stormed off down the hall to the waiting room. I guess he's watching television."

"I brought you a waffle and some coffee." I set the food bag on the bedside table. "I didn't know if I should bring Maum something or not."

"Not," Rizzie said as she opened the container, tore off a fourth of the waffle, and bit into it like a piece of toast. She didn't bother with the packets of butter and syrup.

"Maum can't have anything to eat at all. They're hoping to get an okay for her surgery today. Dr. Midlands came by earlier and said he would operate as soon as the heart doctors let him, even if it's tonight."

"Good," I said as the sheriff walked in, "the sooner, the

better."

Rizzie told Wayne the same information she'd given me while she continued eating the waffle without all the good stuff I like to slather all over mine. When she finished, she dropped the little packets into the drawer of the bedside table, then tossed the bag and the tray into the trash.

I could see that Wayne was about to tell her about the van when Maum's body stiffened and she moaned. Rizzie leaned over and whispered comforting words in her ear while caressing her cheek with one hand and pressing the call button for the nurse with the other. Soon the nurse came in with the hypodermic. She released the medicine into the IV line and within minutes, Maum relaxed and appeared to be sleeping again.

Rizzie popped the top off the cup I'd brought and nodded toward the door. "There's coffee available at the nurses' station if either of you want a cup. I've been drinking it all day."

"No, thanks," I said. I'd been wishing I'd brought her a milkshake or something cold. The room was way too sweltering for anyone to be drinking hot coffee.

"Any doughnuts down there?" Wayne joked and winked at me. I know it's tacky, but I've never denied being tacky sometimes, and I tease him a lot about cops eating doughnuts.

"If there'd been any," Rizzie said. "I wouldn't have inhaled that waffle. There's a snack machine, but it's broken, and I didn't want to be gone from Maum long enough to go to another floor. I was starving."

Wayne motioned toward the empty chair by the bed. "Sit down, Rizzie. I want to talk to you a minute."

"What is it? Don't tell me Ty's in trouble. Maum and I have kept a tight rein on him since he was caught playing hooky last year."

"No, nothing to do with Tyrone," Wayne said. "Do you know of a reason someone would want to do something against you or Tyrone?"

"Not that I know of. What are you talking about?" She panicked. "What's happened?"

"It appears that your running into that pole didn't cause the fire," the sheriff said. "Somebody put a firebomb in your van."

"Was it on a timer? How could they do that?"

"Nothing so fancy as a timer. It was very crude and would have had to be put in right before the fire."

"That's impossible," Rizzie protested.

"Wait a minute," I said. "Didn't Tyrone say he saw someone there?"

"I don't know. I hardly know what *I'm* saying, much less what anyone else says."

"Think about it, and call me if you think of anything that might be related." The sheriff headed toward the door. "I'll stop by the waiting room and ask Tyrone if he saw someone by the van before the fire."

"If I think of anything, anything at all, I'll call you," Rizzie assured Wayne as he left.

I visited with Rizzie before going to the waiting room where I found Tyrone, wearing a sullen expression, slouched on a couch in front of the television, looking for all the world like a grumpy old man.

"Did the sheriff talk to you?"

"Yeah, but I didn't see anyone do anything to the Econoline."

"Well, come on back and tell Rizzie goodbye before we leave," I told him.

"I'm not speaking to her."

"At least go in there and kiss Maum goodnight."

His face crumpled into tears, and, right before my eyes, he changed from rough and tough teenager to a little boy. People talk all the time about pubescent girls and their hormones, but I believe teenaged males are completely unpredictable because of *their* hormones. I tried to put my arm around him, but Tyrone pulled away. Finally, he gained enough control to convert his blubbering to sniffling. He dried his face with the sleeve of his shirt. That wasn't the most courteous thing to do, but at least it wasn't upchuck like Jane had wiped on her arm.

When we reached Room 407, Tyrone told Rizzie, "I'm sorry about the money. I spent it, but I'll pay it back to you as soon as we reopen the restaurant."

"Not to me, to Callie."

I wanted to say, "Forget it," but I kept my mouth shut for a change. Rizzie wasn't as concerned about the money as she was about Tyrone developing a good moral code. We'd discussed that in the past.

Tyrone turned to me. "I'll pay you back, Callie. I promise."

He kissed Rizzie and his grandmother goodnight, then cautioned Rizzie, "Please don't let them operate on Maum without calling me." He looked toward me. "Will you bring me back if she calls?"

"Of course."

Getting into the Mustang, I picked the newspaper up from the seat and showed the front page to Tyrone. "Ever seen him before?" I asked.

"Nope," he lied. I knew he wasn't telling the truth because he answered too fast and he looked over my shoulder instead of at my face. I didn't push the issue because I learned a long time ago that sneakiness works better than confrontation to get information.

"What do you want for dinner?" I asked as we pulled out of the parking lot.

"Are you cooking?"

"No, I thought we'd stop somewhere or pick up something at a drive-through." I was kind of sorry I'd turned down Jane's offer to cook for us.

"If you don't mind driving out to the island, I want to get some more clothes. We need to take Rizzie some of her things, too. She freezes individual dinners when we have leftovers at the diner. We could microwave a couple of plates at the house or take them back to your apartment. In fact, we can pick up some for the next couple of days." He looked at me sheepishly. "I'll still pay you back, but at least that way you don't have to spend money to feed me while I'm staying with you."

I called Daddy to check on him. Mike answered the telephone. Since Bill moved in with Molly when he married her and Frankie stays with Jane most of the time, the only one of my brothers living with Daddy right then was Mike. In the past, all of them except Jim, who's in the Navy, and John, who was happily married and lived in Atlanta, moved in and out of Daddy's house like it had swinging doors anytime they broke up with their wives or girlfriends.

"Yellow," Mike said instead of "hello." He thinks that's funny. I don't know why because I think it's silly, but my brothers aren't known for their cultured behavior.

I could barely hear Mike because Daddy was howling with laughter.

"What's so funny?" I asked.

"Pa's watching TV."

"What show?"

"He's watching a rerun marathon of *Here Comes Honey Boo Boo*. He says that show makes him feel like we're sophisticated."

My daddy is the exact image of a sixty-five-year-old Larry the Cable Guy, including the shirts with no sleeves. I love him, but he's about as classy as a sardine and onion sandwich on mushy white bread.

"Ask him if he wants to talk to me," I instructed Mike.

I heard mumbling and laughing before Mike said, "He says he'll talk to you later. He doesn't want to miss any of his show."

Right before I turned onto the bridge to Surcie Island, Tyrone pointed to the side of the road and said, "Look at that!" The Crime Watch sign by the road had been spray painted with some sort of symbol.

"What's that?" I asked.

"I don't know," he said, and I could tell he was lying again.

Rain began, pattering softly on the rag top, almost as though it were timed to coincide with our reaching the house.

The headlights glared against the front of the building, making the bright blue front door stand out. I hadn't been to their house recently because since Rizzie opened Gastric Gullah, I generally saw her in town.

"When did you paint the door?" I asked.

"Couple of weeks ago. Painted the window trim, too. Maum got upset because she said the blue they were painted had faded to gray. All Gullahs have blue trim on their houses. It's for good luck. Haven't you ever noticed that?"

"Not that I remember. To tell the truth, I've had Gullah friends before, but your family is the only ones I've ever visited on the island."

"You can sit in the car while I go in and get me and Rizzie some clothes and food, lots of food. That way you won't get wet." He got out and dashed to the front porch.

I admit I spent the time he was inside wondering what he'd bring for dinner. I was hungry, and I'd never eaten anything Rizzie or Maum cooked that wasn't delectable.

The teenager must have rushed around inside because he was out fast, loaded down with bags. He had two canned Cokes with him, too.

"I brought us a drink for the ride back to town and a lot of food, so you can pick what you want when we get to your place."

And that's exactly what we did after we took Big Boy out for his usual squatting and walk. Tyrone had brought all kinds of food—oyster pie, Beaufort stew, shrimp bog, and vegetable dishes like potato pone and tomato pie. For dinner, he chose a creole type dish with chicken and shrimp. I picked the oyster pie. I love that stuff.

While Tyrone showered, I called Jane.

"What's going on?" she asked.

When I explained, she told me she'd thought maybe I'd stayed at the hospital with Rizzie.

"No, she's adamant that Tyrone is to be in school every day. He's staying with me while she's at the hospital. What are you and Frankie doing?"

"He just stormed out of here to go to your father's. Probably gonna spend the night there. He's *demanding* I quit my job. I know he's your brother and I shouldn't complain to you about him, but I don't see how I can quit when he's just working part-time here, there, and yonder. Then he suggested we could get married and move into the Parrish house with Mike and Pa. I flatly refused. He got mad and left. I didn't call to complain to you. Just wanted you to know I didn't cook."

She didn't sound upset, but I offered, "Want to come next door for a while?"

"Nope. Roxanne is going to burn this phone up for the rest of the night. I've got to make some money to pay my bills."

I hung up feeling really bad. I'd known this would happen when my best friend hooked up with my brother. When they fuss, I feel guilty. When she makes him mad, I feel sorry for him. When he makes her mad, I feel sorry for her.

Tyrone was taking a long shower, so I called Patel. If I hadn't quit swearing, I'd swear I could *see* him smiling over the telephone, and I don't have one of those fancy phones that can have visual chats.

"I'm glad you called. Did you change your mind or should I start trying to talk you into it?" he said.

"I don't know. Tyrone's getting a shower, and we should stay here and go to bed early, but I thought I'd check and see if you'd already invited someone else to join you for that corndog or if the fair had been rained out."

"No, it's stopped raining here, and I haven't invited anyone else. I don't very often ask women I meet on the fair circuit to join me for dinner at a restaurant or here at the fair. I'm only in town two to three weeks each place. I guess I should make that clear to you, too. I'll only be here another week and a half, but I'd love to show you and the young man around tonight or any night while I'm here."

At least he shoots straight, I thought, *and it might be good to take Tyrone somewhere to get his mind off his grandmother.*

"We've already eaten supper, so we'll pass on the corndog, but when Tyrone comes out of the shower, I'll ask him if he'd like to ride out for a short time. I'll call you back and let you know. Will that be okay?"

"Perfect! And if you've already had dinner, we can have a little dessert. You know—like elephant ears, candied apples, cotton candy, deep fried candy bars, chocolate covered bacon—or anything you think you'd enjoy."

Just then Tyrone came out of the bathroom, so I told Patel to hold on and called to Tyrone, "J. T. Patel, a friend of mine, has invited us to meet him at the fair. We wouldn't be able to stay long, but do you want to go?"

Tyrone's sad face said "no," as he pulled his pockets inside-out, showing me that he had no money.

"You won't need money." My words brightened his face into a smile. I didn't know if Patel would treat for everything, but I had enough in my purse to buy something to eat. I turned back to the telephone. "We'll be there in about thirty minutes."

"Come to the front gate. I'll meet you there."

I postponed my shower but did change clothes. Who wants to go to the fair wearing a black dress and heels? Jeans and a red sweater should be comfortable, and a little extra inflation in my bra put a bounce in my step as well as my bosom. The rain had cooled off the night air, so I grabbed a jacket in case I needed it over the sweater.

Chapter Eight

"Sorry to hear about your grandmother," was the first thing Patel said to Tyrone as he shook hands when I introduced them. "We may not have time to do everything you want, but we'll try. What do you want to do first? Eat, play games, or go on rides?"

Tyrone beamed. "You really mean it?"

"Your choice unless Callie here has an objection." Patel laughed and nodded toward me. "There aren't any girly shows here, so we should be safe letting him choose anything he'd like to do."

"Then let's go through the barns and look at all the farm animals," I teased. "After that, we can visit the exhibit buildings and check out all the prize-winning cakes and pies or jams and jellies."

"She's kidding," Patel assured Tyrone. "Of course, we could go see all the quilts and paintings and stuff like that, but I think we should let this young man tell us what he wants to do."

"Play games," Tyrone said.

"It figures. Young men your age want to play games or ride the tallest, most dangerous rides." He turned onto a sawdust covered walkway. "Come this way."

I've loved carnivals, fairs, and circuses as long as I can remember. When I step through the gates to the fairground, my heart pounds with excitement. Sometimes it beats so hard and fast that I'm afraid I'll pass out before I get to enjoy all the

sights and sounds. I like the smells of foods we don't eat anywhere but there. I'm not talking about cotton candy or pop-
corn. Not even those skinny French fries with vinegar or
cheese sauce. Those are available lots of places these days, and
corndogs, which used to be special, can be bought frozen at the
grocery store and microwaved before swabbing mustard up and
down them.

My favorite foods are the Polish sausages with peppers and
onions like Jane had, and candied apples are good, but apples
dipped in caramel and nuts are even better, and *nobody* does
fried mushrooms like the folks at the fair.

The noise at fairs consists of happy sounds—music from
the rides and voices calling, "Come on in." Of course, that
"come on in" is an invitation to spend money, but it's fun.
When I was a little girl, Daddy took me to the fair every year
and told me, "Everything costs too much. You can't win the
games. The rides and food will give you a belly ache, but it's so
much fun that it's worth the price. We're paying for you to have
a good time, so just enjoy it, and when we get low on funds, I'll
buy you a hat with your name embroidered on it before we go
home." Then, at the end, when we'd ridden and eaten all we
could handle or afford, we'd argue whether to have the person
with the sewing machine and that fancy thread that was yellow
and blue and pink right after each other on the same spool
embroider "Callie" or "Calamine" on my hat that year. I still
have some of those hats in a drawer at Daddy's house.

I'd want to stay a little longer and go into one of those
"Amazing Freaks of Nature" tents, and Daddy would say, "Aw,
Calamine, those are all fakes. The babies in jars are made out of
rubber, but there are some people in real life who are different.
When you do meet someone like that, remember to be kind." I
heard him tell my brother one night after I'd gone to bed that
he didn't want me to ever see those distorted babies in jars
because it might make me have deformed babies when I grew
up. My daddy looks like a redneck, but sometimes he thinks like
a throw-back to some old, superstitious woman.

By the time I was old enough to go without Daddy, the fair that came to Jade County didn't have freak shows anymore. The whole idea of anomalies fascinated me, but instead of seeing different people at the fair, I saw them on television's *The Learning Channel,* and when I did see or meet people different from me, I treated them just like everyone else, which is a very good way for teachers to be. Jane says the success of our friendship since she moved back to St. Mary from the School for the Blind when we were in our early teens has been because I don't treat her different because she's not able to see.

When I lived in Columbia, I'd gone to the South Carolina State Fair. Different attractions had different areas—kiddy rides like Merry Go Rounds in a designated spot, adult rides like the old Round-Up in another. The games had all been set up in a line between the kiddy rides and the side shows. The Jade County Fair was laid out the same way this year. Patel led us to a row of games.

At the booth with "Bushel Basket Balls" over it, the man wearing a pocketed apron motioned toward Tyrone from behind the counter.

"You can win this one. Come on in, and be a winner."

"That carny wants me to throw balls into the baskets," Tyrone said and started toward the stand.

"Game agents," Patel told him. "There's nothing wrong with the word 'carny,' but they prefer to be called game agents. Come over here a minute."

I stepped to the side with him and Tyrone. The game agent continued looking at Tyrone and promising that he could win this one easily and that if he didn't, he could get all his money back and choose any one of the prizes hanging around the booth. I could see why Tyrone was interested in this game. The usual giant stuffed animals were mixed in with iPads and electric guitars.

"The Bushel Basket game," Patel said, "works just like the Tubs of Fun we just passed. He'll tell you that all you have to do is throw two balls into the basket and have them stay and not bounce out. Don't aim at the center of the basket. Throw toward the back rim of the basket."

"Yes, sir," Tyrone looked happier than I'd seen him since Maum's fall.

We stepped back to the game booth. Patel handed the game agent something—I couldn't tell—was it rolled up money or a coupon? The man stuffed it into the pocket on his apron.

"All you have to do is get two balls to stay in the basket," the agent told us. Tyrone aimed carefully and hit the back rim of the basket. The ball went in and stayed. He threw the next ball the same way, and it did the same thing.

"Good job," the agent said, and handed Tyrone a tiny stuffed bear about four inches tall from beneath the counter.

"I thought I was gonna win one of those," Tyrone complained and pointed toward the large prizes.

"You can trade this in for a bigger one when you win again," the agent said and held his open palm out to Tyrone. Patel once again put something in the man's hand.

Again, Tyrone landed both balls in the basket and they stayed. This time he received a stuffed dog about twelve inches high. "I thought you said I could win a big prize."

"You get one of each level, and then you trade them in for your choice of anything we got. Ready to win again?"

"Why not?" Tyrone asked. I thought, *Why not, indeed? It's not your money.*

While Tyrone warmed up his throwing arm with some impressive exercises, Patel whispered to me, "The agent's 'throwing stock to the mark.' Giving away little things called 'slum prizes' to keep the player interested. That's called the 'tiered prize system,' where the payer keeps trading up hoping to get something really big. We'll let this play out. Watch what happens."

Sure enough, Tyrone kept winning, and he kept trading in smaller prizes for bigger ones. The game agent had begun shout-outs to the by-passers, telling them to come watch this winner, and a large crowd gathered.

After what seemed like forever and Tyrone trading in one prize after another, the agent made this big announcement to everyone that "This boy is going to play now for his choice of anything here!" People crowded around cheering Tyrone with shouts of, "Win it!"

Tyrone threw exactly the way he'd done every time from the same place as before. Both balls landed in the basket and stayed causing the game agent to tell Tyrone, "Sorry, Dude, rim shots don't count."

"What? I threw just like I did the other times."

"Yeah, but you leaned over the foul line."

"What foul line?" Patel interrupted.

"Come on, Mr. Patel. Don't start anything. You know how this works."

"I sure do, and I don't appreciate your trying it with me standing here." Both Patel's tone and expression showed he meant business.

Patel and the game agent had a whispered conversation, which ended with Tyrone walking away with an iPad. As we continued around the game circuit, I asked him, "Why did you want another iPad? Don't you have one from the school? You told Rizzie it was in your locker."

"I didn't want to tell her that I don't have it anymore." He looked at Patel. "Can I do that game?" and pointed toward an open tent with "SHOOT OUT THE RED STAR" on a large sign.

"Sure. Let me talk to you about it first."

"Can we get something to eat while we talk and then play the game?" Tyrone asked.

"Don't see why not. Follow me." Patel led us to a Mother Hubbard's Beer Garden, but not the one where I'd found the body.

"Since you've had dinner, let me recommend something that's a cross between a meal and a dessert. Why don't you have an Elvis Burger?"

"What's that?" Tyrone asked before I had a chance.

"It's a hamburger made on Krispy Kreme doughnuts instead of a bun. On that it has a burger and all the trimmings, including bacon and cheese." He breathed in deeply and said the next words like a big announcement. "Plus peanut butter and fried bananas."

Immediately my mind went to Jane. Given the chance, she'd eat that.

"No, thanks," was my reply. Not for me.

"I don't know." Tyrone's expression clouded. "I'm not sure I'd want lettuce and tomato and onions on it. Could I get it without the vegetables but with peanut butter and bananas?"

"No problem," Patel assured him, and then called the server over and requested the special order Elvis Burger and root beer for Tyrone. I asked for fried mushrooms and a Diet Coke while Patel wanted coffee.

Our server had barely walked away when three teenaged boys came in. Tyrone glanced at them and then made a point of looking at Patel and me.

A different female server asked the teenagers, "What would you like?"

"Three draft beers," one of them declared like a king making a proclamation.

"Sorry, we can't serve alcohol to minors."

"I've got ID." The same boy copped an attitude with a smirk.

The server pointed toward our table. "See that man. He's Mr. Patel, the owner. Go show your identification to him and if he accepts it, he'll serve you. I'm not about to give you three any alcohol, ID or not. I can look at you and see you're under-age."

"What the f-word are you supposed to drink in a beer garden?" Substitution of "f-word" is mine; he said the word. I just can't get used to even hearing people say that word out loud in public.

"Take it up with Mr. Patel," the young lady said politely.

"I don't have to. Just get me my beer, bitch."

Patel stood. I knew he was tall, but he looked even bigger now, and the expression on his face would have frightened a bear. He pointed at the boys. "Out!" he said as he walked toward them.

The sassy one opened his mouth, but his buddies tugged on him and urged him to get out of there.

When they were gone, Patel returned to our table and apologized for the interruption. I'd noticed Tyrone's intentionally turning his back to them. "Tyrone, did you know those boys?" I asked.

"Not really. They don't go to my school." He seemed relieved when the server placed the gigantic creation he'd ordered in front of him. He chowed down on doughnuts, meat, cheese, bananas, and peanut butter—keeping his eyes on his food and avoiding eye contact with Patel or me.

"Now, about the Red Star Shooting Game." Patel took a sip of his black coffee. "The goal is to shoot out the star completely so that no red is still there. They'll give you a BB gun and one hundred BBs to do it."

"Is there a trick to it like throwing the ball at the basket rim?" Tyrone was catching on.

"First thing to do is ask to look at the target. You hope the paper is flimsy. The better the grade of paper, the more difficult it is, and the smaller the star, the easier it is. The targets are numbered so that the game agents can account to the owners how many people tried. At the end of the number is a dash followed by a single-digit number, generally a two or three. You want to play this game where the digit is two, which means the star measures one and one-fourth inch. That's the easiest."

"How big is a three?" Tyrone finished the crazy doughnut burger and wiped his mouth on his sleeve.

"One and three-eighths inches."

"That's not much bigger."

"It makes a huge difference."

"What should I do if the target is on thick paper and is a three?"

"Move on to another booth."

"What else?"

I kept eating those mouthwatering mushrooms and listening to Patel's advice.

"Check out the gun and self-zero it. That means shoot the first three or four BBs at the top point of the star. If they hit high and to the right, aim low and to the left. If they hit low and left, aim high and right. You get the idea?"

"Sure. Do they mess up the guns by bending the barrel or something like that?"

"Not necessarily. Maybe some game agents do, but it's generally because the guns are old and have been used a lot. That's what causes them not to aim true. Most marks start shooting at the middle, which is a big mistake."

"What's a mark?"

"You're a mark—the person who's playing the game and paying the man."

"If I shouldn't start in the middle, where do I shoot?"

"Shoot a circle pattern around the star, and don't fire all the BBs fast. Shoot a few, then look to see what you've done before shooting more." Patel looked at the empty plates and bottles in front of Tyrone and me. "Ready to try it?"

Tyrone leaped up like he'd been shot out of a gun barrel himself. He must have remembered how we'd come from the game area because he took the lead. Patel and I followed.

"I doubt this is much fun for you, Callie, but I feel sorry for the young man," Patel said. "You do know that the chances are slim that his grandmother will make a full recovery. About a third of older patients who suffer the trauma of a broken hip and surgery die before they ever get home."

"How do you know that? I thought you ran a restaurant, not a medical center."

"I did, and I do, but I also had a mother."

At the Red Star game, Tyrone methodically followed Patel's instructions while Patel and I stood over to the side. The game agent had been happy to stuff the coupon Patel had given

Tyrone into his apron pocket when Tyrone handed it to him. When Tyrone asked to see the target, the man shot him an unpleasant, questioning glare, but he let the teenager inspect it. He looked even more disagreeable when Tyrone obviously self-zeroed the gun.

That kid shot out the star without even using all one hundred BBs. The game agent looked at the target and pointed at the sign—ALL RED STAR MUST BE SHOT FROM CARD TO WIN A PRIZE. He pulled a large magnifying glass from his apron pocket and held it over the target.

"I see a piece of red at the nine o'clock position. Sorry, but you have to shoot out the entire star."

"I did," Tyrone insisted.

"It doesn't matter what you think. We say if you win or not." The man turned his back on Tyrone and put up another target. "You can try again if you want."

"For free?"

"Of course not. Gimme another coupon or some money."

I kind of expected Patel to step in as he had at the Bushel Basket, but he shook his head, "No," but only slightly, not obvious to anyone watching.

Another coupon went into the apron pocket. I don't know if aim would change so quickly, but Tyrone checked the target and self-zeroed again. Then he shot that star out of the paper, too.

The magnifying glass came out of the pocket, but before the man could even pretend to check the star, Patel stepped forward. "I believe we've got quite a marksman here," he said.

"But there can't be any red showing," the agent protested.

"There isn't." Patel's voice was firm. "And I don't think Bernie will be happy if the young man calls for the police to come over here."

"Pick anything you want," the now hostile agent mumbled, "but you're cut off for tonight. Can't win more than one big prize in one day. Well, really not more than one at this place, so play somewhere else tomorrow."

I fully expected Tyrone to choose something electronic, but he selected a gigantic, fluffy white cat and told us it was for Maum to sleep with. He thought the softness would be warming to her. I didn't comment that the cat was bigger than she was. His grin spilled happiness all around him.

Looking at my watch, I said, "I think we'd best hit the road. Rizzie and Maum will be furious if I don't get him to school tomorrow."

"You treat me like a little kid," Tyrone complained.

"Well, let me get the pretty lady and the sharpshooter some treats to take home." Patel's grin was as big as Tyrone's. He ducked into a different Mother Hubbard's and came out a few minutes later carrying three bags.

"Three?" I asked.

"One for his sister."

Patel walked us to the Mustang, and I kind of wished Tyrone weren't there. Another kiss would have been welcome.

Chapter Nine

Good grief! There was a man sitting in one of the rocking chairs on the front porch when I arrived at work. I grimaced. I'd forgotten I was scheduled to open and hoped Otis nor Odell would know that my arrival was in plenty of time to get my work done, but fifteen minutes late to open.

Nobody had bothered to tell me that Tyrone didn't have classes because of a teachers' inservice day. Last night, I'd been worried about getting him to school today when what I'd really wanted to do was give Tyrone enough of those coupons to play another game somewhere near a place where Patel and I could sit and talk. But I'd been the good babysitter, and we'd gone home at a reasonably decent hour with no private conversation, no kiss, not even a little hand-holding.

Although we'd gone to bed before midnight, I'd had a hard time sleeping. Something kept nibbling at the edges of my mind. I couldn't quite grasp what I was trying to think. It's like when I run into someone I know but can't remember their name and think, "It's right on the tip of my tongue, but not in my brain."

This morning, when I'd told Tyrone to hurry and get ready for school, he'd told me to take him to the hospital instead. By the time I'd fed him breakfast and run inside to take Rizzie a biscuit and check on Maum, who'd been snuggled up to that big, fuzzy white cat since Tyrone walked in, I was late heading to work.

When I saw the man sitting on the verandah, I parked in

the front lot instead of driving around to my spot in back and met the man at the door with my keys in my hand while apologizing for his wait. There's a sign on the door that says we're open from nine to nine, other hours by appointment, and gives a phone number to reach someone at all hours.

I realize the word "dapper" is old-fashioned, but the man was definitely dapper. He exuded a debonair neatness—a tidy little man. Oh, I don't mean a little man like a midget. He was a bit taller than I am, probably five feet, six inches or so, trim and well-dressed in a dark green three-piece suit with a beige and moss green paisley bowtie.

"Is this the funeral home where Miss Gorman is resting?" he asked in a genteel tone.

Now I've heard dead people described as sleeping, and we use the euphemism "slumber room." I know that the expression "Rest in Peace" is used frequently, but no one had ever asked me that question in that way before.

"Yes, sir," I answered and invited him through the door to the tune of "Just As I Am."

"I'm Arthur Richards, an old friend. May I see Miss Gorman?"

"Certainly."

I invited him to sign the register, led him into Slumber Room A, and stayed right by his side as he approached the casket. Miss Nina was still wearing her beige visitation outfit, and I hoped Mr. Richards didn't stay long. I had to change her into the pink dress and restyle her hair before Miss Nila came.

It never pays to second guess what a mourner might do. I've seen them try to lift the decedent from the casket, and I've seen them stand several feet away, scared to be too close to a corpse. I've heard them scream at the top of their voices, and I've not heard them because they were silent as stone. Mr. Richards went to none of these extremes. He stood comfortably near the casket and leaned over close to Miss Nina's face, but he didn't try to reach in. In a polite manner, he puckered his lips and pressed them against her forehead.

Mr. Richards turned his back to Miss Gorman and faced me. "Which one is this?" he said. "I've forgotten what the paper said."

"This is Miss Nina."

"I never could tell them apart. I dated Nina in high school and they used to get a big kick out of tricking me. Sometimes I'd take Nila to the movies thinking she was Nina. I fell in love with them. That was the problem. I was in love with *them*. I would have married either girl, but I couldn't decide which one." He nodded toward the body. "When I realized I'd never be able to convince either of them to marry me and leave the other, I married someone else."

He laughed roguishly. "Maybe if we'd been born fifty years later, I could have lived with both of them."

Not knowing how to reply, I mumbled, "Maybe."

"My wife died last year, and I've been checking obituaries every day since then, waiting for one of the Gormans to die so I could come back to St. Mary and claim the other one."

"I thought you said you dated Nina. She's the one who died."

"It doesn't matter. I told you—half the time when I thought I was dating Nina, she'd send her sister instead. When do you think Nila will be here?"

"The funeral isn't until one o'clock. She won't be coming in for several hours."

I assumed that Miss Nila wouldn't want to see anyone until she was properly dressed for the service, and he made me uncomfortable. Something seemed wrong with a man who didn't care which sister he captured. Who knew? He was still obsessed with the twins all these years later, but Miss Nila might not be interested at all. She could despise him for running out on her sister so long ago, or she might have disliked him back then and still feel that way.

"I guess I'll leave and come back closer to one o'clock."

He smiled and actually made a courtly bow to me before he

left.

"Do you remember Arthur Richards?" I asked Miss Nila as I used a curling iron on her hair. I'd finished with Miss Nina just in time for Odell to help me re-casket her and wheel her back to Slumber Room A.

"Artie Richards?" Her face lit up. "Of course I remember him."

"He came in this morning. I told him you wouldn't be here until almost time for the services. I didn't think you'd want to see anyone before you dressed."

"You were exactly right. I wonder what that old coot is going to have to say after all these years."

I grinned. "He's a widower. I have an idea he wants to court you."

"I couldn't do that. I'm buying a lot of new black clothes, and I'm going to be in widow's weeds for a year. I think losing your identical twin you've been with since before you were born has to be as traumatic as losing a man. I certainly don't plan to start dating my sister's boyfriend right after she died."

Odell and Otis had taken Miss Nina to the chapel while Miss Nila dressed. When we went in, several people were already sitting there, including my brother Bill and his wife Molly, who was Nina and Nila's niece. Each of them came to the surviving sister and offered condolences.

Otis approached me with an apologetic expression. "I know you want to go to Rizzie and Tyrone, but we're going to need you at graveside until it's over."

I'd hoped I could leave as soon as I'd finished with Miss Nila's makeup and hair. I wanted desperately to go to the hospital. Surely they would soon be able to operate on Maum's hip, and I felt I should be there with her family. On the other hand, the interaction between Miss Nila and Mr. Richards promised to be interesting. I wasn't disappointed on that score.

He showed up in a tuxedo and carrying roses!

• • •

Mr. Richards sat beside Miss Nila in the folding chairs under the canvas awning at the Baptist church cemetery. He'd managed to worm his way in front of her relatives and acted as though he hadn't been gone all those years. As we'd walked from the family car, he'd held her elbow like some men do. I hate that! I always feel like the man is going to surprise me by jerking my arm up. One of my brothers probably did that to me when I was a little girl.

Rev. Brandon was to the "ashes to ashes, dust to dust" part when tiny raindrops sprinkled the casket and those of us not under the tent. We've had thunderstorms spring up during funerals, and personally, I hate rain, even a gentle shower, during the graveside service. Everyone looked up at the sky. Not a dark, dismal, overcast day. Bright rays of sun. There's an old saying that when it rains while the sun shines, it means the devil is beating his wife. I don't believe that stuff. Sun signifies happiness. Why would the sun shine during domestic violence, even in Hades?

A gigantic hot-air balloon floated slowly, ever so slowly, not really very far above the church steeple. People standing in the basket leaned against the wicker sides and peered out at us. As we watched, the brightly striped red, blue, orange, and yellow balloon moved over to the church yard beside the cemetery as a slightly aged pickup truck and a shiny new minibus with a picture of a hot-air balloon on the side pulled up. The gondola settled to the earth with unhurried grace. I'd always thought the basket would be bigger than it was in comparison to the balloon.

Several fellows who'd piled out of the truck lowered and deflated the balloon before placing a stepstool beside the basket and beginning to assist passengers out. The bus driver stood by the bus sheltering himself from the increasing rain with a large umbrella with the same bright stripes as the balloon. Seems that hot-air balloon baskets would have an opening of some kind for riders to use. Not so. No doors. Each passenger climbed over the side of the basket, which was about four feet tall. The oldest and fattest people used the stepstool while workers helped them.

Before the balloon landed in the church yard, I'd wondered if this were some kind of homage to Miss Gorman, maybe arranged by Mr. Richards. Now that I saw so many passengers and that the older man, who appeared to be the pilot, wore a khaki jump suit with "Cloud Nine Balloons" on the back, I realized it was a commercial balloon ride. I'd seen Cloud Nine advertised on television and in the paper offering "unforgettable adventures, an opportunity to see the world from the heavens." They also promised champagne toasts and photographs at the end of their rides.

"What the hell do you think you're doing?" Odell shouted as he rushed to the basket. "We're in the middle of a funeral here." Arthur Richards jumped from his chair and ran right behind him.

Guess Odell didn't stop to think that a funeral director screaming across the graveyard wasn't any more dignified than a hot-air balloon landing during a service. I don't know what in the dickens Richards thought.

"I'm sorry," said the pilot. He was supervising loading the deflated balloon and the basket into the truck. "We don't fly except with good weather conditions. Just got word that this little rain is at the head of a storm front. We had to get these people down and back safely to their cars. It was all I could do not to land on top of a tombstone."

The church cemetery wasn't perpetual care, not limited to flat tributes. Angels and other marble and stone tributes watched over the graves. One obelisk was shaped like the Washington Monument. I imagine landing on that would tear a hole in the basket.

"Well, I don't appreciate you disrupting the service," Odell sputtered.

"The funeral of someone I loved," Richards grumbled.

"We have some control," the balloon pilot responded, "but when the wind isn't cooperating, I have to put this baby down where I can. You'd better finish up here, too. Our weather radio says we're going to have a big storm real soon." He looked up at the sky, which had now darkened with gray and black clouds, and then turned his back on Odell and Richards.

I knew it was coming. Like Jane, Odell doesn't like being told what to do, and to him, the man's turning his back on him was an insult. I could see where this was headed by the way the muscles on the side of Odell's face tightened and released, tightened and released.

"I don't need you to tell me how to handle a funeral," Odell barked and stepped forward toward the balloon pilot, who turned around then. That's when I noticed both of them had clenched their hands into fists.

I wished Otis were supervising this funeral instead of his brother. Odell isn't as polished as Otis. I've been told that, years ago, they looked identical and acted more similar, but time has changed both of them.

The other difference between the twin brothers is that Odell has a harder time maintaining the calm, controlled manner preferred in a funeral director, but he generally manages a professional composure. I feared this might be an exception.

Odell drew his fist back. I expected him to hit the pilot, but at the last moment, he pulled the punch, and then dropped his arm to his side.

Not so Arthur Richards. His fist shot out and landed squarely on the balloon man's chin. The blow brought a shocked look to both Odell and the pilot, but only for a few seconds. Odell grabbed Richards and was holding him to stop the altercation, but the balloon man hit back. His fist landed on Arthur's nose, and blood spurted down the front of his white tuxedo shirt.

I rushed toward them, hoping I could stop the fight with words. I certainly didn't plan to jump between them. By the time I reached the disturbance, the burly young men who'd loaded the basket and balloon on the truck had pulled the pilot away while Odell restrained Arthur Richards.

"I'm going to sue you," Odell declared. "You have no right to disrupt religious rites and show such disrespect for a cemetery and the people who are laid to rest here." He puffed up like a big old bullfrog.

"I'll sue you." The balloon pilot yelled. "Your employee hit me first."

I've seen my daddy turn the hose on fighting dogs. Water works wonders. About that time, the clouds opened up and dumped a flood of gigantic, biting raindrops. Before we could get all the mourners into their cars and the balloon people could get their passengers into the bus, the rain turned to hail— huge pellets of ice. I didn't see any sign of champagne toasts or photo opportunities. Guess Cloud Nine saved that for later.

As Odell slid into the driver's seat of the family car, he shook his fist and yelled at the balloon man. "Cloud Nine Balloon Rides. I know your name and you'll be hearing from my lawyer."

"You don't own this graveyard, but I see your sign on that tent, too—Middleton's Mortuary. You'll hear from my lawyer before you even have time to call yours. That man hit me first, and you're responsible for your employee's actions."

Odell didn't bother to explain that Arthur Richards didn't work for Middleton's. He put the family car in gear, and we wound our way out of the cemetery slowly because of the hail. In the seat behind Odell and me, Miss Nila dabbed tissues against the blood spots on Arthur's pleated shirt front.

"Excuse me, sir." Richards leaned forward and touched Odell lightly on the shoulder. "I'm an attorney, and I'll be glad to handle this for you."

"You're damn right you'll handle it," Odell snapped. "You hit him first, and you don't work for me." The rest of the ride was silent except for the hammering of hailstones on the roof of the funeral home's new Lincoln Town Car.

Chapter Ten

"How is everything?" I asked Rizzie when I called her first thing back at Middleton's. The storm had moved rapidly away, and its only remains were a steady rain.

"About the same. With the pain meds, Maum is sleeping a lot, and Ty's been on his iPad since you dropped him off. Thanks for buying him the new cover for it." I hadn't bought him anything. The cover on the iPad he'd won last night came with it, but I didn't tell Rizzie that.

"It's a little late for lunch, but I can get you both something to eat."

"No, Jane and Frankie came by a couple of hours ago and brought homemade lasagna and chocolate cheesecake for both of us. I'd been drinking Cokes, but she brought a gallon of sweet ice tea. We're fine. You shouldn't be out driving in this weather anyway. Why don't you take a couple of hours for yourself? Come later and you can just take Ty with you when you leave."

"Are you sure there's nothing I can do?"

"Positive."

Next call was to Jane to thank her for taking lunch to Rizzie and Tyrone. "You don't have to thank me," she said. "They're my friends, too."

"I'm glad Frankie's back. Did you two work things out?"

"Kinda. I promised to look into some other kind of work. Would that make you happy, too?"

"What do you mean? I've never had a problem with your

job. Roxanne earns you better money than you've ever made anywhere else and solves a lot of problems with transportation. You're my friend no matter what you do." I hesitated, then added, "I was even your friend back when you went shop-lifting."

"I don't do that anymore."

"And I'm glad, but I'd still be your friend regardless, and I guess I thanked you for taking lunch to Rizzie and Tyrone because it gives me some free time."

"What'cha gonna do? It's not really shopping weather, but if you do that, I'll go with you."

"Afraid not. I'm going to call Patel and see if that hail storm has shut down the fair for the afternoon." The elusive thoughts that had kept me awake during the night had finally surfaced.

"You go, girl!"

In some ways, I'm as modern as a girl can be. Ex-scuuze me, a *woman* can be. But as redneck and free-wheeling as Daddy was with the boys, my father raised me strict and expected me to act like a lady—his idea of a lady. It's taken several years for me to become comfortable calling men after only one or two dates unless, like last night, I was returning a call. I overcame that restriction over a year ago, so I called Patel.

"Yes," he answered instead of "Hello." At least he didn't say "Yellow" like Mike does.

"What's the question?" I asked.

"Callie, so good to hear from you. I've been thinking of calling you all day, but things are pretty messed up out here now. How are you?"

"Fine. What's wrong?"

"Vandalism. Somebody got past our security guards and splashed paint on several tents—mainly Mother Hubbard's places. It happened last night after we shut down. The sheriff's department was on the way when that big storm came through.

There are some deputies here now."

"Is Sheriff Harmon there?"

"No, some of his deputies." He hesitated. "I don't guess you could get away a while and come out? I'd invite myself into town, but I don't think it's advisable right now."

"Actually, I do have time. The funeral is finished, and I've talked to Rizzie. Everything's the same at the hospital. I thought of a couple of things I wanted to ask you. Are you certain I won't be in your way?"

"Positive. Just call me back on the cell when you're almost here, and I'll meet you at the gate so you don't have to pay to come in."

Of course, I went by my apartment to put on fresh makeup and change into khaki cargo pants and a black pullover turtleneck sweater. I pumped up my bra just a little more before I headed to the fairgrounds. When I was parked and called Patel, he assured me, "I'm on my way right now," and in a couple of minutes, he met me.

The Mother Hubbard's Beer Garden closest to the front gate was visible when we went inside. One whole side of the tent had been splashed with red, blue, orange, and yellow paint. It looked like the colors on the Cloud Nine hot-air balloon, but not neat like the stripes had been on the balloon. Someone had printed profanity—not kindergarten cussing, but *real* vulgarity—in those bright colors. I turned away to keep from even looking at "FU Badell."

"The deputy is sending a sketch artist back and wants me help them with pictures of those teenagers last night, the ones who gave the server trouble while you were here. Jill called me by name, and 'Badell' is probably how those kids heard 'Patel.' Didn't Tyrone say he'd seen them around?"

"Said he'd seen them around but that he didn't know them." I smiled my sweetest, most comforting smile. It had to be upsetting to Patel, seeing his property damaged like that, especially since the vandals had singled him out by writing their version of his name.

"I haven't had lunch. Would you like something to eat?"

"I haven't eaten, but I'd settle for a Diet Coke and more of those fried mushrooms for lunch."

We walked to another Mother Hubbard's Beer Garden tent because Patel had closed the one nearest the gate. We sat at a table near the kitchen area. A server I hadn't seen before took the order, and Patel slid back in his folding chair. "I'm glad to see you." His tone said as much as his words. "I confess this disturbs me, both the fact it happened and that it's exposed for everyone to see right at the entrance to the fair, but that storm makes it impossible to take that tent down yet. I have a spare because we set up more stations at some fairs that are larger than this, but I can't dismantle wet canvas."

"I'm so sorry." I almost added, "for your loss." It's a habit.

"What did you want to talk about?"

"That Red Star game. Do they ever use real guns instead of BB guns?"

"Not since I started working the circuit. I understand that many years ago, some game owners allowed shooters to use their own rifles, but not these days. Letting marks bring guns onto the grounds would be asking for trouble, not just from stray bullets, but we still have an occasional fight, and we don't need any more trouble than we get under normal circumstances. "

"It occurred to me that maybe the shot that killed that man in your kitchen was a stray bullet from another game, but I guess that's not possible."

"It might have been years ago, but not now. The forensics technicians made a big deal of checking the canvas all around that storage area for holes that would indicate the bullet was fired from a distance. To be honest with you, I can't figure how the man was shot in that small area of the tent."

"How big is the storage area?" I laughed. "Or should I call it Mother Hubbard's cupboard?"

His turn to laugh. "It's adequate, but not large enough to count a bullet fired inside as 'from a distance.' Would you like to see the size? I can show you how the tents are partitioned."

"Is this one just like the one where we found the body?"

"Exactly the same."

"Then, sure, I'd like to have a look."

Patel led me through the opening in the canvas between the dining area and the kitchen. The tent was a huge square with almost three-fourths of it taken up by dining area furnished with small tables and folding chairs. The back fourth was officially kitchen with over two-thirds of that space containing gas burners and refrigeration units.

On the far left side, which would have been comparable to directly behind where Jane sat in the other tent, a canvas wall divided the back area, creating a separate storage room stacked with cases of beer, crates of bread, and other supplies. If the killer had been inside that closed off section, no one would have seen him, but how and why would the victim or the shooter have gotten into the area without workers seeing him? Besides, the sheriff had said the bullet was fired from a distance longer than the inside of the storage zone, yet Patel told me that forensics people had checked the canvas walls and found no holes where the bullet had penetrated while traveling to the victim's body.

"And you're sure that the other tent is the same?" I asked.

"That's what I said." Patel's voice wasn't angry, but he didn't sound pleased that I'd question him about something he'd already answered.

We went back to our table and talked about the teenaged boys we'd seen last night. I asked him to tell the sketch artist that if he needed me also, just let me or Sheriff Harmon know.

I said that, but I didn't really want to be there when the artist arrived. He might tie me up with sketches that could take a significant amount of time. I didn't mind doing it, just not right then. I'd learned what I wanted to know, and I was ready to get back to the hospital and check on the Profit family. When I explained to Patel, he told our server to bring us a bag of food for me to take to "her friend in the hospital." I added that we only needed enough for one because Tyrone would be leaving with me, and we'd eat later.

Patel reached across the table and took my hand. "I'm sorry about your friends and their grandmother's accident, and I understand you need to go, but I do hope we'll see each other several more times before I leave." He released my hand when the server brought the food back to me.

"I'd like that, too, but this is a bad patch of time for me with my work and being responsible for Tyrone. You made him very happy last night, and he hasn't had much joy recently."

"He seems to be a good kid, and he listens, which is important. He showed that by how he followed my instructions at both games. I wonder if he knows more about those boys last night than he says though. Did you notice that he made a conscious effort not to look at them?"

"I saw that." I glanced down at my watch before standing. Patel walked me out of the tent. "I really have to go. Call and let me know if you learn anymore about who put that paint on your tent." I touched his arm. *Dalmation!* I was impressed by the hard muscle I felt. "I'm sorry this happened in our town." I stepped forward to walk back to the gate, but Patel stopped me, and the look in those dark brown eyes was as sincere as any I've ever seen.

"I want to tell you something. From the moment I saw you, I couldn't stop looking. I would have come out and introduced myself if someone hadn't needed me at another concession. You make me feel like a teenager myself—a sixteen year old who can't keep his mind off a girl. I really want to see you again before we leave this town. Will you let me know if your friend's condition improves and you have any time available to spend with me?"

Speechless. I'm hardly ever without something, sometimes too much, to say, but his declarations left me wordless for a minute or so. Finally, I nodded, and said, "I'll do that."

Chapter Eleven

"Gone."

Just like that ancient Ferlin Husky song Daddy used to listen to on his tape player.

They were missing.

When I walked into Maum's room, she was gone.

No Rizzie or Tyrone either.

My heart dropped to my stomach, and I thought I would hurl. What happened?

A nurse stuck her head in the door. "They just left for pre-op," she said and gave me directions to get there. I dropped the bag of food on the chair and tried to follow her instructions.

I only got lost twice on the way, but everyone I asked answered courteously just like the employees at Publix when I ask how to find some unusual grocery item for some new recipe Jane wants to cook. When I reached the pre-op cubicle, Maum lay on a narrow bed with Rizzie standing on one side and Tyrone on the other. She was awake and she looked as scared as I felt. Maum was ninety years old—not a great age to undergo a major operation.

"Dr. Redmond, the cardiologist, has okayed the surgery, but he doesn't want her to have general anesthetic." Rizzie's voice squeaked. When I'm scared, I get nauseated. Usually throw up. When Rizzie is frightened, her tone rises steadily. "He's sure a nice doctor. Acts like he really cares about her. He teased her that she'll be dancing in no time, and he winked at her. She smiled."

Maum shuddered and said something, but her voice was so soft that I didn't understand. I leaned over close to her. "They're going to cut me while I'm awake," she whispered, and her fear was so thick I felt like I could touch it.

"You won't know it," Tyrone assured his grandmother. "The anesthesiologist said they'll be giving you medicine so you can't feel a thing below the waist."

"What if the building catches on fire while I can't feel anything? I won't be able to get out." Maum looked more frightened by the moment.

Tyrone laughed. "First, it's not gonna happen. Second, if it did, they'd carry you out just like they would if you were asleep." He paused. "If they didn't, I would."

A very tall man in scrubs came in and stood at the foot of the bed. "I'm Dr. Sparrow," he said. "You can remember my name by thinking of a bird. I'll be doing Mrs. Profit's surgery."

"I didn't know they scheduled surgery this late," I commented.

"Surgeries take place twenty-four, seven," the doctor said, and then frowned and added, "but I'm glad this is my last one for today."

"Are you assisting Dr. Midlands?" Rizzie's tone mimicked her puzzled expression.

"No," Dr. Sparrow answered, "we both finished cases about the same time. I ran into him in the hall and told him about my last one for today which is a very difficult procedure that I know he's had quite a bit of luck with in the past. He said that this was a simple hip replacement, and I talked him into trading."

I didn't like it. Not one little bit.

I didn't like those doctors switching patients like little kids swap marbles, and I didn't like him referring to "luck" with operations. Luck wouldn't do any good if the surgeon were less than competent. But Maum needed the surgery as soon as possible, and like so many people, I'm a little in awe of medical professionals. Besides, as much as I loved Maum, I wasn't related, so, contrary to my usual behavior, I kept my mouth shut while the doctor walked out.

When I'd been with relatives before they went to the operating room, medicine was injected into their IV lines to make them groggy before they went under. Since Maum wasn't being put to sleep, I wasn't surprised when masked and gowned attendants took her away on her gurney while still wide awake. I assumed that in addition to her lower body being numbed, Maum would have some of that medicine that makes the patient forget without going to sleep.

"Come with me," a nurse told us. "I'll show you the waiting room. The doctor will come out and talk to you there as soon as the surgery is over. Mrs. Profit will go to recovery when it's completed, and you'll be able to see her for a few minutes then."

Don't know where I got the idea that surgery was a nine-to-five job. The waiting room was full of families watching television and pacing around the room. A gentleman asked us the name of our patient and gave Rizzie a slip of paper with a number on it.

Suspended from the wall was a television screen with patient numbers in a column on the left. Beside their numbers, messages showed like "in prep," "in surgery," or "in recovery." A lot of them displayed "back in room." Using the number Rizzie had, we could track Maum's progress.

"Is there a cafeteria here?" Tyrone asked the lady at the desk.

"It's closed, and I'm sorry to tell you the snack machine is empty, but there's a drink machine over there." She pointed.

"I'm starving," Tyrone complained.

"There's a bag of food up in Maum's room. Patel sent it to Rizzie," I said.

"Did you bring me one?" he asked.

"No, I thought you and I were going home and have dinner together."

"Go back and get the bag," Rizzie told him. "I'm still full

of the food Jane and Frankie brought us this afternoon when they stopped by."

The surgery took forever. The clock didn't say that, but it lied.

"What's happened?" Tyrone said when he brought the bag of goodies down from Maum's room. "There are people in the room packing up Maum's stuff." He burst into tears. "Did she die?"

"No," I consoled him. "They'd tell us if something like that happened."

An older man on the couch beside where we sat looked over at us, obviously listening to every word.

"What floor was the patient on?" he asked.

"Fourth, the cardiac floor."

"Did I hear y'all say she's having a hip replacement?"

"That's right."

"They'll move her up to the orthopedic floor then. It's been remodeled and is extra nice. She'll go there from recovery. Don't worry. They'll tell you where she's going before she comes out of recovery."

"How do you know?" Tyrone asked, and Rizzie must have thought his questioning the man was rude even though Tyrone's tone wasn't disrespectful, because she frowned at him.

"I know since my wife has heart trouble and had her left hip replaced last year, but she fell again, and now she's getting a new right one, too." He sighed. "The worst part of it is rehab. She'll have to go back to a rehab center for physical rehabilitation. Last time, she just wanted to go home so bad, but she had to do rehab. They always make hip replacement patients go to rehab."

"Is it here in the hospital?" Rizzie asked.

"No, there are several places for it. The social worker will go over what's available with you, and the family or next of kin gets to decide which one."

Next of kin? That brought thoughts I didn't want to think.

I was hoping the man would tell us more, but a woman in

green scrubs came and told him his wife was in recovery and he could see her, so he followed the attendant away.

Tyrone wolfed down a corndog and a sausage dog while Rizzie and I watched some boring documentaries on television. The three of us jumped up when Dr. Sparrow came into the room and looked around. He spotted us but didn't walk over to us. He spoke from a distance.

"Oh, there you are," he said. "The surgery is over. She did fine, and she's in recovery now. Once they get her situated, a nurse will come for you and you can see her for a few minutes."

"Did . . ." Rizzie began.

"I'll see you tomorrow," the bird said and left. His name was "Sparrow," and he was a big, tall man, and he made me think of a buzzard.

We waited and waited, then waited some more. Finally, someone came and told us to follow him to recovery.

Maum tried to smile when she saw us, but she wasn't very successful. "I could hear it," she said softly. She grimaced. "I could hear them sawing my bone." A tear slipped down her cheek. "And now I can't move my legs."

"You'll be able to move your legs when the medicine wears off, but it's over now," Rizzie said. "They've fixed your hip. When that heals, you'll get some rehab and be good as new."

"Rehab? Rehab?" Maum whimpered. "That's a nursing home. I don't want to go to a nursing home. I want to go to our house."

"Don't worry. We'll get you home just as soon as possible."

A nurse checked the monitors that showed Maum's blood pressure and all kinds of things. They'd put a morphine pump on her, and it was obvious Maum didn't understand about pressing the button when her pain was too bad. Maum kept trying to touch her nostrils. The oxygen prongs in her nose must have been uncomfortable.

I didn't see what harm we were doing just standing there, but after a few minutes, the nurse hurried us out. As we left, I heard Maum say, "Can't they stay with me just a little longer? I don't want to be alone."

"Don't worry, Maum. We'll be waiting for you," Rizzie called back to her as they hustled us out and told us Maum had been assigned to room 803 and to go up there and wait for her.

When we got off the elevator, we saw a small open alcove with drink and snack machines. They worked, and we bought a ton of stuff to eat and drink.

Good heavens! The room on the orthopedic floor was like a hotel suite. Not that I've ever stayed in a hotel that big or fancy, not even on my honeymoon. Instead of just a bedside table and one chair beside the patient's bed, this was an L-shaped room with two recliners, a love seat, a full couch that opened into a double bed, and a little round table with a Tiffany lamp on it.

Plus more closet and drawer space than I have in my entire apartment, and a bathroom big enough for a party. I looked around to see if there was one of those locked refrigerators that have mini-bottles, imported beers, and snacks in it. I stayed in a motel with one of those and when I checked out, they charged me an arm and a leg for a beer and a little bag of pretzels.

Rizzie stretched out on the couch while I curled up on the love seat with several pillows and Tyrone kicked back in a re-cliner holding the television remote and flipping from channel to channel.

When the attendants brought Maum back, we all gathered around her to be sure she knew we were there, but she was asleep.

"She was awake in recovery, but we adjusted her pain meds on the pump just before we came to the room," one of the men told us. They attached the automatic blood pressure cuff to her arm, adjusted the oxygen prongs in her nose, and filled her water bottle before leaving us alone with her.

"Go on home," Rizzie said. "I'm staying through the night, but there's no reason for all of us to stay here."

"Are you sure?"

"Positive. I'm just going to stretch out and watch TV."

"Will you put the top down?" Tyrone asked before we reached the elevator. I agreed, and then he questioned, "Is it too late to go to your dad's? When Jane and Frankie brought the food, they said your brother John is still in town, and they're going to play music again tonight."

"No," I answered, "it's not too late. They'll be picking until at least midnight."

The ugliest house in the county—that's what I call the house I grew up in because it has dark gray shingles and black trim—the colors on sale when Daddy redid the exterior. By looks, it would be the perfect home for the Adams Family, but it was more like those happy sit-coms because when I was a child, and even now, that house was always filled with love, laughter, and music.

I parked behind John's BMW, and as Tyrone and I walked up to the porch, music spilled out of the open front door. Daddy and all of my brothers play guitar, and several of them play mandolin, bass, and Dobro or the resophonic guitar as some folks insist on calling it because Dobro is a brand name, but in our case, the one at the house actually is a Dobro brand, so I just keep calling it the Dobro like we always have. Our only fiddler is John, and Daddy and I are the only ones who play banjo. I hadn't bothered to stop by my apartment for my banjo because Daddy has lots of spare instruments.

Besides music, the smell of food wafted out, too. I recognized that odor—Daddy's catfish stew. He makes all kinds of stews, including squirrel with potatoes and gravy, but my favorite is his catfish.

A lot of the music played at the Parrish place is bluegrass, but we mix in a little folk and country as well as gospel. Tyrone and I walked into "Uncle Pen," with Daddy, John, Mike, and Bill picking and singing. When they finished the song, they welcomed Tyrone and asked about his grandmother. I got

Tyrone and me each a bowl of stew and a couple of slices of bread. Some people in the South eat crackers or cornbread with catfish, but our family eats sliced bread.

Daddy and The Boys were all drinking beer, and a cold one would have been perfect with the stew, but I got Tyrone a Coke and me a Diet Coke.

"Do you think your dad would let me have a beer?" Tyrone asked when I handed the can to him.

"Are you out of your mind?" I said. "No way would he let you drink beer at his house. You're underage, and he might not even if you were old enough. I'm way past the legal age to drink, and he doesn't let me have beer when I'm around him."

"I've seen you and Rizzie drink beer," Tyrone protested.

"Not in front of my daddy, you haven't," I answered.

"Hurry up eating and grab a banjo," John called. He's my oldest brother and the one I'm closest to. I hadn't known he was coming up from Atlanta. I looked around for Miriam and their two kids, but they weren't there. John had been feeling unloved and unappreciated recently, and I hoped he'd just come for a visit and not because he was leaving his, at least up until now, first and only wife.

Jim's in the Navy and never been married, but track records for the rest of us aren't good. Frank, Mike, Bill, and I have all been divorced—two times for Mike. At least none of us had kids that we knew of. Well, I would have known, but so far as we knew, John's son and daughter were Daddy's only grandchildren. Of course, that might be about to change for Frankie, and maybe down the road for Bill. He married again not long ago, but unless Molly straightens him out, she'll kick him to the curb before they celebrate their first anniversary.

When I'd finished eating and Tyrone had begun his second bowl of stew, I grabbed Daddy's banjo, but John took it out of my hand and gave me a guitar.

"Before you play banjo, sing 'One of These Days' for me," he said. That's an old song written by Earl Montgomery and recorded by several artists, but my favorite is the one by

Emmylou Harris with the Nitty Gritty Dirt Band. My brothers all say I sound like Emmylou, but I think they just say that 'cause they love me. She recorded it long before I was married, but I played the dickens out of that song for months before I got my divorce and changed jobs. Then, when I moved home for a while, I sang it every time we picked. That song said exactly what I felt at that time.

Mike had been playing doghouse bass, but he leaned it up against the corner and grabbed the electric bass. Daddy took mandolin; Bill, on Dobro; John, on fiddle; and I had Daddy's Martin guitar. With me singing lead and The Boys backing me up, we sounded pretty good even though Frankie's tenor voice would have added a lot. I assumed he was somewhere with Jane and that Bill's wife Molly was with her family since they'd just buried her aunt. Bill probably should have been with her. He is definitely not the most thoughtful husband, but then, I'd rather make music with my family than hang around with in-laws, too. We tore that song up:

I won't have to chop no wood
I can be bad or I can be good
I can be anyway that I feel
One of these days

Might be a woman that's dressed in black
Be a hobo by the railroad track
I'll be gone like the wayward wind one of these days
One of these days it will soon be all over cut and dry
And I won't have this urge to go all bottled up inside
One of these days I'll look back and say I left in time
Cause somewhere for me, I know there's peace of mind

I might someday walk across this land
Carrying the Lord's Book in my hand
Going cross the country singing loud as I can
One of these days

But I won't have trouble on my back
Cuttin' like the devil with a choppin' axe
Got to shake it off my back one of these days
One of these days it will soon be all over, cut and dry
And I won't have this urge to go all bottled up inside
One of these days I'll look back and say I left in time
Cause somewhere for me, I know there's peace of mind
There's gonna be peace of mind for me, one of these days

"Are you crying, son?" Daddy asked.

I looked to see who he was talking to and I'd have dropped my teeth if they'd been store-bought when I saw that John wasn't picking and singing. He was picking and crying.

"Are you okay?" I asked.

"I got something in my eye," John mumbled and wiped his face with the back of his hand. "But I understand now," he mumbled. "I understand why Callie played and sang that song so much when she left Donnie and moved back from Columbia." He attempted a smile, but it didn't really work. "Callie, you've become a woman in black like it says in the song. Tell us, Callie, do you have peace of mind now?"

Speechless seldom describes me, but it did then. Was I happier than I was at the end of my marriage to Donnie? Yes, but the qualifier was that I was happier than before, but not *really* happy. I didn't admit it, but I was like almost every woman my age. I wanted to be wanted, but not for any fly-by-night affair. Recently, I'd thought that my new Donald and I were finding peace of mind together, but I hadn't heard from him in almost three weeks. I smiled and lied, "Yes, I believe so."

Mike laughed, "While we've got you talking, tell us if you're being bad or being good these days."

I faked a slap at him and said, "What's next?"

"I want to do 'Will the Circle Be Unbroken,'" John said. "I'll take the lead."

I traded the guitar for a banjo and we broke into that old standard by A. P. Carter that's been recorded by danged near everybody including the Allman Brothers years ago. John started off strong.

I was standing by my window
On one cold and cloudy day
When I saw that hearse come rolling
For to carry my mother away

Will the circle be unbroken
By and by, Lord, by and by
There's a better home a'waiting
In the sky, Lord, in the sky

I said to that undertaker
Undertaker, please drive slow
For this lady you are carrying
Lord, I hate to see her go

Will the circle be unbroken
By and by, Lord, by and by

John's voice cracked and he broke down sobbing. We all stopped, and Bill went to his side. "What's wrong?" he asked.

"I miss her so bad," John said, "I just miss her so bad."

"Then you should have brought her with you," Daddy said.

"What are you talking about?" John.

"Miriam. If you miss her so bad, you shouldn't have left her home." Daddy.

"I don't miss Miriam at all. I miss Mama. Am I the only one who misses Mama? Nobody ever even mentions her. Do you even remember her?" John.

Daddy said, "It's been over thirty years, but I still miss her. Why do you think I stayed home and raised you young'uns instead of running around with women? Calamine and the young ones can't possibly remember your mama, but I think about her every day. That's why I don't look for someone to court now. How can I when my mind's never far away from your mama?"

John slumped down on the couch, and we all gathered around him. Tyrone asked me, "What's wrong?"

"John's my oldest brother. He was twelve when our mother died, and he's missing her tonight."

"I didn't know your mama was dead. I just knew she wasn't here. Thought maybe she'd gone off to someplace more exciting than here like my ma did. I'm lucky my Maum was here to take care of me." Then, a tear trickled down his cheek.

What to do? I'm surrounded by sensitive men who cry, but who can blame anyone for crying over the death or absence of a mother?

John wiped his face with a dish towel Mike handed him and stood up. "Let's pick some songs that don't wring my heart out like a wet rag. How about 'She'll Be Coming Round the Mountain?' That'll work, won't it?"

Tyrone joined in singing that and the others he knew like "There's a Hole in the Bucket, Dear Liza." I was just glad nobody mentioned "Sweeter than the Flowers" by the Stanley Brothers. That song about "Oh, no, Mother, we'll never forget you, and someday we'll meet you up there" could bring tears to my own eyes, and I never knew my mother because she died giving birth to me.

Rain had begun before we left, and I wanted to get on the road before it turned into a storm. Daddy seemed to have a hard time letting us leave. He kept saying things that delayed us. Then he filled two big jars with catfish stew—one to take to my place and one for Jane and Frankie. He also promised Tyrone he'd teach him to play guitar and insisted on lending us a guitar to take home with us so I could show the teenager a few chords before they got together for a lesson. No, the one he lent us wasn't a Martin, but it sounded good anyway.

Chapter Twelve

Spooky. I can't deny that I got a creepy feeling every time I had to go out to the new casket warehouse behind Middleton's. It wasn't the coffins. I used to go upstairs without that weird feeling when we stored them on the second floor of the house, but since Otis and Odell had the pre-fab building put in back, I did *not* like going back there, and I did *not* want to take Mr. Nathaniel Haeden in there to pick up a Gates Exquisite bronze with satin cream interior.

Not that the Middletons sent me in there very often. Most families select a casket from photographs Otis and Odell show them during the planning session. We kept the most popular choices in stock and Otis or Odell would bring what we needed from the warehouse. Occasionally, we "borrowed" something from a nearby funeral home. Of course, we didn't return that exact coffin. We'd order a replacement to return to the lender. Most of the time, I didn't see a casket until it showed up in my workroom waiting for the decedent I was working on.

The first time I went into the warehouse, I expected it to be set up like the display room had been upstairs with caskets open so customers could see the beautiful interiors. Not so in the warehouse. The caskets were closed and then covered with what Otis called "dust covers," but they were really packing blankets. I knew because I'm the one who wrote the check to pay for them.

Enough backstory about that big building jammed plum full of closed caskets draped with blue blankets. The next morning, after I dropped Tyrone off at school, Odell met me at the employee entrance. "Doofus (Odelleze for his brother) agreed to let Mr. Haeden from Haeden's Funeral Home in Beaufort get a Gates model 111399 Exquisite from us.

"They'll be sending a funeral coach (Funeraleze for hearse and Otis and Odell's preferred word) sometime this morning, but Otis and I are going to see our lawyer because that damn fool at the hot-air balloon place is suing us. They think the man who hit their pilot works for us. I don't even know who he is."

"I know his name."

"Good!" He pulled a scratch pad from his pocket and handed it to me with a ballpoint pen. "Write his name down but don't tell me what it is." I wrote "Arthur Richards" on the paper. He folded the pad closed without looking at it and shoved it into his inside suit coat pocket. "I want to be able to honestly say I don't know that man's name, but if this gets too deep, I'll sic the lawyers on the idiot who did the hitting." He scowled, but I knew it wasn't *at* me—it was *for* me, to show me his displeasure at having to deal with the situation.

"When someone comes from Haeden's in Beaufort, let them in and make sure they pick up the right model. I put a tag on it last night. Doofus and I should be back before too long, but you know how lawyers are. This might take some time."

Sure enough, the Middletons hadn't been gone ten minutes before "The Old Rugged Cross" announced someone in the front hall.

Mr. Nathaniel Haeden himself had come to get the casket. I'd seen him before, and he was one of those men that women don't get tired of seeing—broad shouldered, slim hipped and a constant smile. The only thing wrong with Mr. Haeden was his left hand. He wore a wide gold band on his ring finger. I shouldn't say "only" thing. He had an annoying habit of saying "You know?" after almost every statement.

"Morning, Miss Parrish. Good to see you, you know. May I see Otis or Odell?"

"They had to go out on business, but I'm authorized to

release the Gates Exquisite to you."

"Fine. Where should I take the hearse? Will we be loading it from the rear dock like the last time?"

"No, sir. We have a new warehouse in back. Pull around and you'll see it. We'll bring it out through the garage doors."

"I'll do that." He gave me a quizzical look. "Otis and Odell didn't happen to go to Beaufort for a pick-up, did they?"

"No, sir. It's a business matter, not a pick-up."

"I really shouldn't have even asked that, you know, but I saw in the paper that Nila Gorman used Middleton's for her sister Nina's services. You know, they actually lived in Beaufort, and I'd assumed we'd be who they called, you know. If we're doing something at Haeden's that's driving our customers to Middleton's, we want to correct it, you know."

Memory of Miss Nila telling me she'd come to Middleton's because she liked the way I did makeup filled me with pride. If my dress had buttoned up the front, I could have burst those buttons loose even without my wonderful bra, which I'd fully inflated this morning before heading out of the house. I really wanted to tell Mr. Haeden what Miss Nila had said, but I had enough sense not to brag on myself to Middleton's competition.

I detoured by my office for the garage door clicker, and then went out through the employee door while Mr. Haeden backed his funeral coach up to the wide automatic doors of the warehouse. He opened the back of the vehicle and pulled out the church truck, which isn't a vehicle. It's a portable stand that's used to transfer caskets to and from funeral coaches.

"Be careful walking," Mr. Haeden said. "The ground's still muddy from last night's rain, you know."

Seeing no need to enter the building through the office door, I stood between Mr. Haeden and the church truck, pointed the remote control, and pressed "open."

Shih tzu! I gasped in astonishment while Mr. Haeden spouted profanity that wasn't anywhere near kindergarten cussing. Matter of fact, it was post-graduate level profanity. The warehouse was a mess! The blue blankets that had covered each casket lay crumpled on the floor beside them. Lids stood open. Bright red paint defaced almost every one of the coffins—ruining even those with only a small spatter. Who wants to bury a loved one in a vandalized casket?

Three men stood inside the warehouse. I can't say that they looked like deer caught in headlights because I couldn't see their eyes very well with the ski masks covering their faces. Frozen in shock, we all just stood there—three people dressed in black with their faces covered and their gloved hands holding spray cans of paint. Mr. Haeden and I also wore black, but he had on a suit and I had on my Middleton's uniform—black dress and low heels.

A few minutes, or perhaps only a few seconds, we stood facing each other in disbelief. Suddenly, one of the masked three screamed, "Run!"

Just my luck—I stood between the door and the open space of the outdoors because the funeral coach blocked most of the way.

Whap! A runner knocked me over. I fell onto the open door of Haeden's hearse and then down to the ground. Mr. Haeden started to lift me to a standing position but stopped, pulled out his cell phone, and punched 911.

"Send an ambulance to Middleton's Mortuary," he shouted into the telephone.

"I don't need an ambulance," I protested. "Just help me up."

"No, you're bleeding, you know. Something could be broken, you know."

I managed to pull myself up by holding onto the hearse. I looked down. Blood saturated the front of my dress and had smeared onto the funeral coach. I wiped my face and said, "It's okay, Mr. Haeden. Just a bloody nose."

Too late. I could already hear the sirens screaming their way to us. Ambulance, fire truck, sheriff's deputy—they all arrived at the same time.

Mr. Haeden insisted on telling the paramedics that I needed to go to the ER. "She hit the corner of the back door of the hearse really hard, you know. She could have a broken bone or internal injuries, you know. I'd really like to have her checked out because technically she was injured by my hearse, you know."

Whoooosh. The sound was slow and drawn-out, kind of like the noise a balloon makes, not when it pops, but when it's leaking. *What's that?* I thought, and then I realized what it was.

My boob had sprung a leak. Well, not really one of The Girls. It was the bra.

I looked down and saw that I was lop-sided. The left side of my chest appeared round and firm and fully packed, but the right side was rapidly going flat. I felt like wrapping my arms around my chest so all the emergency workers couldn't see me, but I had to hold the gauze pad the paramedic had given me pressed to my nose. It still streamed blood which was landing on my chest, directing everyone's eyes to my uneven bosom. This was extremely upsetting. Whenever I wear my inflatable bras, I always measure to be sure The Girls are equal. At least with all the blood, the mud on my dress was barely noticeable, but my one-sided chest was definitely obvious.

"Callie Parrish!" The fireman we'd seen in the ER parking lot when Rizzie's van was on fire spoke around the fat cigar in his mouth. His eyes twinkled, and I knew he was amused rather than sympathetic.

"Dixon, I believe," I said.

"You got it. We're sent out anytime the ambulance goes, but I don't think you need a fire engine even if you do look like a hot mess."

"You'd better examine her, you know. I don't want any injuries showing up later, you know."

"The EMTs will check her out." Dixon laughed so hard the cigar shot out of his mouth. "Perhaps they have a pump that might help her."

"A pump? I don't understand, you know."

Dixon roared. "Don't you hear the air coming out of her chest?"

"Oh, my God! Does she have a punctured lung?"

"No, I think she'd be having trouble breathing if that happened." Dixon picked up his cigar from the ground, wiped it off, and put it back into his mouth. He waved to the other firemen and called, "We aren't needed here. Let's go."

I didn't think I needed to go to the ER, but I didn't want to stand out there where everyone could see my bosom (or at least the half that was still there) either, so when the paramedic wanted me to get in the ambulance, I climbed in and obediently lay down on the gurney. Just then, the deputy decided he needed me to answer a few questions so he could fill out his incident report.

Dalmation! He climbed up beside me.

"Let Mr. Haeden tell you what happened," I insisted. "I don't know any more than he does. We opened the warehouse door and three men came running out."

The deputy wrote that on his paper and asked, "You could see they were male?"

"I didn't really see they were men, but they moved like it. Young men because of the way they sprinted."

"So you're telling me they were men because of how they ran?"

"Yes, and they were all flat-chested, too."

"All the way flat-chested or just half-way?" The deputy laughed as long and loud as the fireman had.

"Out," the paramedic ordered. "We're taking her in to have a chest X-ray. She must have taken a hard blow there."

"Wait a minute," I said, wanting to defend my position on the gender of the vandals. "The one who yelled, 'Run,' definitely sounded male. Matter of fact, the voice seemed familiar."

"You're interfering with her medical treatment," the other ambulance guy said.

The deputy got out and the EMTs closed the ambulance with one of them in the back with me and one up front to drive.

"A chest X-ray?" I asked.

The man with me smiled. "Your brothers are friends of mine. I figured you wanted to get out of there—considering your wardrobe malfunction."

I admit I wondered if Dr. Donald Walters would magically appear when I reached the emergency room. He always had before, but not this time.

Going to the hospital wasn't as ridiculous as it seemed because they had to cauterize a blood vessel in my nose to stop the gushing blood. I removed the faulty bra when I put on the little hospital gown thingy for a chest X-ray and a head scan, both of which turned out to be totally negative. They dismissed me.

Too bad I'd gone to Jade County Hospital instead of Healing Heart where Maum was. I could have gone to her room to check on her, but, on second thought, I wouldn't want Rizzie to see me all bloody. I called Frankie and he showed up with Jane. He went bonkers that I'd been hurt. The blood all down the front of my dress scared him even though I assured both of them I was fine. At least he didn't see my lop-sided boobs because I'd put my bra into the bag the hospital gave me for my belongings while I wore the little open-back gown that let my tush peep out but didn't expose my pathetically flat chest.

As we left the hospital, in walked J. T. Patel.

"Well, hello," I said in the most chipper voice I could muster.

"Are you all right?" He didn't seem to mind the bloody dress, flat chest, and mussed up hair. "I called you and whoever answered your telephone said you'd come here by ambulance."

I confess that I'm not the most conscientious person when it comes to my cell phone. I had no idea where I'd left it, probably on my desk.

"I'm fine," I lied. I definitely wasn't fine about him seeing me like I looked. I turned toward Frankie and Jane. "Patel, this is my brother Frankie and his girlfriend Jane." I introduced them.

"I remember Jane. How are you today?" Patel responded.

"Thank you for buying my sausage dog that day," Jane answered. I knew Jane well enough to realize that was her way of letting him know she remembered him, too.

Patel laughed. "I apologize for offending you. I meant to be helpful, not insulting."

"I understand you and Callie went to Andre's," Jane continued, letting him know that I shared my life with her.

"It's a wonderful restaurant. Perhaps the four of us can have dinner there together one night before I leave." Patel turned on the charm.

Frankie's eyes about popped out of his head and he spouted, "Double-date to Andre's? Afraid not. I'm not a carny making tons of money off poor hicks at the fair. Can't afford a place like Andre's."

I was tired. I was still upset about the warehouse. My head had begun to hurt. I was embarrassed to be seen all flat-chested and bloody. Those are some of the reasons I slapped my brother in front of everybody going in and out of the emergency room that afternoon. Only some of the reasons, the main one was because I was ashamed of him, humiliated that a member of my family would be so rude to someone that was a total stranger to him but was someone that I liked more and more every time I saw him.

Frankie exploded, probably as much out of embarrassment as pain. I hadn't hit him hard, but I knew I was totally in the wrong to hit him at all. We weren't little kids anymore. Adults shouldn't go around slapping each other. Well, actually, neither should children, but it's more forgivable if it's not grown-ups. I had to confess, Frankie's explosion was in general, not directly aimed at me. "What's this all about?" he screeched.

"She's not herself. Let it be," Jane tried to intervene. "And if you touch her, we're finished."

"I'm not going to do anything to her, but I'm not taking her home either. Come on, we're leaving." Frankie grabbed Jane by the arm, and they walked toward the parking lot—quickly.

PMS. That's my explanation for what happened next, and I'm sticking to it, though I doubt that had anything to do with my actions. People falsely accuse PMS all the time, so I might as well do it, too. I burst into tears that turned to loud, gut-wrenching sobs. Patel reached out and took my hand.

"Come on, I'll take you home."

"Is there room for both of us in that little tiny car you drive?" I tried to joke, but the words got lost in the crying.

Big Boy was excited to see me in the middle of the day and just as happy to make a new friend. He licked Patel's hands over and over and couldn't get enough of him.

"He really likes you," I said after inviting Patel to have a seat on my tan-colored suede couch that Big Boy knows perfectly well is off-limits to him.

All the way from the hospital to my apartment, I'd apologized to Patel for the Parrish family showing our behinds in front of him.

"My turn to apologize," Patel said. "When the man where you work answered your cell phone and said you'd been hurt and taken to the hospital by ambulance, I rushed out of Mother Hubbard's without washing up. I probably smell like a great big corndog."

I laughed. Couldn't help saying, "Better a corndog than a horndog."

Big Boy presented his leash to Patel, who scratched his ears and asked, "Does he want to go out? If you want, I'll take him for a walk while you get a shower."

When I came back into the living room almost an hour later, Patel and Big Boy were watching television while the man fed the dog tiny pieces of banana MoonPie.

"I hope it's okay to let him eat this. He kept going to that cabinet and when I looked in, the only foods in there were MoonPies, and I didn't think you'd let him eat chocolate, so I got him one of these."

"They're for him." I noticed the smile on Patel's face and was happy that I'd taken the time to actually "do" my hair and makeup as well as dressing in another of my black work dresses.

"Would you mind taking me to Middleton's to pick up my car?" I asked.

"Not at all. Are you taking the rest of the day off? You probably should."

"That will depend on what Otis and Odell need. I definitely want to go to Healing Heart Medical Center and check on my friend and her grandmother."

Shih tzu! I thought it, didn't say it. "What time is it?"

"Almost five."

"I was supposed to pick up Tyrone at the school at three-thirty. May I use your telephone?"

He handed me his cell, and I dialed Rizzie's number.

She answered with, "Who is this?"

"It's Callie. My phone's at work and I've done something awful."

"Yeah, I heard that you've had quite a day. Busted your boob and hit your brother after trying to block three trespassers at work."

"All that and a bag of chips. I forgot about picking Tyrone up from school. Have you heard from him?"

"Otis picked him up and brought him over. He told us about the break-in at Middleton's. I think Ty's developed an attachment for you. He got all upset about you being hurt, and I was glad that he called a friend to pick him up from here. They're going to the arcade and Ty's spending the night with him, so you won't have to take Ty to school tomorrow either."

"I don't mind watching out for Tyrone, but he does need to see his friends. We have to remember he's a kid. I've got a ride back to work to get my car. If Otis and Odell don't need me, I'll come see you. If I have to stay there, I'll call you."

"Don't forget workmen's compensation. You were hurt on the job. Otis said Harmon wants to talk to you again, too." She laughed. "Better hope Frankie doesn't want to charge you with assault."

"Did Otis tell you about that? How did he know about me slapping Frankie?"

"He didn't. Jane called and told me. She said the man from the fair showed up at the hospital, too. Is he still with you?"

I ignored her question and asked one of my own. "Is Jane mad at me?"

"No, she thinks it's funny, said she'd felt like hitting him a few times herself.

Chapter between
Twelve and Fourteen

Anyone who's read a Callie Parrish Mystery knows I've never written a thirteenth chapter. I'm not superstitious, but I, Calamine Lotion Parrish, have not and will not write a Chapter Thirteen. This started with my first book when I thought about buildings with no thirteenth floor and why that might be.

When I was a child and went to Charleston or Columbia with Daddy, we rode in elevators. He always let me press the button for the floor we needed. I didn't realize there was no floor called the thirteenth. I thought they just left out the number between twelve and fourteen. I believed the thirteenth floor existed, but it must have been a place of secrets. That fascination with hidden doings behind closed doors and the slight fear those thoughts triggered probably account for my enjoying horror stories along with the mysteries I've loved since my first *Encyclopedia Brown* and *Trixie Belden* books.

This time, I have a really good reason for refusing to write a Chapter Thirteen. I just finished reading *The Thirteenth Child* by David Dean. I'm telling you: When I got to the last fifty pages of that book, I wet my panties. I'm not kidding. Problem was where I was reading. In bed. I was snuggled all cozy under the blankets reading when my bladder protested being full of Diet Coke, and I was too scared to get up and go to the bathroom by myself.

All one hundred and forty pounds of my full-grown dog Big Boy slept like a puppy on the rug beside the bed, but by the time I woke him up to go with me, it was too late. Of course, then I had to go to the bathroom for a shower, to the kitchen

to put the wet things in the clothes washer, and to the linen
closet for dry sheets. By the time we did all that, Big Boy had to
go potty, so I took him outside. He thought we'd go for a walk,
too, but I only let him hide behind the oak tree to do his girl-
dog squat like he always does. Made him come right back
inside. I felt a little guilty about refusing to walk him, so I gave
Big Boy a banana MoonPie.

    I'm not telling anyone why David Dean chose *The
Thirteenth Child* as the title of the book. Let 'em read it, and find
out for themselves. I will say it was a good decision, and I'm
going to read it again. I might read it in the bathtub so that I
won't have so far to go if it scares the—oops! I'd better not go
there.

Chapter Fourteen

"You understand that your grandmother will have to go to a rehab center for a few weeks, right?"

Rizzie nodded at Dr. Sparrow. He had arrived shortly after I did, and I could see that she didn't like the way he stood way across the room while he talked to her. He'd come into the room and never once looked at Maum even though she was awake. He didn't speak to her either. Just stood away from them, talked *at* Rizzie, and seemed in a hurry to leave.

"The social worker will give you a brochure describing local rehabilitation centers. She'll work it all out with you and arrange an ambulance to take the patient there, probably tomorrow, no later than the next day." He stepped toward the door. I didn't like the way he never called Maum by name, referred to her as "your grandmother" and "the patient."

"Excuse me, I have a question about Maum's stitches," Rizzie said and moved toward him.

"Save it for later. I'm in a hurry." He closed the door behind him.

"What do you want to know about her stitches?" I asked Rizzie.

"When do the stitches come out? Do we bring Maum back here?"

Cajones, chutzpah—whatever you call it, since Maum's accident, I had more of it at five feet, four inches than Rizzie had at almost five, eleven. I followed the bird to the nurses' station where he was chatting with a blonde who looked like her hooters might burst through the buttons on her uniform at any minute.

"Ex-scuuze me," I said. "Before you rushed out to chat with Blondie here, my friend wanted to know when Mrs. Profit's stitches will come out."

The doctor didn't look happy to be confronted, but he didn't tell me he was too busy to answer. "Ten days," he said. "My policy is ten days before the bandage is removed to look at the incision and remove the stitches."

I know I was out of line, but then, today seemed to be my day to be offensive, as I'd shown by slapping my brother. In for a dime, in for a dollar, so I continued. "That seems like a long time."

"And where did you earn your medical degree?" sarcasm dripped from Sparrow. "Infection is always a danger with surgery, and I wait ten days before opening the bandage in order to keep the incision site sterile."

"And will we need to bring Mrs. Profit back to the hospital or to your office to have the stitches out?"

"Neither. The rehab center will have someone on the premises to remove stitches."

His expression clearly showed that I'd irritated him and he'd had enough of me. He walked quickly to the elevator without a goodbye and left.

An hour or so later, a sweet-faced lady came into Maum's room. "Hello, is this Mrs. Profit?" she asked and smiled toward the bed.

"Yes, ma'am." Rizzie has good manners.

"I'm Natasha Marchant, the social worker. I've brought you a list of places that Mrs. Profit can go for her rehab." She handed a manila envelope to Rizzie. "Some descriptions and brochures are included in the packet. Look them over. Visit some. If you have any questions, call me. I've put a check by the ones your insurance will cover. When you decide which one you want to use, call me, and I'll see if there's a bed available."

She patted Maum on the arm and smiled again. "I hope

you feel better soon, Mrs. Profit."

Maum moaned and grimaced as Ms. Marchant left. Rizzie pressed the button on the morphine pump, and soon Maum was asleep. Rizzie and I sat at the little table and began looking at the list.

"Listen to this," Rizzie laughed and pointed toward one of the brochures. "This one has in-house movies, weekly live entertainment, and a gourmet restaurant, but it isn't checked on our list."

"Peaceful Pines has a check," I commented. "A friend's aunt was there. The family seemed pleased with it, and it's near Gastric Gullah."

"Doesn't matter if it's near the restaurant. I'm not going back to work until Maum is at home."

"Why don't I stay here with Maum and you ride over and take a look at Peaceful Pines?" I suggested. "I'd want to see the place before I committed to Daddy or one of my brothers going there."

"Even Frankie?" Rizzie teased.

"Even Frankie."

"I don't want to leave Maum. You go look at it. Should we call for an appointment?"

"I've been told that it's better to just show up unannounced."

"What if we choose Peaceful Pines and they don't have an opening?"

"Then we look somewhere else."

"You're right, Callie. It's just that Maum's so weak and feels so bad that I don't understand putting her out of the hospital only two or three days after surgery."

"It's the times, Rizzie. That's how it works these days."

I handed Rizzie the keys to the Mustang and settled into the recliner to watch television while Maum slept her morphine-induced sleep and Rizzie visited Peaceful Pines.

When she returned, Rizzie called Ms. Marchant's office and left a message on her machine.

Less than an hour later, a tall, slim gentleman wearing khakis and a brown striped shirt arrived. "I'm Bret Johnson. Ms. Marchant tells me that you've selected Peaceful Pines Health and Rehab for Mrs. Profit's rehabilitation. We do have a bed available for your grandmother, and I'm here to answer any questions you may have."

"When are visiting hours?" I asked. I've been in and out of a lot of nursing homes for body pick-ups, and any place that restricts when a patient can see their friends and relatives is suspect in my book.

"Twenty-four, seven. We encourage visitors at all times. You will be welcome to come in whenever you like, to sit in on rehab sessions, and guests may eat meals along with the patients. Of course, there's a charge for food, but it's reasonable. We take good care of our clients, and relatives don't need to spend the night with them, but if you want to stay, we provide a cot in the room. There's no extra charge for that. Do you have any more questions?"

"What about clothes? Will she need to wear anything special?" I could almost see Rizzie's brain clicking along, trying to process all of this. At the same time, I found it hard to picture Maum in a jogging suit.

"No, she can wear her regular clothing. Of course, you'll want to bring gowns or pajamas and a robe for nightwear, but since our goal is to help patients get back to normal daily life, we like for them to dress in regular clothing each day." He smiled. "Shall I hold the available bed for Mrs. Profit?"

"Yes," Rizzie answered.

"I'll stop by Ms. Marchant's office and let her know we're holding the bed and she can make arrangements for transportation."

"How soon?"

"That's up to the doctor."

I had agreed to get in touch with Patel after I left the hospital.

He'd suggested taking Tyrone and me to dinner. I really liked Patel, and I would have enjoyed an evening with him without Tyrone, but my headache had steadily grown worse during the afternoon and evening. I didn't mind having Tyrone at the house, but, to be truthful, I'd lived alone long enough that I cherished time alone.

As always, Big Boy met me at the door, all excited as well as eager to go out for bathroom business. I clipped his leash on and took him for an extra long walk. We were barely back inside my apartment when I heard a knock on the door. Okay, so I had a momentary negative thought. Had Patel shown up without calling since he'd learned where I lived? I don't like unexpected visitors. I peeked through the tiny hole in the door. Sheriff Wayne Harmon.

I opened the door, protesting immediately. "Not tonight, Wayne. I've got a bad headache."

The sheriff laughed. "Not tonight. I've got a headache. Who do you think you are? My wife?"

I laughed then, too, because the reason Wayne was divorced was that his ex-wife had turned out to be a nympho who'd never had a headache that prevented her being in the mood, whether Wayne was there or some other guy. For a long time, Wayne had been unable to even talk about her. It was good that he'd reached the point he could joke about her faults.

"Come in and sit down, but I honestly don't feel like giving you a statement tonight. Can't it wait until tomorrow?"

"I didn't come for a statement." That's when I noticed he held a pizza box pressed up against his side with his left arm while his hand clutched a paper bag. That right hand was virtually useless with the casts on every finger.

"For me?" I asked in a silly, little girl tone that came way too close to being a Magnolia Mouth accent and pointed toward the box.

"Yep, and look what else I have." He sat the box and bag on my kitchen table, then opened the bag. A six pack of Michelob, my favorite brand.

"Did they give you any pain meds?" Wayne asked as he tore off two sheets of paper towel and put them on the table to use for plates.

"No, I didn't have the headache then. Really, they just stopped my nose bleed and did some X-rays and a scan. No sign of anything broken and no sign of concussion." I knew that was what he'd been thinking because I've had several concussions in the past.

"Then I guess you can have one of these," he said and popped the top off two of the beers. He opened the pizza box and drew an imaginary line down the center of the pizza with his finger.

"That side's yours," he said pointing to the side closest to me. "I let them put those anchovies you like on it because I know you love them though I don't understand how anyone would want sardines on pizza."

We consumed that pizza in no time, and Wayne insisted on cleaning up after we ate. Not that dropping paper towels and beer bottles into the trash can takes a whole lot of time or energy. He put the rest of the beers in my refrigerator.

"Want another one?" I asked and pointed toward the closed refrigerator door.

"Nope. I'm driving."

We moved to the couch and I waited for the inquisition, but he didn't ask anything except did I need anything.

"No, what do you mean?"

"Well, I came to talk you into letting me take you to your dad's to spend the night. Whether you admit it or not, that business at the warehouse had to have been very upsetting or you would never have smacked Frankie. You wouldn't have done that otherwise."

"Does everyone in town know about that? Frankie embarrassed me in front of someone I didn't want to think I come from a family of rude rednecks."

"So you reacted like a rude redneck and socked him?"

"Yes, I did, but I'm not proud of it. I may even call and

apologize tomorrow."

"There's something else I want to tell you. Remember how whoever splashed paint all over the Mother Hubbard tent at the fairgrounds had tried to write Mr. Patel's name?

"Yes, but they misspelled it."

"Well, they didn't spell your name correctly, either. On one of the caskets way in the back, they wrote, 'For Calee Paris.'"

"What?"

"They tried to spray paint your name on a coffin."

"Oh, - - - -," and once again, I forgot to kindergarten cuss.

"Would you consider going over to your dad's now?"

"No, I think Big Boy would let me know if anyone comes here looking for trouble, and I've got a gun, you know."

"You know?" Wayne smirked. "Did you spend too much time with Mr. Haeden this morning? I talked with him and he just 'bout 'you know'ed' me to death."

"Listen, I'm really tired and now that my stomach's full of pizza and beer, I'd like to get a shower and go to bed. Would you mind?"

"Mind going to bed with you?"

"No, leaving so I can go to bed *alone*. What's got into you with all these suggestive remarks? You know I think of you like a brother."

"And I think of you as my little sister—most of the time. Speaking of brothers, I have a message for you from one of yours."

"Not from Frankie, I hope."

"No, from John." He hesitated and stared at me. "Don't get all upset. I know you're aware that he's been going through some kind of mid-life crisis, but I have good news from him. Before he headed back to Atlanta, I talked to him about counseling. My marriage didn't work and I don't think it was fixable, but John and Miriam's relationship has been too strong all these years to let it fall apart now. I also pointed out to him that he's been going through more difficulty about losing your mother, but if he leaves Miriam, he'll be doing something similar to his kids. He called me today and said that he's found a counselor who will work with him individually as well as work with the family as a group."

"That's the best news I've heard all day—not just today, but in a long time." I yawned right in his face. "Now my stomach's full and my mind's at ease about John, I hate to be rude, but could you leave and let me go to bed?"

"Yes, but I do want you to be cautious, watch what you do, and be aware of your surroundings."

"You've given me that lecture before. I know all that and about keeping my doors locked both at home and when driving as well as always looking through the peep-hole before letting anyone inside." I considered the whole thing for a minute or so. "I think this paint business is just teenagers pulling pranks."

"Some pretty expensive pranks. Mr. Patel's tent wasn't cheap, but the financial damage to Middleton's by ruining all those caskets is going to be astronomical, and Otis doesn't know how much insurance will cover."

"I still think it's just kids."

"That's what I'm afraid of."

When Wayne left, I walked Big Boy again, being very conscious of my surroundings. I'd made the decision not to see Patel that night, so I took a long, hot bath in peach-scented bath oil and put on that warm, comforting night gown. I climbed into bed and pulled the covers up to my chin the way Maum likes them before putting Patel's number on speed dial and using it to call him. I looked forward to just lying there all warm and secure and talking to him, but he didn't answer his telephone.

No answer at all.

I knew I should have called him earlier, and I had no claim on him to be upset if he didn't answer when I called several hours later than he probably expected to hear from me. I knew that, but it didn't make me feel any better. I just lay there and felt sorry for myself. Dr. Donald dumped me. Was Patel dumping me before we even got started?

We? There is no we. He'll be gone the end of the week.

It was all I could do not to get up and go into the kitchen to get the box of MoonPies.

Chapter Fifteen

The next day brought a wonderful surprise. Odell called before I was even out of bed and told me he and Otis had decided to give me a week off to "recuperate from that horrible thing that happened yesterday."

I called Rizzie and offered to pick up waffles for both of us and have breakfast with her at the hospital.

"No, don't pick up waffles. Bring doughnuts." Rizzie sounded excited. "Maum says she feels like a glazed Krispy Kreme."

This was also great news because Maum hadn't eaten much at all since she fell. I was out of the apartment in a flash and picked up an assorted half dozen doughnuts. Two of them were glazed; two, my favorites which were Boston crème with chocolate frosting; and two of Rizzie's preference, frosted maples with sprinkles.

My heart filled with happiness as I watched Maum eat a glazed doughnut. She didn't feel like feeding herself, so Rizzie pinched off tiny bite-sized pieces and fed them to her between sips of milk through a bendable straw. I noticed they'd given her two percent milk and wondered if the dietician really thought it necessary to limit the tiny woman's calorie intake. Then I realized the milk was low-fat because of her heart condition, not out of fear she'd gain weight.

Maum only ate one, but Rizzie and I both scoffed up two doughnuts apiece. I'd bought a newspaper, so Rizzie and I settled into comfortable seats, divided the *St. Mary News* between us, and read while Maum took a nap.

Our peaceful morning was interrupted by the arrival of the bird. I declare, it was hard to think of Dr. Sparrow by his name or as "the bird," when I considered him a buzzard.

Again, he stood in the doorway, not getting near any of us and not even looking at Maum.

"I've signed the papers for your grandmother to move to the nursing home for rehab," he said to Rizzie, without really looking at her either.

"When?" I asked.

"Today. Just as soon as the social worker can arrange transportation." He left without saying goodbye or anything else.

Apparently, Maum hadn't been in as deep a sleep as I'd thought. She sniffled.

"What is it, Maum?" Rizzie asked as she patted her grand-mother's hand.

The waterworks began. Not a few tears, waterfalls. Maum sobbed. She'd heard the bird say that she'd be going to Peaceful Pines Health and Rehab. The nurse came in and removed the morphine pump. She told us that the ambulance would be there at eleven o'clock to move her. Maum was more awake now than she'd been since the operation. In fact, she was wide awake.

"Peaceful Pines sounds like a graveyard," Maum said. "If I'm going to a graveyard, I want to go to Surcie Island and lie beside Paw Paw."

"It's not a cemetery. It's a place to help you learn to walk again."

"I don't need nobody to show me how to walk. Pull me up and I'll show you." She lifted her arms toward Rizzie, and it was obvious that just that little bit of exertion exhausted her.

"We'll follow the ambulance in my car," I said.

"You follow. I'm going to ride with her."

A little after ten, two men in uniform came to the room with a gurney. One of them held a clipboard, which he read from, "Mrs. Profit?"

"Yes," Maum answered for herself.

"We'll be taking you to Peaceful Pines."

I began rushing around trying to gather up flowers and other things we'd accumulated in the room in those few days. "We're not ready," I said. "They told us eleven. The nurse said she'd take out the IV's, and she hasn't yet."

The younger man laughed. "They told us ten, and I was afraid we were late. It's no problem. We'll wait at the nurses' desk while you get packed."

When we called them back in, they were as gentle as if Maum had been their own grandmother. They flirted with her tenderly, teasing her about her being a cougar and their date for the morning. She actually smiled a little, but the tears came again when the older one told her that Rizzie couldn't ride in the back of the ambulance with her. The younger one quickly assured her he would be right by her side and Rizzie could ride up front with the driver.

I followed them in the service elevator down to the ER exit and watched the men slide the gurney into the back of the ambulance. Then I went back upstairs and finished emptying the room of the Profits' belongings.

At Peaceful Pines, the CNAs welcomed Maum and helped settle her in Room 107. I'd finally managed to remember that CNA stands for "Certified Nursing Assistant." The room was a double, and the lady sharing the room with Maum smiled and said, "Hello, Roommate. I'm Hennie Owens. Glad to meet' cha."

There was some confusion about the bird's orders. When the nurse practitioner came in, she asked what pain medicine Maum had been receiving. She seemed surprised that Dr. Sparrow had sent Maum without pain med orders when they'd just taken off the morphine pump. She also questioned the fact that Maum was running an elevated temperature but had not been getting any kind of antibiotics. She assured us that she would check with Dr. Sparrow and get these matters corrected.

Maum's pain increased significantly during the afternoon while Peaceful Pines attempted to get additional orders from Dr. Sparrow. Finally, the nurse practitioner ordered Lortab for pain and the antibiotic Keflex until the bird responded.

We'd brought Maum to Peaceful Pines for rehabilitation, but I had a strong feeling that she'd been sent too soon. In the next few days, I spent more and more time with Rizzie by Maum's side with interruptions only to pick up Tyrone from school and bring him back to sit with us. I had the time off, and I hadn't heard from Patel. Sometimes I wondered if he'd gotten sick or hurt, but most of the time, I just wrote him off as not being as interested as I had thought or hoped.

After only three days at Peaceful Pines and only five days since her surgery, it was obvious that the Lortab wasn't controlling Maum's pain, which seemed to be worsening not by the day, but by the hour. Miss Hennie didn't bother us, stayed quiet in her bed or out in the day room in her slanted wheel chair. On the third day, as I waved to her in the day room when I entered Peaceful Pines, she motioned me over.

"I'm an old lady, and I try to mind my own business, but I want to tell you some things that you and Mrs. Profit's family might not know. I'm not a nurse, but they should be turning her every two hours to keep her from getting bed sores. Maybe the CNAs think you and your friend are turning her, but it's their job, and I'm not sure her grandchildren know how important it is. The other thing is that if she misses three days of rehab, they have to move her to the rest home part of the building. She hasn't been well enough for physical therapy, and she seems to be in more and more pain. That nurse practitioner is good. She takes care of me, but if I were Mrs. Profit's children, I would *insist* they have the staff doctor see her. That's within their rights."

I thanked her, went straight to Rizzie, and repeated everything Miss Hennie had told me. We didn't wait for the nurse practitioner to ask her for a doctor. Rizzie wanted me to go for her, but I insisted we go together. After all, I wasn't a relative.

We had just a bit of trouble finding out who to tell we wanted a doctor.

At the nurse's desk, I asked, "Who's the top person in charge here?"

"What's wrong?" was the response.

"I just want to know who's in charge?"

"Of what?"

"Okay, who's in charge of the nursing staff?"

"Is something wrong?"

"What do I have to do to get an answer to my question? If I need to scream it out loud, I will," I threatened.

I had to wonder if the charge nurse had heard of some of my shenanigans, because she told me to see the head of staff and where that office was situated. We went there where, when I asked if it would be possible for the staff doctor to see Maum, we were told that they were following the orders that came from Mrs. Profit's surgeon.

"I didn't ask you what the surgeon said!" I tried really hard to hold on to my temper. I hate, absolutely *hate* people who won't answer a direct question, people who don't seem to understand, but are really simply trying to redirect the questioner. It's a politician's trick that has no place in real life.

After a lot of discussion and my showing my flat behind because I hadn't worn my fanny panties that day to boost me up like Lopez or a Kardashian, the head nurse called the staff doctor and requested that he see Mrs. Profit that day. Rizzie and I went back to Maum's side and waited, and waited, and waited.

I was ready to go down the hall and show more of my butt than I already had when a pleasant young man came in and asked, "Is this Mrs. Profit?"

"Yes," Maum managed to say through a grimace.

"What seems to be the problem?" he asked.

"I hurt. I hurt so bad I wish I would die." Maum's weak voice could barely be heard.

The doctor turned to Rizzie and me. "I think we should

unbandage that incision and see what's going on."

What *was* going on was massive infection as well as an allergic reaction to the adhesive of the bandage. No wonder poor Maum was in so much pain. Her whole hip was deep scarlet, blistered, and oozing ugly stuff.

The staff doctor changed Maum to a stronger antibiotic and pain medicine, both to be given by IV. He also put her on nutritional milkshakes between meals and ordered her incision dressings to be changed and medicated several times each day.

Rizzie and I were optimistic these changes would put Maum on the road to recovery, but at the end of the week when I went back to work, we couldn't see much change in Maum's progress. About the only thing we'd really accomplished during the time I was off was to rent Rizzie a car. She'd insisted she didn't need one, but I wanted her to be able to leave Peaceful Pines if something happened to Maum when I wasn't there. I still hadn't heard from Patel, and I'd stopped calling his number.

Tyrone spent most of his time at Peaceful Pines when he wasn't in school. The patients in the day room seemed to like him. He spoke to all of them when he came and went, and they smiled at him every time they saw him.

The night I went back to work, Patel called.

"I owe you another apology," he began.

"For what? Standing me up?" I seemed to have forgotten that I'd been hours late calling him back that night. I also didn't seem to remember how angry I was when my brother was rude to him because now I was equally discourteous.

"No, for letting too much of my feelings show. I have to be honest. You remind me too much of Shea, my wife. You look a lot like her except her hair was darker, and your actions make me think of her. I realized the day you went to the ER that I was getting too involved with you too quickly. It wouldn't be honest to keep seeing you, knowing that some of my attraction to you had to do with Shea."

I didn't tell him that my hair is naturally darker than I was wearing it. I didn't really say much at all. Just thanked him for letting me know what had happened, disconnected the telephone, and cried.

Chapter Sixteen

"Callie, can you come to Peaceful Pines this afternoon?" Rizzie's voice sounded pathetic on the telephone. "They've scheduled a meeting about Maum at two o'clock. I'm so scared they're going to say she can't stay here. What am I going to do? I don't think I can take good enough care of her at home."

"I'll be there. Do you want me to get Tyrone out of school for the meeting?"

"No, I don't want him here."

No physical therapy during the weeks she'd been at Peaceful Pines. That suited Maum fine. She'd given up on ever walking again, and she'd grown tired of the occupational people wanting to guide her hands to brush her hair and teeth. "Nobody needs to show me how to use a brush. I been doing that ninety years. I broke my hip, not my head," she'd say. "I'm tired. If my hair needs combing, Rizzie or Callie will do it."

I'd been so excited the day she ate the doughnut, but when I took her doughnuts again, she refused them. She'd been turning down the mealtime trays, too. Even when they offered something she liked, Maum would only eat a bite or so and that had to be spoon-fed to her. She'd eaten that doughnut like she loved it, and she'd grinned when she finished it, though she refused a second one that day or thereafter.

I made it a point to get to Peaceful Pines early so I could visit with Rizzie and Maum before the meeting. When I went into her room, I was, as every time I saw her now, shocked at how tiny and frail she was. She'd always been slight, but now she seemed swallowed in the bed with the covers all tucked in around her neck to keep her warm. She liked to have her big white fluffy cat Tyrone had brought her across her feet. Said the stuffed animal kept her feet warm. I thought of her telling me, "Old bones are cold bones," the first time I met her.

The round table in the conference room reminded me of the ones we have in planning rooms at the funeral home. The ladies sitting there identified themselves: nurse, dietician, head physical therapist, and social worker. The one man was a financial adviser. Rizzie introduced herself, though she'd spent so much time with Maum that they all knew her. She presented me as "Ms. Parrish, my sister." That got a rise from several sets of eyebrows.

"Ms. Profit, we're here to discuss your grandmother. As you've seen, her condition is not improving." The tone struck me as accusatory, but it couldn't have been. Rizzie had done everything expected and more. I think I just felt defensive. I wondered if Rizzie was experiencing the same emotions.

They took turns speaking, and none of it was good. Maum's intake was far too low, even with the supplement shakes. The therapist said that there was nothing more they could do. "We feel that she's a candidate for Hospice Care," the nurse told us.

Rizzie's eyes bugged, and I'm sure mine did, too.

"Hospice? You mean she's dying?" Rizzie could barely be heard.

"Hospice is no longer called in just before death. It's now for people who aren't benefitting from medical efforts to cure them. Generally, that does occur about six months or so before death, but we've had patients who received Hospice care and then got so much better that they were removed from the Hospice program," the nurse explained.

"What would be different if Maum had Hospice?" I asked since Rizzie seemed speechless. "Are you saying she'd be moved from here but that someone would come in to help care for her?"

"No, she won't have to leave here if the family chooses to apply for Hospice care. She'll stay right here, but her treatment will be aimed toward keeping her comfortable. She hates the IV, and Hospice will remove it and give her meds by mouth. Recognizing that she can't be cured, her care will be aimed toward making her as comfortable as possible. Instead of whichever CNA is on duty giving her a bath and feeding her, she would have her own Hospice nursing assistant, the same one each day. She'll also have a Hospice nurse and doctor. I guess what Hospice really does is provide personalized services and support for the patient and family."

Rizzie still seemed in shock, so I continued asking the questions. "I thought Hospice was just for cancer and stroke patients. What is Maum's diagnosis? Infection and complications?"

"Technically, Mrs. Profit's diagnosis is Adult Failure to Thrive, which just means that she's not getting better."

"Does she qualify for Hospice?" Rizzie finally found her voice.

"Yes, she does, and the doctor here is willing to recommend her."

"Then do it." Rizzie paused. "What about the cost?"

The male financial adviser addressed that issue in length, but what it boiled down to was that with government medical assistance and the insurance Rizzie had blessedly purchased the week before Maum's fall, her Hospice charges would be covered.

"Then do it," Rizzie repeated.

The next day, Linda showed up.

Linda: petite, blonde, mid to late thirties, and an angel. She leaned over Maum and spoke in a loud, but soothing, voice.

"I'm Linda, and I'm your own CNA from now on. I'll be here every weekday morning to help take care of you."

She handled Maum's tiny body tenderly while bathing and

dressing her, and then shamed me by giving her a manicure that very first day. I'd neglected what should have been my responsibility. After that, for the first time since the fall, Rizzie could leave Maum for brief periods without worry or feeling guilty—so long as Linda was there.

I became optimistic. Maybe Maum wouldn't get well, but perhaps she'd stay the same or improve just a little.

It wasn't to be.

On Sunday, I took Tyrone out to Daddy's for the day. My father had taken a real shine to the teenager and was teaching him to play the guitar. In turn, Tyrone was showing Daddy and Mike how to cook some of the dishes served at the restaurant, which was still closed.

I almost waited until afternoon to go to Peaceful Pines. I really needed to do laundry, and the apartment wasn't exactly immaculate either. Not that it ever is. Cleaning is not what I do best. Come to think of it, I hadn't been doing what I think I do best very regularly since I moved back to St. Mary.

Instead of turning left off Highway 21 toward my apartment on Oak Street, I turned right and went to Peaceful Pines. They'd changed the code again, so instead of being able to punch in the numbers on the key pad to open the door, I had to wait for an attendant to let me in.

The sound was soft, but I heard it in the hall—Rizzie crying.

She was curled up in the chair beside the bed with Maum lying on it looking dead. The big, fluffy cat Tyrone had won for her at the fair lay across the foot of the bed as usual. I've seen enough bodies to recognize that look, but I saw that her chest was rising and falling slightly. Assuming that it had all just caught up with Rizzie, I hugged her.

"She's dying," she whispered.

"What makes you think that?"

"The Hospice doctor came in. He told me Maum is in something called the 'active stage of dying.' She called out for Paw Paw all last night. The not eating at all and sleeping so much are both part of it. Her body's just shutting down."

I spend a lot of time with people who are already dead, but I admit that I'd never experienced death, never been there when someone actually died. I couldn't see much difference between today and the past few days except that Maum lay even more still and was less responsive when Rizzie or I spoke to her.

Lots of people accuse me of being flippant, a smart aleck, and my mouth does get away from me often, but for once in my life, I had nothing cheeky to say. Buh-leeve me. My mind was in serious mode and my heart ached with pain.

"Don't you think I should get Tyrone?" I asked.

"No, just bring him this afternoon like we planned. They say this will probably take several days."

By the time I returned with Tyrone that afternoon, Miss Owens had been moved to another room. In place of her bed, there were three more chairs—one for each of us plus a spare. Maum was quiet and still. Rizzie didn't say anything to Tyrone about the prognosis.

As we left Peaceful Pines, Tyrone said, "Don't you think she might be just a little better? She wasn't crying and calling out like she has been."

I think my next words were the hardest I've ever spoken. "No, Tyrone," I said, "Maum's not better. She's weaker. She probably won't last much longer." Though she'd looked frail for some time, her condition was now more apparent—Maum was wasting away.

He was silent all the way to the apartment and had little to say that night through dinner and television. At bedtime, he asked, "Do you think we should go back and stay with Rizzie?"

"She told me that she'll let us know when she needs us and that your and my job is to see that you're in school every day, which reminds me. Have you done your homework?"

"Callie, it's Sunday. You know teachers don't assign homework on weekends."

The following days weren't very different until early Wednesday morning. I'd stopped by Peaceful Pines after dropping Tyrone off at school. Maum and Rizzie appeared to be sleeping. Rizzie had lowered the hospital bed and straightened the reclining chair so they were level with each other. She lay in the chair with her arm reached out holding Maum's hand as they slept, and they both seemed peaceful.

Linda came in quietly. Rizzie looked up and asked, "Oh, is it morning?"

I stayed in the room while Linda bathed and dressed Maum. She talked to Maum the whole time she worked with her, complimenting her and saying, "Gotta keep that beautiful skin soft and pretty," while she rubbed in lotion. She'd shown us how to hold a finger over the top of a straw and dip it into water to suction liquid into it. The liquid falls into the patient's mouth when the straw is put there and the finger is taken off. At first, that worked well to get a few drops into Maum's mouth, and she'd swallow. Now she didn't swallow at all. The straw had to be put far enough in the back of her throat to drip down like when the nurse gave Maum the morphine she was back on from a syringe. The morphine came at more frequent intervals and with regular increases in the dosage.

Maum's face contorted, and Linda pressed the call button. The nurse came immediately and squirted the morphine into the back of Maum's mouth. "Call me if there's any change," she said.

I'd brought coffee and pumpkin spice muffins, planning to eat with Rizzie, then head to the funeral home, but before we'd finished eating, Maum's breathing changed. I knew what that was. I'd never heard it before, but I've heard *of* the death rattle often enough to recognize it. Maum sounded like she was choking. I pressed the call button.

"I'll get some atropine for her," the nurse said. "The rattle is caused by saliva accumulating in her throat because she's not able to swallow. A few drops of atropine will clear it up."

Sure enough, she came back in a few minutes with another dropper, which she used to give Maum the medicine way back in her throat. The rattle eased and then stopped.

Rizzie is an impressive woman, usually confident and sure of herself. Right then, she looked like a confused little girl.

"It's really happening, Callie. She's leaving us," Rizzie whispered. She added, "The night nurse said they think hearing is the last thing to go, so I don't want to talk about her dying loud enough for her to hear me."

She stroked Maum's forehead and leaned close to her. "I love you," she said, "You're the best grandmother anyone could ever want."

"I'm going for Tyrone." I was scared to wait until school let out that afternoon.

"It may be several more days," Rizzie protested, but not adamantly, "and Maum wouldn't want him missing school."

"He has the right to be here and tell her how he feels about her." I've heard too many mourners at Middleton's wish they'd had a chance to say goodbye.

On the way to the high school, I called and explained to Otis why I hadn't arrived at work.

"Stay with those kids. I'll cover for you." His tone was as kind as his words.

Those kids? Rizzie and I are in our early thirties—grown women to elderly men who want to be our sugar daddies, kids to men like my daddy and the Middletons who view us as needing protection.

When the school secretary called Tyrone to the office, he must have thought Maum was already dead. Sorrow and disbelief filled his face.

"Did my grandmother die?" he asked.

"No," I answered, "but she's worse. The time is near, and I

knew you'd want to see her to tell her goodbye."

"Is she dying now?"

"The nurse said it could be another day or so, but she's definitely worse."

Maum's rattle was so loud that we heard it before we opened the door to her room.

Rizzie looked up. She was standing by the bed with her arm under Maum's neck, supporting her head.

"The atropine's not helping anymore. The nurse has gone to get an electrical suction pump to clear the saliva." She stroked Maum's forehead and said into her ear again, "I love you, Maum. You're the best mama and grandmamma anyone could ever have. Tyrone and Callie are here with me. We all love you." She motioned to Tyrone. He stepped to the other side of the bed and said, "I love you, too, Maum," while stroking her hand.

The death rattle stopped.

"The atropine must be working," Rizzie said.

I looked warily at Maum's chest and face for what seemed like several minutes but could probably be measured in seconds.

"No," I said, "she's gone."

We all stood motionless—Rizzie and Tyrone on each side and me at the foot of the bed. I'd thought Maum looked dead earlier, but now I saw the difference. I'd said she was gone, and she was. The essence of Maum was no longer there.

The nurse hurried in carrying a small pump.

"She left us a few minutes ago," I said. The nurse looked surprised, but she set the pump down on the bedside table and removed her stethoscope from around her neck. She listened to Maum's chest for several minutes, then said, "Her heart's stopped."

Tyrone shrieked. His face contorted, not in sorrow, but in rage. His fists clenched rock-hard. He stepped back away from the bed.

"I'm gonna *kill* that doctor!" Tyrone roared. "That bird surgeon did this. He didn't take care of her operation. I *hate* him. *I'll kill him!*"

Rizzie and I both moved to embrace Tyrone, to comfort him, but he shoved us away and stumbled toward the door. His balled-up right fist shot out and smashed a hole in the wall. A security guard ran up and grabbed the teenager, trying to restrain him, but Tyrone broke away from him and stormed through the lobby headed outside. Sight of the key pad by the door stopped him. He didn't know the new code. He crumpled to the floor and wailed. The elderly patients in their wheel chairs directed sympathetic smiles at him. They'd been around life long enough not to be surprised or scared of genuine grief.

Chapter Seventeen

Late Wednesday afternoon, Lizzie, Tyrone, Otis, and I sat around the conference table and planned the funeral. Since Rizzie wanted to combine Gullah traditions with some modern burial practices, I needed to e-mail Maum's obituary to the newspaper and post it on our Internet site as quickly as possible. The telephone had been ringing constantly as Gastric Gullah customers inquired about plans, beginning almost before we got Maum to the funeral home. In a lot of ways, St. Mary still functions like little towns of yesteryear. Someone at Peaceful Pines must have spread the word.

As soon as we'd filled in the form with details needed for the obituary, I excused myself from the planning session. Since Rizzie and I were friends, I didn't think it was my business to listen to the financial arrangements, but Otis had already told me he planned to give the Profits a discount. He knew Rizzie's restaurant had been closed during Maum's illness, but it was also good business for Middleton's. We'd never had many dealings with the Gullah community. Doing exactly what Rizzie wanted and being financially reasonable would benefit Middleton's in the long run.

Besides, I needed to get the announcements written. The newspaper obit would come out Thursday morning, but the information on our web page should be made available immediately.

The write-up was different from most of the ones I do. For one thing, though they knew that Maum's name was Hattie

Mae, neither knew her last name before marriage. Rizzie nor Tyrone knew the names of Maum's parents. I asked how they'd gotten past that requirement at the hospital and was told, "We said we didn't know." Chalk up a duh for me.

What we did know was that there would be no visitation at a church or Middleton's. The family would receive friends and relatives at their home Thursday night. A procession from the house to the Surcie Island Gullah Cemetery would begin at eleven o'clock Friday morning.

By the time I'd posted and e-mailed Maum's obituary, Rizzie had left. I drove one of Middleton's vans with chairs in it to Surcie Island to deliver a guest register even though Rizzie had declined any folding chairs. She refused them again at the house. The first thing she did was hand me a new red silk dress for Maum. I put it in the van so I wouldn't forget it.

"I need some information about the cemetery," I said. "We'll need to mark the grave that's to be opened."

"Well, walk over there with Ty and me now. I need to check it out anyway."

Large conch shells with deep pink throats outlined areas covered with crushed oyster shells. Though they varied in size, all the bordered patches were rectangular, the shape of graves. Some had homemade wooden markers or big stones with names and dates painted on them. Only one had a granite headstone—small, but obviously professionally made and engraved. Rizzie had told me the first time I'd been there a few years back that Maum had ordered the marker and had it brought to the island by row boat.

Each site was topped with lots of "gifts." A cornhusk doll and tiny wooden bowl sat on the smallest grave. Liquor bottles, homemade pipes, tools, perfume bottles, baskets, and broken pottery covered many of the adult graves. On my first visit, Rizzie had explained that the pottery was broken and scattered around intentionally. The handmade sweetgrass baskets were filled with weathered packages of snuff, chewing tobacco, and other small offerings. She had also stressed that Gullah people would never steal grave gifts out of respect for the dead and fear of supernatural retaliation.

Rizzie led the way to the only spot that was marked with a granite headstone. She looked down.

"This is my grandfather's grave," she said. "Maum will be laid to rest beside him." She looked around. "I've been negligent putting grave gifts here. Before Maum began working at Gastric Gullah, she brought presents to Paw Paw here every week or so.

I leaned over the one granite marker and silently read that Methusalah Profit had been dead over twenty-seven years. I thought again of the first time I'd seen this graveyard. Until then, I'd thought Rizzie's name was "Prophet," but she'd explained that it was P-r-o-f-i-t. Slaves had no last name before emancipation. When they were freed, some of them took their owners' names while others simply chose a name they wanted. Lizzie claimed her family chose Profit because they wanted to make money. Another time, she said that was a joke and "Profit" was a misspelling of the word "Prophet" because her ancestors could foresee the future.

She waved her arms around and told Tyrone, "We'll get the weed-eater and clip these plants and grass tomorrow morning. Can't have this place looking like this." He nodded yes, and she continued, "You're lucky, Ty. Years ago, we would have had to use a sling-blade."

"I can have the men clean the cemetery when they come to open the grave," I said.

"Not necessary. Our people have always dug our graves by hand. The islanders will do it out of respect for Maum. I'll add some gifts for Paw Paw, too, before Maum's service. Come on. Let's go back to the house. I wouldn't mind being here after dark, but it might bother you."

"Rizzie, if I work with dead people all the time, why would I be scared of a cemetery?"

"Never know."

As we walked, I asked, "Are you sure you don't want Middleton's to open the grave? You know we can take care of everything."

"I don't need *everything*. We've always buried our own, and that's what Maum would want, but like I said, I do want her embalmed. I bought the red outfit, and I want you to dress her and polish her nails to match. Our men sometimes build wooden coffins for our people, but I picked one at Middleton's. I want Maum brought to the house in her casket tomorrow. Our people will spend tomorrow night at the house singing and sharing stories about Maum, and in the morning, we'll bring her here. I understand that staying the night with her is called a wake and that embalming is necessary to do that. Traditionally, our funerals are quicker because we haven't embalmed. I want everyone to see how pretty Maum looks wearing red." Her dark eyes filled with emotion, and she sniffled. "Of course, most of her friends have already passed."

"Then you'll need the hearse back Friday morning?" I asked.

Tyrone answered. "The Gullah don't need a hearse to bring Maum from the house to her grave. The men will carry her." He cut a look at Rizzie. "I know I'm not quite old enough, but I want to be a carrier."

"Of course," Rizzie said. "I think Maum would like that."

"Can I make a basket of grave gifts?" I asked.

"Sure. I'll give you one of my best baskets. You go on back to town. Ty and I are going to clean up the house. Maum would have fits if anyone saw the house not looking spic and span. Call us in the morning when we can see her."

"I want to be with my friends," Tyrone pleaded. "Can I go off tonight?"

"If we get the house clean before too late, you can see your friends. I know it's been hard on you spending so much time away."

"Do you want me to come back and help clean?" I asked,

though everybody knows that if I ever win the lottery, the first thing I'll do is hire a maid.

"No, thanks. Ty can help with the heavy cleaning, and I'll finish up while he hangs out with his friends. I'd kind of like to be alone."

I'd like to say I had a date that night, but I didn't. I could have gone over to Jane's or out to Daddy's, but I spent the evening reading and talking to Big Boy about everything that was on my mind including Maum's death and why both Dr. Donald and Patel had dropped me. I watched the news on television, but it was just more about vandalism around town. I felt old because I thought, *What have times come to?*

Chapter Eighteen

I take pride in taking pride in my work, but I believe I tried harder for perfection with Maum than I ever have with anyone. I wanted her nails to be perfect; her skin, a warm dark mahogany; her hair, a soft, silvery gray. Rizzie hadn't said anything about it, but I added a touch of red lipstick after I put the red silk dress on her.

The telephone rang and when no one else answered it, I did. There's an extension in my workroom.

"Hello. Middleton's Mortuary. Callie Parrish speaking. How may I help you?"

"This is Dr. Walter Marshall Graham. I'm calling to inquire about the services for Mrs. Profit."

I opened my mouth to respond, but he'd only paused to take a breath. He continued without giving me time to utter a single word.

"The newspaper said you're handling the funeral but the family will gather at the Profit home for a wake Thursday night and process to the Surcie Island Gullah Cemetery Friday morning at eleven."

Again I opened my mouth. Again he spoke before I had a chance.

"That doesn't make sense. If they're going to bury her on that wretched island with all those broken dishes and old liquor bottles lying around, why is a mortuary involved?"

Finally he stopped long enough for me to talk. "Mrs. Profit's family requested that Middleton's take care of certain aspects of the service while also following some of their traditional customs."

"What exactly are you doing?"

"Sir, I'm not allowed to give out additional information. The obituary includes all the information that I'm allowed to tell the public." That was the truth. Anything more than what's in the obituary is private.

"I'm not the public. She's my older sister." He paused. I assume to let me think about it, and then he added, "And her name is spelled incorrectly in the paper and on your website. It's spelled H-a-d-d-i-e space M-a-u-d-e, not Hattie Mae. I'm coming over there to see her."

"Dr. Graham, we can't let you see her until her family okays it. Nobody can view her until then."

"I told you that I *am* her family. I haven't seen her in over twenty-five years, so I can understand not being named as a survivor, but she is, or *was* my sister!"

"Then you may see her after her grandchildren okay it." I said it as politely as I possibly could. I will never understand why people show up after their kinfolk die even if they haven't been around for years. Seems it would make more sense to be there while the loved one was alive. I'd never heard Rizzie nor Maum mention a surviving member of their family. They always talked like the three of them were the only ones remaining.

"I'm on the way over there *now*." He disconnected the phone, and I went back to work.

Rizzie and Tyrone had selected a pine casket with shirred crepe, cream-colored interior and swing-bar handles, which are long rods along both sides of the casket instead of individual hand holds. After Odell helped me casket Maum and place her in Slumber Room A, I pulled the door closed. I didn't bother to post Maum's name on the sign in the hall beside it because she wasn't going to stay there for visitation nor the service. I called Rizzie to tell her to come see if everything was to her satisfaction before we transported Maum to the house.

"Be there in about an hour," she said.

Recent days had been stressful, and I appreciated having some time in my office without a pressing responsibility. I was making a list of things I wanted to put in a grave gift basket for Maum when there was a sharp rap on the door.

"Come in," I said, wondering how Rizzie had arrived so quickly.

"Are you busy?" Sheriff Harmon asked.

"Not right now. Have a seat."

He pulled out his ever-present mini tape recorder as he sat down. "I understand Rizzie's brother threw a hissy fit when their grandmother died."

"Hissy fit" is Southernese for tantrum. Wayne's got a college degree and a whole lot of criminal courses beyond that, but it's hard to educate the Southern vernacular out of a true born and bred South Carolinian's vocabulary.

"I guess you could say that."

"Describe it. I've already talked to people at Peaceful Pines."

"Since when is it against the law for a boy to be upset when the only mama he's ever known dies?" Yes, my tone sounded defensive.

"How many times do I have to tell you? I ask the questions. It's your place to answer them, not ask more. Describe the boy's actions and words when his grandmother died."

"First, he fell all to pieces, crying and sobbing. Then he got mad. Tyrone blames Dr. Sparrow for Maum's death. He screamed that he hated him and he knocked a hole in the wall, but Rizzie is paying for that.

"Later, when Rizzie and I explained that Maum's age and general health made it hard for her to endure the trauma and surgery, he said he wasn't mad about that. Said he hated the way the doctor 'dissed' Maum by never looking at her or moving into the room. Said the doctor should have checked her incision, and Rizzie nor I could convince him that the doctor thought he was avoiding Maum having infection by not having the dressing changed." I thought for a moment. "But then, of course, when they finally opened the bandage, the wound was horribly infected."

"Did you see any of what he called 'dissing'?"

"I agree that doctor has the worst bedside manner I've ever seen. He'd step inside and stand right at the door. Never looked anyone in the face, never said 'hello' or 'good morning.' One time when Rizzie tried to ask a question about Maum, he told her he didn't have time to talk to her, he was in a hurry."

"Now think carefully, Callie. Did Tyrone threaten Dr. Sparrow?

I didn't want to say it, but Wayne's known me since I was a little girl, and he'd be able to tell if I lied to him. I said, "I told you he screamed he wanted to kill the doctor, but you know how kids are, especially at his age and as stressed as he's been."

"Where was Tyrone last night?"

"Rizzie let him go off with his friends. He needed to get away. Why are you asking all this?"

"Someone shot Dr. Sparrow last night."

I confess I wasn't overly shocked or overly sad about that. I hadn't liked the doctor either. Maybe a little pain and suffering would make him more sympathetic with his patients.

"How is he?" I asked out of nothing more than curiosity.

"Dead." Wayne went silent for a moment. I guess he was letting that word sink in. "Since it's a homicide, I sent him to Charleston as soon as he was pronounced and forensics had finished photographing. The body will probably come back here until his wife chooses a mortuary."

Otis and Odell need all the business they can get, but I have to confess I hoped Mrs. Sparrow didn't use Middleton's when the law released her husband's body. I'd disliked that man almost as much as Tyrone did, and I didn't want to work on him. I do the best possible job on anyone I work with, but, frankly, I didn't care how that doctor looked in his casket. Didn't matter to me if he even had a casket. Just throw him in a deep hole and cover him up.

"When is Maum's funeral?" Wayne's words brought me to the present.

"Tomorrow morning. We're taking her to the house this afternoon. They'll have a wake there all night. The funeral will be at the Gullah cemetery tomorrow."

"I hate to do it before they've buried Mrs. Profit, but if Tyrone threatened Dr. Sparrow, I need to talk to the boy as soon as possible."

"He's at the graveyard, cleaning it for his grandmother's funeral."

Wayne brushed his left hand across his forehead, making me hope he'd have the casts off his right hand soon. "I'll talk to you later," he said and turned toward the door before he stopped and looked back at me. "Have you ever seen the boy with a gun?" he asked.

I said, "Not really," and that wasn't a lie. I'd never actually seen Tyrone with a *real* weapon, but I'd seen him shoot stars out of targets with a BB gun at the fair, and I'd eaten meals at the Profit home where the main dish came from animals Tyrone had brought home from hunting, probably with a gun. I'd bet he hadn't been hunting with a bow and arrow, but some things are better left unsaid. Don't get me wrong. If I had any idea at all that Tyrone had actually shot someone, I would have told the sheriff, but I didn't think the teenager would hurt anyone, and I didn't want to add to his and Rizzie's grief.

The sheriff hadn't been gone long before "A Mighty Fortress Is Our God" played over the intercom. I was glad Wayne left before Rizzie came. I didn't put any stock in Tyrone's threat, but I felt that she didn't need to be worried about Tyrone being questioned about a murder.

Standing inside the front hall was a tall, trim man who looked like a black Andy Griffith on the old *Matlock* television series. Daddy is a big fan of *Mayberry*, and I'd grown up seeing him watch anything with Andy Griffith in it. The man wore a light gray, maybe even some shade of white, pin-striped seersucker suit. Seersucker is summer wear, but he looked like he probably wore it year-round, a part of his image. With his right hand, he twirled a fancy walking stick with a carved ivory handle. I can't swear that it was real ivory. Could have been plastic, but it looked antique enough to have been made before elephant tusks became protected.

"I'm Dr. Graham, and I've come to see my sister." His haughty tone matched his pompous appearance. His thinning white hair was partially covered by a white Southern gentleman's hat, and a diamond on his left little finger glistened.

"I told you on the telephone that I can't allow anyone to see Mrs. Profit until after her children come." This man flustered me. I admit that.

"They aren't her *children*. Teresa is her grandchild. I have no idea who this Tyrone might be. Is he Teresa's child?"

I almost explained who Tyrone was, but I realized that would be a violation of our privacy policy also.

"When will Teresa be here?"

"Any time now."

"I'll stay. I'd like to wait in the room with my sister."

"That's not possible."

"Then I'll just sit here." He almost gave me a heart attack when he stepped toward Slumber Room A where Maum lay, but he stopped by the door and sat in the ivory satin striped wingback chair.

Maybe I should have stayed there and talked to him, but I didn't want to. He made me nervous, and I was afraid his being there would upset Tyrone and Rizzie. I didn't know for sure that he wasn't lying. Rizzie had indicated she and Tyrone were Maum's only immediate family. I stepped down the hall, paused, and acted like I was adjusting a silk floral arrangement on a small antique table by the door to Slumber Room B.

Dr. Graham appeared very self-assured, but after a few minutes, he began to squirm. A little while longer, and he propped his cane against the wall and reached inside his jacket. I wasn't surprised when he brought out a silver flask. He unscrewed the lid, tipped the flask to his mouth, and then held it away from his face, staring at it. He placed the flask back to his lips. As he moved it down, his hand trembled, and he dropped the flask on the chair seat. I saw a little spill of amber liquid.

Appalled, he glared at it, and then screwed the top back on the flask and returned it to his inside coat pocket. He leaned over and examined the discoloration on the upholstery. Using a handkerchief from his pocket, he rubbed the stain vigorously while looking around to see if anyone were watching. Wiping it hadn't made the spot disappear. I could still see it from where I stood.

I made it a point to appear totally involved with adjusting each stem in the floral arrangement. Dr. Graham's anxious look changed to relief when he spotted a mauve throw pillow on the chair across from him. He stepped across the hall, grabbed the pillow, and carefully positioned it to cover the spot on his chair. Picking up his cane, he moved to the opposite chair.

Dr. Graham was barely seated when the front door opened to the notes of "Peace in the Valley." Tyrone entered beside Rizzie. He handed me an oval-shaped sweetgrass basket with an intricate handle and said, "Rizzie told me to choose a basket for you. Will this one do?"

"It's beautiful. Thank you," I said.

Several people I didn't know followed Rizzie and Tyrone in. Nowadays, most of the Gullah people dress just like everyone else, but, for this occasion, a lot of them wore African garb like Rizzie wears sometimes for Gastric Gullah's special catered events and other Gullahs wear on the roadside during tourist season in St. Mary when they sell their handmade baskets. The men who weren't wearing dashiki shirts had on modern suits but had added scarves and kufi caps, either knitted, made of Kente cloth, or embroidered. The women wore beautiful traditional print long dresses or skirts with fancy blouses.

"Tyrone and I want to go in first," Rizzie informed me and waved her arm at the folks behind her. "Our friends here will come in after we have a few minutes alone with Maum."

"Teresa?" Dr. Graham stood and walked toward Rizzie. He didn't use his walking stick. Must have been window dressing.

"Yes. Do I know you?" Teresa's expression questioned. She extended her hand as though expecting a handshake. Instead, Dr. Graham put his arms around her and tried to pull her into a tight embrace. Rizzie didn't pull away, but she didn't hug him back either. No smashing of the hooters against this stranger.

"I'm your uncle, Dr. Walter Marshall Graham."

"I don't know any Grahams."

"I changed my name when I left the island. Your grandmother was my sister, a lot older, more than twenty years." He actually had the audacity to look offended. "You were just a little girl the last time I went on Surcie to see my sister and her family."

"Wally?" Rizzie asked incredulously. "Wally? You're Maum's brother Wally? She thought you must have died when she never heard from you. She used to cry when she talked about you."

"I always meant to come back so she could see how well I've done in the outside world. I earned a doctorate and teach English on the college level." I guess that explained why he didn't have a Gullah accent. Must have taken a lot of work.

He spread his arms wide, delicately, as though he might perform a pirouette. "I'm the gentleman I always wanted to be." He patted his inside coat pocket as if assuring himself the flask was there. "I came as soon as I saw Haddie Maude died. I read the *St. Mary News* every morning on the Internet."

"She's been really sick. You would have thrilled her if you'd come to see her."

"I was so busy becoming successful that I just never made it." Pretentious pride oozed out of him. He turned toward Tyrone. "And who is this young man?"

"Ty is your nephew. Maum was raising him like she did me."

"Since I'm here now, I'll go over your plans for her rites. If she had insurance, there's no reason to bury Haddie Maude out on Surcie. I'm sure there's somewhere nicer here in town." He'd gotten rid of not just the Gullah accent; he didn't even sound Southern though he made such an effort to project that Southern gentleman image. More refined, but the same controlling tone that Jane complained about with Frankie.

"Didn't I read that she'd been working at some business? Gastric Gullah I believe it said." He chuckled. "I admit I could never have imagined Haddie Maude leaving Surcie Island, but I don't see why you'd take her back there. I'd like you to give her a nice funeral here in town."

Rizzie was speechless, but Tyrone wasn't.

"Uncle or not, you don't have anything to say about Maum's funeral. We still live in the house on Surcie Island. Maum wanted to be buried beside Paw Paw, and that's where she'll be. Right now, Rizzie and I are going in to see her." He stepped around Dr. Graham and toward Slumber Room A.

"I want to see her, too, but *this girl* wouldn't let me see my own sister."

"Just wait right here. You can come in with the others in a few minutes," Rizzie answered.

"I'm her next of kin."

"No, Ty and I are all of her kin. Everyone else has either died or run away like you did."

"Follow me," I said and led Rizzie and Tyrone to Maum's casket. Dr. Graham remained in the hall with the others.

"She looks perfect," Rizzie said. "You can call them in." She gestured toward the door.

I led the whole crowd into Slumber Room A where they *oo'ed* and *ah'ed* at the beautiful lady in the red dress with bright red polish on her fingernails. I get really irritated at people who say, "She looks just like she's sleeping." There's no way that I can work that magic, but in this case, it was true. Maum looked like she might sit up and ask for another blanket any minute.

Dr. Graham made a big production of his feelings—talking

to the body as though he'd just returned from a few days away. Rizzie held herself together well until they were about ready to leave, and then she burst into tears.

"I should have bought her that dress long ago," she sobbed.

"She wouldn't have worn it," Tyrone said. "She wanted it for this." He put his arm around Rizzie and kissed her on the cheek. And to think this was the kid the sheriff wanted to question about a murder!

Returning a loved one's body to the house for visitation used to be standard in the South; now it's only done occasionally. Whenever the family wants the body placed in the home for visitation, a representative of Middleton's stays with the decedent. Both Otis and Odell offered to spend the night at the Profit home, but I planned to be there the whole time anyway, so I volunteered to represent Middleton's as well as myself. I also asked that I not be paid for the time and that Rizzie not be charged for my attendance.

With my little overnight bag; Maum's basket full of manicure tools, hand cream, cuticle remover, and several shades of red polish; and a bouquet of red roses beside me, I rode in the front of the hearse with Odell to take Maum home for the last time. Yes, we played the CD player, and not hymns, but he would turn it off when we were near the house.

"What's with the guy in the white suit?' Odell asked.

"He's Maum's long lost brother who showed up wanting to take over everything."

"I don't think I'd try to take over *anything* from Rizzie or Tyrone Profit. They're strong people," Odell said. Mentally, I agreed with Odell that the Profits were normally resilient, but Maum's illness and death had knocked a big hole into their strength reserves.

Silence is rare between me and Odell, and my escape into my own world of thought must have bothered him. "Did Otis tell you that we're getting the man who died at the fairgrounds until he's identified?" Odell asked.

"No, will I be working on him?"

"Not until he's either released to his family or sent to a potter's field."

I'd never been to a potter's field burial where they put poor people who either have no relatives or their family won't claim them. Odell's continued words brought me back from my thoughts. "For now," he said, "we'll be keeping him in the cooler."

"Not going to embalm him like Spaghetti?" I asked.

"What do you know about Spaghetti?" he asked.

"Otis told me about him, and then I researched him on the Internet," I said.

"Okay, tell me what you know about him."

I grinned. I hadn't just casually looked it up. The story had fascinated me, and I'd known a lot about it from reading many articles about it.

"Spaghetti was the nickname for an Italian carnival worker who died during a fight in Laurinburg, North Carolina, in 1911," I said.

"Exactly right," Odell said. "Do you know the rest of the story?"

"Yes, his father came and gave McDougald Funeral Home ten dollars for embalming with a promise to come back and pay for a funeral. He never came back and McDougald kept the body there and let people look at it until an Italian man had Spaghetti buried."

"How much time did the body stay at the funeral home?"

"Sixty-one years. From 1911 to 1972."

"You are one smart lady," Odell said. "You should let Otis and me send you to mortuary school in Greenwood. We like your work, and one of these days, Doofus and I won't be wanting to go in and embalm all the decedents. You know neither of us has children either." He laughed and added, "At least, not any that we know of."

I shuddered. "I've said before, I don't even want to watch a prep, much less do it myself."

"Think about it." Odell paused. "What do you know about 'The Alton Mummy'?"

"Never heard of it."

"It's a lot like Spaghetti's story, but this man's nickname was 'Deaf Bill.' He was a hard-of-hearing fisherman who had a drinking problem and liked to get inebriated and preach on the Missouri and Illinois riverbanks. He was friendly with a Mr. Bauer, who owned a funeral home in Madison, Missouri."

"What happened?"

"Deaf Bill's drinking had him going down-hill and Mr. Bauer helped him get into the poor farm."

"What's a poor farm?"

"It's like what they used to call poor houses, and I guess the poor houses and poor farms were society's way to deal with homelessness way back when." Odell harrumphed, which is a sound he makes frequently. "If you go down to the Clark Creek Bridge, you'll see that St. Mary has a few homeless people these days."

"The sheriff said there are some problems that St. Mary has now that we didn't have before. Is that what he's talking about?"

"I don't know." He frowned, and I guessed that he was a little irritated that I'd changed the subject.

"What happened after Deaf Bill went to the poor farm?" I urged.

"Deaf Bill's condition had gotten so bad that he couldn't support himself fishing, so he went to the poor farm, and he died there. Bauer took the body and decided to hold it until he could locate Deaf Bill's family. That was in 1915 and they didn't bury the man until 1996, eighty-one years later."

"Wow!" I couldn't say the word I wanted to without breaking my vow not to curse, and I'd been slipping and using some non-kindergarten-cussing lately. When I taught school, I collected "Little Johnny" teacher jokes. Otis and Odell were too respectful to tell jokes about funeral homes, but they both seemed to have hundreds of anecdotes to tell me when we rode any distance.

We crossed the bridge onto the island, and Odell turned off the CD player. I thought about a horrible time a few years back when Jane was kidnapped from Happy Jack's Campground on Surcie Island, but we turned away from that part of the island and traveled the dirt road to the house. Rizzie had been watching for us because when we drove up, she came out followed by a lot of people.

It's customary to go into the house and check out where the casket is to be, so I did that. Rizzie had cleared a perfect spot right near where Maum always liked to sit in her rocking chair. She'd also tied a red ribbon from arm to arm of the rocker to keep anyone from sitting in her grandmother's chair. I slipped the roses onto the seat behind the ribbon. I remembered Maum telling us many times that she wanted her rocking chair placed on her grave.

With the mechanics of the hearse and the church truck (Funeraleze for a collapsible aluminum bier on wheels used to move the coffin to and from the hearse and sometimes used as a bier by attaching a skirt around it), Odell and I wouldn't have had any trouble carrying the casket in, but as soon as we were ready to roll, nine men and Tyrone stepped forward and stood with the casket—four men on each side, Tyrone at the head, and an elderly man at the foot. I noticed Dr. Graham didn't offer to help. The carriers took hold of the casket and had no trouble carrying Maum up the steps. Odell rolled the bier in, and the carriers set the casket on it. When he'd locked the casket onto the bier and opened the lid, I stepped forward to double-check that everything was okay inside the coffin.

I work at a mortuary.

I deal with dead people all the time.

I am a professional.

I cried like a baby.

Chapter Nineteen

Starving. I realize that's an exaggeration, but it's how I felt. Besides, hyperbole is my habit. The delicious smells of a ton of foods on the kitchen counters and table tantalized and reminded me I'd skipped lunch. Well, not really two thousand pounds of food, but a whole lot. I'd known that the Gullah people prepare a big meal for after a funeral, but apparently, the guests had brought dishes for tonight, too. Rizzie hadn't had time to do all that cooking.

Even though the Profits and I were good friends, as a representative of Middleton's, I couldn't just walk in and grab a plate of food. Odell circulated around the room, shaking hands and nodding his head in response to comments from the mourners. I looked around for somewhere to set my basket and overnight case. Tyrone solved the problem by taking them from me and putting them in Maum's bedroom. I followed him there and noticed that the dresser mirror was turned backward. I knew this was a custom in several cultures.

About an hour after Odell left, I realized that there would be no official meal; people just ate whenever they wanted. I filled a paper plate with Gullah food though there were all kinds of things that weren't Gullah. I'd missed Rizzie and Maum's cooking since Gastric Gullah had been closed despite the fact that Tyrone and I had eaten a lot of their dishes out of Rizzie's freezer. I hoped their friends were as good at cooking as the Profits. I sat on the floor in the kitchen. Rizzie had declined the funeral home's offer to deliver folding chairs, and every seat in the house was occupied by someone near Maum's age. Younger people all stood or sat on the floor. Dr. Graham looked around. Seeing no place to sit, he dropped the bouquet of roses on the floor and reached for the red ribbon across the seat of Maum's rocking chair.

"No!" Tyrone shouted. "Don't sit there."

I noticed that when Dr. Graham dropped the flowers to the floor, a few petals fell off. They looked like even the roses were crying or bleeding for Maum.

A big man wearing African clothing offered his seat on the couch to Graham. I had to stop feeling so negative about the man. He wasn't young, probably in his seventies, and I'd always been taught to respect my elders. After eating, I tried to listen to the tales and yarns about Maum. Her long-lost brother told stories about when he was a child, but since there was twenty years difference between him and Maum, they sounded more like anecdotes of a mother and son.

I must have looked tired. Rizzie told me that they would stay up all night, but that I could lie down in Maum's room.

"Won't your uncle be there?" I asked.

"If he needs to rest, he can take a nap in Ty's room."

About midnight, I excused myself and lay down on Maum's bed. Technically, as a representative of Middleton's, I should have stayed awake and within sight of the casket, but I didn't think there would be any problems if I took a nap.

The next morning, a lot of people had gone home to change clothes for the funeral.

Rizzie and Tyrone were polite enough to let me shower first in their one bathroom. I put on my work uniform—a fresh black dress and low heels, then I sat in the main room and welcomed guests while Rizzie and Tyrone got ready. Uncle Wally was the last one to use the restroom. He came out wearing the same suit he'd worn the day before. Most of the people who'd been there the night before were back, freshly dressed in either traditional Gullah garb or Sunday best clothes.

The clock's hands crept closer and closer to eleven. A few

minutes before the minute hand reached twelve, Rizzie stood by the casket and said, "If anyone wants to tell Maum goodbye, come now before we close the coffin."

I certainly didn't correct her and explain the difference between a casket and a coffin. I know the difference and use the words interchangeably myself. Everyone lined up and passed by Maum. When they'd all gone by, Rizzie and Tyrone stood by the casket for several minutes. They both kissed Maum on the cheek, then Rizzie turned and looked at me. I stepped forward and closed the lid just as Odell came in. He walked over to Rizzie and asked, "Are you sure you don't want to use the hearse?"

"No. Carrying our loved ones to their graves is a sign of respect." She turned toward me and said, "Get your basket, Callie."

The same men who had carried Maum into the house the day before took their places beside the casket with Tyrone at the front. I followed them outside and was surprised to see a white stretch limousine parked in the drive.

If I didn't worry it would be disrespectful, I'd say people poured out of that vehicle like clowns out of a car at the circus. Some Gullah, some not, but all wearing red shirts. Rizzie's mouth stretched into a tremendous smile.

"Who are they?" I asked her.

"Customers," she answered. "Maum used to tell everyone how much she loved the color red."

She turned toward the red shirts and called out, "Welcome. Thank you for coming."

The procession was led by Tyrone at the front of the casket, followed by Rizzie and some of the people who had been at the house, many carrying baskets or white ceramic bowls and pitchers. A big, muscular man between the people from the house and the red shirt people at the back carried Maum's rocking chair.

When we reached the edge of the cemetery, Tyrone stopped. He called out *Sez weh leh weh maa'ch een,* which was a

Gullah request for permission to enter the graveyard. They all paused for a few minutes, then walked toward the open grave. *We Maum w'ary. Wa dey een heaven. Weh peeceubble mo'nuh. Keep we fom ebil, bad mout'.* Rizzie said in a chanting tone. I knew what it meant. She'd said that Maum was weary and had gone to heaven, and that the mourners were peaceful and she requested that the mourners not be victims of evil spells or a curse. Then she added, *Yuh him,* and waved her hand toward the casket. I knew that this was her way of saying, "Here she is." "Him" is used for both males and females in Gullah. Rizzie had released Maum to go to her rest.

Even though the grave had been dug by hand, Middleton's had put our casket-lowering equipment and a canvas awning in place, but no seats. Rizzie must have told Otis or Odell, "No chairs," for there as she had for the house.

The Gullah mourners went forward and smashed bottles, bowls, and the ceramic pitchers around the grave site. Rizzie had told me this would happen. She'd said, "The broken glass and dishes 'break the chain,' so no one else in our family will die soon."

Under Odell's direction, Tyrone and the men placed the casket on the equipment. Rizzie and her friends spoke to the crowd, sometimes in Gullah, sometimes not. Odell lowered the casket, and the mourners took turns with shovels until the ground was level over the grave. The man carrying Maum's rocking chair with the roses back in place in the seat placed it at the head of the grave, right beside Paw Paw's marker. Those of us with baskets placed them on the grave. These were gifts for Maum in the afterlife.

A few more words in Gullah, and the procession reversed itself and returned to the house. Even more food had been added, and this time, the food was served as a meal with everyone sitting anywhere they could including on the front and back porches. I was on the front porch. Good grief! I knew Rizzie's a great cook, but it must be in the blood. Everything I tasted was delicious.

I noticed a plate piled high with food on the porch railing. No one touched it, so when I started back inside, I picked it up.

"Oh, no!" several people said. An elderly man in traditional clothing took the plate from me and set it back on the porch. *Saraka,* he said. "That is the food for the departed."

When Sheriff Wayne Harmon came in, I assumed he'd come to express his condolences. I could have kicked him when he went over to Rizzie and said, "I hate to ask this, but I really need to talk to Tyrone about where he was night before last."

"Can't this wait?" I asked with what I'm sure was a hateful look.

"It's all right," Rizzie said. "We'll go into Maum's room and talk there. I know I can be with Tyrone while you question him since he's underage and I suppose I'm his guardian now that Maum's gone. Can Callie sit in with us?"

"It's not usual, but I'd rather let her than argue with her about it."

"I'm Ty's guardian, and I'm asking her to be there," Rizzie said.

"That's something else we need to talk about," Wayne said. "So far as I'm concerned, you're an adult and head of this household now, so you're in charge of him, but you might want to see a lawyer and make guardianship legal."

"Ty," Rizzie called. "Come here a minute." The teenager's face showed dried tear tracks, but he smiled.

"What is it?" he asked. "Do I need to do something?"

"The sheriff wants to talk with you. Let's go in Maum's room."

The smile disappeared off Tyrone's face. The three of us went into the bedroom and closed the door.

"First, I'm not arresting you," Wayne said to Tyrone, "so you don't need the Miranda rights."

"Miranda rights? Arresting him?" Rizzie exploded so loud the mourners probably heard her in the front room.

"No, I just said I'm not. Tyrone, have you heard that Dr.

Parrot was shot the night your grandmother died?"

"Serves him right."

"I understand you threatened Dr. Sparrow at the nursing home.

"I hate him. I want him dead. If he'd taken better care of Maum, she wouldn't have died."

"Ty, we've talked about that," I interrupted. "Your grandmother was just too old and fragile to endure that break and surgery."

"I don't care. I hope that doctor *dies*."

"He did," the sheriff said. "Dr. Sparrow died on the steps of the hospital. A really fine shot in the front of his head. As hunters would say, "A clean kill.""

"Do we need a lawyer?" Rizzie asked.

"I hope not," Wayne answered, "but Tyrone needs to tell me where he was that night after your grandmother died, and I need to see all of his weapons."

The teenager's face fell. "I didn't shoot the doctor. I never even thought about that. I was gonna hire a root worker and pay for a spell."

"Tyrone Methusalah Profit! Don't you dare even think of finding a root doctor! You have no idea what you'd be messing with!" Rizzie's horror showed on her face.

"Maybe the root worker told you to hoodoo the doctor yourself with a bullet," Wayne suggested.

"I never found anyone who'd tell me where to find someone to work a spell. That's where I went that night. I heard there was a hag or worker on the next island over, but nobody would tell me anything."

"You said you were going out with your friends," Rizzie accused. "You told me you were meeting someone when you left walking. Tell the sheriff who took you looking for somebody to put a mojo on that doctor."

"Nobody. I walked."

"So you have no way to confirm where you were that night after you threatened to kill the doctor?" The sheriff looked worried.

"No, sir."

"Show me your gun."

"I can't."

"What do you mean you can't?" Rizzie demanded.

"I heard about somebody shooting Dr. Sparrow, and I knew someone would tell you about me threatening him, so I threw my gun off the bridge."

Chapter Twenty

If it hadn't been for Big Boy, I would have felt lonely. I'd grown used to having Donald at my place, and then he'd dropped off the face of the earth with no calls or anything. Immediately after that, Tyrone had stayed with me while Rizzie sat at the hospital, then the rehab center, with Maum during her illness. This afternoon, I was not only home with no one except my dog, I couldn't even go next door to visit Jane. She'd finally relented and let Frankie take her to the doctor to confirm her pregnancy.

One thing about my dog, he doesn't need any encouragement to show his affection. He couldn't get enough of having me all to himself. I'd curled up on the couch with a mystery novel, a Diet Coke, and a MoonPie, but Big Boy kept nuzzling his nose between my face and the book. I rubbed him in his favored spot. Well, it might not be his *very favorite* place, but it was his preferred location that I was willing to stroke—between his ears. All that did was encourage him to try to climb into my lap while he slobbered all over my book. Buh-leeve me. Almost a hundred and fifty pounds of Great Dane is too much to sit on me.

When he licked my cheek, I realized that Big Boy's teeth hadn't been brushed recently. That's when I thought about how long it had been since I'd washed or groomed him. As a tiny puppy, I'd sometimes taken Big Boy into the shower with me. That stopped when he was only a couple of months old for two reasons. He grew too big and he grew too old. Maybe spending my girlhood in that house of testosterone I called home created an overly active sense of modesty in me, but it seemed weird to be naked in the tub with Big Boy after he was older. Oh, I don't mean I'm overly modest when I'm doing the deed, but I definitely felt that way about bathing with my dog. It's like that time when he was a puppy and Donald and I were all hot and bothered, but I put a stop to everything because puppy Big Boy was watching us.

My bathing method for him now was to coerce the dog into the tub where I soap him up, then use the shower extension to rinse him. He tolerates this, but he's definitely not fond of it. I use his leash when I'm washing him because it gives me better control. I clipped it to his collar and led him into the bathroom. Smart? That dog's a genius when it comes to bathing. He seems to know whenever I even think about putting him in the tub and sometimes he runs from me or tries to hide. Of course, Big Boy doesn't play hide and seek very well. He can't seem to grasp how large he is and that whatever he chooses to take cover behind usually leaves his back end exposed.

I man-handled Big Boy into the tub and convinced him to sit. He looked just like a black and white spotted Scooby Doo. I opened the liquid soap with one hand while holding tight to his leash up near his neck. Talking to him the entire time, I covered him with suds. That big dog looked kind of cute, almost fuzzy. Just as I reached for the shower extension, Big Boy barked at a deafening volume and jerked loose from my hold on the leash. I grabbed for him, but slipped on the tile. He took off running out of the bathroom, barking like a mad dog.

Big Boy loped from room to room, barking constantly, and stopping occasionally to shake in that funny, almost spastic, way dogs do when they're wet and don't like it. I darted right behind him, shouting his name and grabbing for the dog or the leash. My living room furniture is suede. Imagine that after it's speckled with suds.

He dashed to the front door and pawed at it frantically, barking even louder. I finally caught his leash again. Possibly the least thought-out thing I could do was to open the front door, but I wasn't thinking at all. I threw the door open and Big Boy flew through it. He pulled the leash from my hand and took off down the street dragging it behind him while I sputtered his name mixed with some prize kindergarten cussing.

I had a friend back in Columbia who used to say, "I couldn't keep that dog under my porch," every time she broke up with one of the smooth-talking, womanizing bad boys that always caught her attention. Well, I couldn't keep this dog on my porch, in my yard, or on my street. I couldn't catch him. He ran off, dragging his leash behind him. My brothers had warned me that I needed to have Big Boy neutered because I wouldn't be able to hold him back if he encountered a female dog ready to mate. I wished I'd listened to them. Finally, I gave up and walked back to my yard.

Forget the kindergarten cussing. I let loose with a stream of at least college level, probably post-graduate, words that I wouldn't want my daddy or brothers to know I'd ever heard of, much less said.

Somebody keyed my car—a 1966 vintage Mustang convertible, the only thing I'd received from my divorce because my then husband was saddled with a ton of student loans he'd borrowed during his medical school education while I fed and supported him. I'd grown to love this car which now wore long, deep scratches into both blue sides. Most of the cuts were unformed slashes, but a few of them formed letters that spelled words as bad as the ones that poured from my mouth and the words I'd seen painted on the Mother Hubbard's Beer Garden tent.

I fingered the marks. They cut deeper than just into the paint. I had an idea that those gashes would be obvious even after the sides were sanded. No wonder Big Boy had been so rowdy in the tub. He probably heard whoever was in our yard vandalizing my car, and his sprint down the street was in pursuit of the culprit.

Trying hard not to cry, I went inside and called Wayne. I

know not to dial 911 for anything that isn't an emergency, and I wasn't quite sure if this qualified. It was a crime, but no person had been injured, just my blue baby.

When I got him on the telephone, Wayne said, "It's okay to call 911 to report something like a keyed car, but you can call me personally anytime. It doesn't have to be a homicide and there doesn't have to be a corpse." He chuckled and assured me he'd come over himself.

I've already confessed that I wasn't thinking very clearly. What if there was a body out there? With my track record, that wouldn't be a surprise. I decided to go back to the car and check it more carefully, then try to find Big Boy.

Not a body in the back seat. Not a body in the trunk. No bodies anywhere, but a weapon on the driver's seat—an ice pick, a regular ice pick like people used in my granny's youth to chip ice blocks in old timey ice boxes before refrigerators became common.

Two patrol cars pulled up in front of the apartment. Wayne got out first, followed by a deputy. They inspected the Mustang.

"Somebody did a real job on this," the deputy said. "Worst case of keying I've ever seen." They looked at the ice pick lying on the seat, but neither reached for it.

"Callie," Wayne said, "I can't stay. Officer Aaron here is going to fill out the report. I got a call right after I talked to you." He turned toward the deputy. "I know we would normally just do some printing ourselves, but with everything going on these days, call for forensics. We want this checked out thoroughly, especially that ice pick." He hugged me casually around the shoulders and left.

"What does the sheriff mean about everything going on these days?" I asked.

"Just more vandalism than this town's ever had before." The deputy turned away from me and used his radio to call for assistance from St. Mary's equivalent of CSI. Then he turned back and offered, "When we finish the report and the tech arrives, I'll help you search for your dog."

If I hadn't known better, I would have thought I *had* found a body in the car. The technician handled that ice pick as though it were a murder weapon. He photographed it from a dozen angles, fingerprinted it, and finally bagged it for evidence without ever touching it with his hands. His thorough examination of my car involved lots of photographs and black fingerprint dust.

"When you report this to your insurance adjustor, be sure to point out these holes in the roof of the car," he told me and pointed to some spots so small I hadn't seen them. Whoever had used the ice pick on the sides of the car had pierced openings through the ragtop cover.

Just as the deputy and technician prepared to leave, Jane and Frankie pulled into the driveway on their side of the duplex. My brother had forgiven me for slapping him and seemed genuinely concerned that something had happened to me that required law enforcement.

"What's going on?" Frankie called as they got out of the truck.

"Somebody keyed my car and poked holes in the top," I answered.

"It's a wonder they didn't flatten your tires while they were at it," Frankie commented.

"I thought that, too," the deputy said. "I'm thinking that whoever did this was scared off by the dog barking." He turned toward me. "You said your dog barked, probably while this was happening, right?"

"Yes." I didn't want to talk about it anymore. I didn't want to look at my poor blue baby right then. I reached out for Jane's hand. "What did the doctor say?" I asked.

"Who's here?" she asked. "When we came up, Frankie said he saw policemen."

"Just a sheriff's deputy and a forensics technician. Somebody keyed my car." I grinned at her and squeezed her hand. "What did the doctor say?" I repeated. "Am I going to be an aunt again?"

"We'll talk about it inside. Give me ten minutes, then come over, and we'll talk." Using her cane, Jane took herself to the door, pulled her key from her pocket and let herself into her apartment. Frankie stayed outside talking to the deputy.

"I'll help you look for Big Boy," my brother told me, but that proved unnecessary. Big Boy came home with his tail between his legs, squatted behind the tree to tee tee like a girl dog, then went to the front door.

I hadn't realized what he was doing, but my dog had tried to protect me and my car. I took him inside and gave him a banana MoonPie.

"I'm not pregnant. I'm crazy." Jane's staccato words surprised me. I'd decided that her moodiness, excess hunger, and morning sickness at all times of day meant she was going to have a baby. Her refusal to see a doctor before now had convinced me she just wasn't ready to deal with it. She'd always said that motherhood wasn't for her.

"That's not what the doctor meant," Frankie said, not in a mean way, but not in a loving tone either.

"He said it in nicer words, but what do you think he was insinuating when he advised me to see a counselor? You know what kind of 'counselor' he was talking about? A head doctor. A shrink."

"Calm down," I said, hoping to quiet her agitation while thinking about John and wondering if counseling was helping him.

"I don't want to calm down," she argued.

"It's that job of hers, that Roxanne. That's why she's always so stressed." Thank heaven Jane couldn't see that smug, superior expression on Frankie's face.

"My job pays my bills," Jane snapped. "And if there had been a baby, Roxanne would have had to pay for it."

"I work," Frankie defended.

"Whenever you feel like it."

I couldn't stand up for my brother on that one. He won't hold a regular job. Somebody always hurts his feelings or makes him mad, so he quits and works with Daddy when he needs him and does odd jobs for other people whenever they're available. John has suggested Frankie start a handyman business, but Frankie would rather live day to day.

"You've had physical symptoms of pregnancy," I offered. "What did the doctor say about that?"

"He gave me pills to regulate my cycle, and, like I said, he wants me to see a counselor."

"And that's what we'll do." I've never wanted to think one of my brothers could be a control freak, but I have to admit, Frankie sounded too authoritative when he said that.

"What can I do for you?" I asked. "Want me to order a pizza or something?"

"No, what everyone can do for me is go away. I'd like to be alone for a while. At first, I hated the idea of having a baby. I know visual handicaps don't keep women from being good mothers, but I was afraid. What if something happened to it because I couldn't see? What if I couldn't buy what it needed because Frankie doesn't have a regular job? There were all kinds of reasons why I didn't want to be pregnant."

She sniffled. "Now that I'm not going to have a baby, I wish I was. I know it's not reasonable, but because I didn't want children, I almost feel like I killed my baby."

"You have to remind yourself that you didn't *lose* the baby. There never *was* a baby," I tried to console.

"So why am I so sad?" Jane paused. "What I'd really like now is for everyone to go away and leave me alone."

"I'll cook dinner," Frankie offered.

"No, please just go to your father's house and stay there tonight. We'll talk tomorrow."

Nothing Frankie or I said convinced Jane to change her mind. He left to go to Daddy's with instructions to Jane, "Call me if you change your mind." The problem was that even that sounded bossy.

Chapter Twenty-One

Fully expecting to hear Jane crying through the night, I respected her wishes and went to my side of the duplex after Frankie left. Big Boy waited for me at my door with his leash between his teeth, and we headed outside for his business and a walk.

We were almost back to the apartment when the sheriff pulled up in his cruiser. "Hi," he said. "I looked at the report on your car. You're lucky the perp didn't get to your tires. My deputy thinks Big Boy scared them off."

"I wish he'd barked in time to scare them off before they did what they did," I answered. "Then again, maybe he did, and I just thought he was mad about the bath. Why did the technicians make such a big deal with the ice pick?"

"Ice picks have been used for homicides. Used to be thought to be a weapon of the Mafia. I wondered if the ice pick in your car might have been used to kill the kid at the fair."

"Was it?"

"I've been checking out a theft at a downtown church, but I did take time to call Charleston and ask the ME if that wound in the unknown's back could have been made with an ice pick."

"Could it?"

"Don't know if it could have, but it didn't. I felt like a fool when I remembered that the medical examiner recovered a .308 Winchester bullet that went from his back straight through to his heart. Barely stopped short of making an exit wound. I'm overworked and under staffed with all that's going on in this town."

"Maybe the ice pick didn't kill him, but the fingerprints may lead to solving some other vandalism like the churches."

"Robbing these churches isn't simple vandalism. The one I was at tonight had a bunch of silver stolen—candlesticks, offering plates, communion ware—over two thousand dollars makes it grand theft."

"I don't know a dollar amount, but repairing my Mustang is going to cost big bucks," I complained, "and the top will have to be patched, or probably replaced, unless I want to ride around with rain dripping on my head."

"You're right. Those holes will leak."

Wayne followed Big Boy and me back to the duplex and stepped out of the cruiser. "I want you to be extra careful with all that's going on these days."

"And who saved whom?" I asked and pointed to the cast on his right hand. I knew that was dirty pool to remind him that I'd shot the man who smashed five of his fingers with a sledge hammer, but I did it anyway.

"Are you carrying a gun today?"

"No."

"Enough said. Let's tell Jane to be extra careful. I'm glad Frankie is with her," he told me.

"Frankie's not with her," I said. "She found out she's not pregnant, and she wanted to be alone. She sent him home to Daddy's house."

"Maybe she'll let you stay with her. Let's talk to her about being cautious." He parked the car and walked up to Jane's porch with me.

We knocked. No answer. We knocked again. No answer. Wayne pounded the door with his left fist and yelled, "Jade County Sheriff's Department. Open up!"

Jane's voice asked, "Who is it with the sheriff's department? I need your name."

"It's Wayne Harmon."

"And I'm with him," I said, knowing she'd recognize my

voice.

A crack appeared between the door and the frame, and Jane's face peeked out. Well, it appeared. She can't peek.

"We came to advise you to be especially careful about opening your door," Wayne said, "but it seems you already are. Would you consider spending the night with Callie? I'd feel better about you two girls if neither of you is alone."

"*Girls?*" Jane shrieked. "We're both full grown women, and we can take care of ourselves."

"Can we come in?" I asked.

"Not unless the sheriff says I have to let you in," she answered. "I'm working, trying to earn enough to pay my bills."

At midnight, when I turned off my television, I didn't hear Jane weeping next door. I heard her purring. Actually, Roxanne was the one making that sound. I put a pillow over my head and went to sleep with Big Boy lying on the bedside rug.

"I Feel Good," James Brown awoke me.

"Hello," I probably said it with a question mark at the end. It was three o'clock in the morning.

"Callie, get dressed. I'm coming to pick you up." The sheriff sounded all business.

"What is it?" I panicked. "Has Daddy had another heart attack?"

"No, and I'm trying to keep him from having one."

"Where are we going?" I asked as I pulled on a pair of jeans and a shirt.

"We're going to Jade County Hospital, and I'll tell you about it in the car."

I knew Wayne had worked all day. What had him still out so late at night? I tugged on socks and shoes.

The doorbell rang, and I ran into the living room and opened the door.

"What if it hadn't been me?" Wayne's look matched his worried tone of voice. "You didn't even ask who was there."

"You said you were coming." I tried to justify my actions, but I knew I'd goofed.

"That doesn't mean someone else couldn't have been standing on your porch."

Just then, Jane's door opened and she stepped out. "What's going on?"

"You're not pregnant?" Wayne questioned.

"No, what's that got to do with anything?" Jane asked.

"I came for Callie to take her to the hospital, but since it's Frank, you may as well come, too."

"Frankie? What's happened?" I screamed while Jane yelled, "What's wrong?"

"He's been shot."

"Is he dead?" I demanded, thinking of the young man at Mother Hubbard's Beer Garden and Dr. Sparrow.

"He's not dead. They're cleaning out the wound. He did something stupid and it earned him a trip to the ER, a tetanus shot, some pain meds both there and later for home, and what's going to be one heck of a sore place when the anesthetic wears off. The surgeon says he'll need to stay at the hospital a few days, but I think he needs a relative there when he wakes up in recovery. Mike and I don't think your father is well enough to handle this tonight. I'm taking you to the hospital so Mike can go back to the house. Your daddy can see his dumb son to-morrow. Probably figures Frank went back to your house, Jane."

Wayne opened the door of his cruiser for Jane and me and then got in the car himself and headed off, I assumed toward the hospital, but I was too upset to notice.

"The hospital has to notify my department any time someone comes in with a gunshot wound. The dispatcher called me at home because he knew I'm longtime friends with the Parrish family."

"What happened?"

"It was a freak accident, but it wouldn't have happened if he'd been sober." Wayne frowned. "You know that old car your dad has down by the lake?"

"Sure. I keep telling him that if they can't repair the car, he needs to have it hauled away. Nothing trashier than old junk cars in people's yards, and I consider by the lake a part of Daddy's yard."

The sheriff continued. "Well, Frank went drinking tonight. Somebody in the bar told him that a .45 would crack an engine block. Since he had access to a .45 and an engine block, Frank went to the lake and shot one with your daddy's 1911. It didn't crack the block, but it came back and hit him in the groin."

"In the *groin?*" I couldn't help wondering if Jane's reaction was out of fear for his condition or fear of what damage the shot might do to his future chances of fatherhood.

"Don't worry." Wayne smirked an embarrassed grin. "The surgeon says his package is safe, but he's going to have to stay a few days. Mike was with him and took him to the hospital, but I'm sending him home to take care of your father."

"You mean the bullet ricocheted back at Frankie?"

"Sure did. A ricocheted bullet isn't as rare as some people think. The determining factors are the angle of impact and the nature of the surface it hits. A bullet can ricochet off water if it hits the water at the right minor angle, kind of like skipping stones across the pond. The problem is that a ricocheted bullet will commonly tumble in its path through the air and sometimes makes an entrance wound that's larger and more irregular because the bullet is deformed and has a significant amount of energy."

"I don't care about all that." Jane shook visibly. "How is Frankie going to be?"

"The doctor says he'll be okay."

We arrived at the hospital before Frankie went to recovery. The three of us sat around in the waiting room drinking coffee from a machine.

"Danged fool! I oughta beat his butt, and I just might

when he gets better." I knew that voice before I saw him. Daddy. He and Mike sat down with us.

"Thought we were going to tell him about this tomorrow," Wayne said to Mike.

"Pa reads me like a book." Mike shrugged his shoulders. "He knew something was wrong when I went in the house. He's always been able to do that to me. I never got away with anything growing up."

I'll say this for Frankie. When he woke up in recovery, he took it like a man. Both Daddy and the sheriff read him the riot act for stupidity and he made no effort to defend himself against their tirades. Jane didn't have much to say. I couldn't tell if, like me, she was just glad he was okay or if she were too mad to speak to him. For his part, Frankie apologized to everyone for doing something so foolish and making us all spend the night at the hospital instead of in our beds sleeping.

When I finally got home, I called Otis and told him I needed the day off. I seldom do that, but he did something he's never done before. He said, "No, I need you here today. Sleep a few hours, then come on in."

Chapter Twenty-Two

"Why me?" Okay, I confess. I grumbled. Otis and Odell stood there, glaring at me. Neither of them can stand whining. They both knew I'd spent most of the night at the hospital with my stupid brother before going home with my BFF to spend hours assuring her that Frankie's getting shot wasn't her fault. They knew all that, but they're both believers in strong work ethics and meeting responsibilities.

"Because it's your job," Odell growled and pointed to the sheet-covered corpse on my work table. Like I didn't know a body lay there.

"It's your responsibility." Otis tried to soften his brother's impact.

"I know Dr. Sparrow didn't kill Maum, but I never liked him, and I don't want to cosmetize him." My tone turned from complaining to pleading. "Are you going to fire me if I refuse?"

"We won't dismiss you for not cosmetizing Dr. Sparrow, but we might find someone who's more willing to do the work she's told to do around here," Odell grumbled. "It's your job, and neither Otis nor I would do as good a job hiding that bullet hole in his face as you will."

I remembered when I'd been scared that Otis's ex-wife was going to take over my job because I really didn't want to go back to teaching kindergarten. Besides, I'd let my certification expire and would need a graduate college course for recertification. I wanted to work in a beauty shop even less than I wanted to cosmetize Dr. Sparrow. One thing I did know for sure. Regardless of how I felt about the man, if I had to prepare him for his visitation, I would do absolutely the best job possible. I take pride in my work.

"Well, Callie," Otis said, "are you a professional or not?"

"I'll do it," I managed to say in a civil tone without rolling my eyes.

"Call me when you're ready to dress him, and I'll come help you," Odell said, and they both left me alone with the only doctor I've ever despised. That's a lie! My ex-husband was a doctor, and most of the time I despised him, too. I acknowledge that I'm not automatically in awe of doctors or lawyers. Like everybody else, there are good ones and bad ones.

Not much to do except makeup. Dr. Sparrow's hygiene and grooming were excellent. He obviously took good care of his hands, probably with professional manicures, because his cuticles were perfectly clipped and his nails were buffed. I guess a surgeon would be conscious of his hands. I wondered what kind of lotion he'd used. The skin was in good condition, especially considering all that hand washing he'd had to do.

The same with his head. His haircut was recent and well-done, and there were no stray hairs that needed clipping in his eyebrows or peeking out of his nose or ears. Mrs. Sparrow had provided a recent photo, but I remembered how his hair had been combed from seeing him at the hospital.

After all that complaining and whining, I was finished in hardly any time and called Otis in. We dressed the doctor in his expensive charcoal gray suit, white shirt, and red and gray striped necktie. When we'd finished, Dr. Sparrow looked for all the world like a politician.

Mrs. Sparrow had selected one of our most luxurious caskets from all the new stock since the warehouse break-in: high gloss finished solid cherry wood half couch with gold hardware and gold trim. The inside was pale blue velvet with an adjustable bed and mattress. Only the best for the bird. When the doctor was casketed, Otis and I wheeled the bier into the hall and down to the slumber rooms. I assumed we were going to A, but Otis said, "No, Mrs. Irvin's in there until her service this afternoon." Mrs. Irvin was an elderly lady we'd brought in from Lazy Days Nursing Home.

"I assumed that since Mrs. Sparrow chose a top of the line casket, she'd want Slumber Room A." It's a little bigger than B.

"We'll move Dr. Sparrow after Mrs. Irvin's funeral. Don't you think it would be disrespectful to move her before her service just because the doctor's family bought a more expensive casket?"

That's why I like working for Otis and Odell. They might argue between themselves sometimes, and Odell calls Otis "Doofus" when no one else is around, but at heart, they're both thoughtful of others.

We positioned Dr. Sparrow in Slumber Room B, and I returned to my office to call Mrs. Sparrow and let her know she could come see him whenever she liked. It's SOP for the next of kin to see the body before anyone else is allowed.

"I'll be there this afternoon. I don't know what time," she said. Didn't sound like she was as eager as a lot of our families are to see their loved ones.

I hadn't had much reading time lately, so I got a mug of coffee from the kitchen. Back in my office, I pulled the door closed, propped my feet on my desk, and pulled out one of my favorite mysteries with Judith and Renie by Mary Daheim. I can read those books over and over.

Half an hour before time to take Mrs. Irvin to the church, Odell opened my door and peeked in.

"Do you want me to attend Mrs. Irvin's service?" I asked. "Attend" in Funeraleze means "work" a funeral, but we never refer to our presence there as part of our job.

"No, stay here. You can read your book, but be on the lookout for Mrs. Sparrow."

"I wasn't here when she made arrangements. What does she look like?"

"Tall, slim, blonde—arm candy. She looks like a rich doctor's trophy wife."

The funeral home is kind of nice when it's all mine. I know it's hard to believe anyone could actually enjoy hanging out alone in a mortuary, but I do. The music is soft classical except when the instrumental hymns override it to let us know the front door is open. The temperature is always cool and comfortable. My office isn't as luxurious as the furniture in the conference and slumber rooms, but it's far from shabby.

Fully expecting the doctor's arm candy, I went to the main hall when "It Is No Secret" announced that the door had opened. I about had a heart attack when I saw Dr. Donald Walters standing just inside the front door. He looked just as good as he did the first time I ever saw him, and he moved quickly to where I stood at the back of the hall.

"Long time no see." Now, if I had to think forever about what to say to a man who'd chased me, woo'ed me, and finally won his way into my heart and bed only to drop me like the proverbial hot potato, it couldn't have been any worse than that.

He reached his arms out as though expecting me to fall into them for a warm embrace. I didn't. Took a step backward instead.

Normally, I'm only rude to my brothers and impolite to them just when they give me reason, but my response to Dr. Donald's intended hug was, "What do you want?"

"To apologize." He had a sheepish grin. "I heard that Rizzie's grandmother died, and I know you've had a hard time."

"Yes, Maum died after going through a medical hell, Tyrone may be in trouble, and my brother Frankie got shot last night." My words tumbled out on top of each other. "Oh, and somebody keyed my car and punched holes in the top that can't be repaired. I had to special order a new ragtop, and I'm praying the weather stays clear because I've got the holes patched with bandages until the new top comes in. Let's see. Is there anything else? I interrupted a break-in at Middleton's and wound up bleeding all over the emergency room. Yes, life has been exciting since you dumped me. How about you? Just moved right on to your next conquest?"

"I saw a report on the news about the caskets at Middleton's being ruined, but I didn't know about Frankie. What's going on? Jane accidentally poisoned him that time using the bug spray in place of aerosol shortening. Did she shoot him, too?"

"No. It was an accident."

"Well, for your information, I haven't moved on to another woman. I told you that I'm over skirt-chasing. I just got scared that we were moving too fast. I guess I'm commitment-shy." He grinned that handsome smile of his. "Are you going to give me another chance?"

"Not right now," I answered softly.

He actually had the gall to look shocked. Dr. Donald Walters fully thought he could just waltz back into my life when he'd been gone during a time I really needed somebody. One reason I'd wound up with him after Bill and Molly's wedding was because he'd been around during most of my crisis periods since I'd met him. These past few weeks, he'd ignored me even when I tried calling him, and now he wanted to just pick up where we'd left off. Having spent some time with Patel made turning down Dr. Donald easier, but knowing Patel was gone made rejecting Dr. Donald harder.

"I don't know. I need time." Spiteful. That's how I felt. "And before you get back with me beyond a casual friendship, you're going to need some blood-work."

"What?"

"I don't care what you say about being scared of commitment. I think you saw someone else you wanted, and it didn't work out, so you're back here after me. You're a doctor. You ought to know what I'm talking about."

"STDs?"

"Yes."

"You've changed," he accused.

"I'm just getting smarter."

An instrumental version of "In the Garden" announced

that someone was at the front door.

I could have guessed the lady standing there was Mrs. Sparrow. Tall and slender with a high-dollar multi-blond color job on a pricey haircut, she wore pale cream-colored slacks and a sweater that probably cost more than I had invested in my entire wardrobe. Heck, more than the value of all my clothes and Jane's added together.

Dr. Donald stepped around her to get out the door, but not before he checked her out with a big smile.

"Welcome to Middleton's," I said. "I'm Callie Parrish. May I help you?"

"I'm Robin Sparrow," the woman said and broke into a loud laugh. She turned toward the man with her and tittered, "I hate saying that. I should have thought of how it would sound before I married him."

"I've told you how to solve that. Call yourself Robbie." Stereotypes seem like a form of bias to me, so I seldom use them, but this handsome man's appearance was a perfect type-cast for a gigolo tennis pro. He wasn't wearing tennis shorts, but his slim white slacks, fitted navy blue knit shirt, golden tan, sandy hair, and super white teeth all fit the picture.

"Robbie doesn't really suit me. The kind of woman I am should have a name like Tiffany or Paris."

"Absolutely right," the man agreed, and then turned to me. "I'm Mickey Thompson. We've come to see Dr. Sparrow."

"Yes, right this way." I led them to Slumber Room B and stood toward the rear of the room because I wanted to give them privacy. If either of them had seemed the type to become hysterical and try to grab the body, I would have stayed closer. I assumed Mr. Handsome was the widow's brother. They kind of matched each other. Who knew? Maybe his hair was natural, but I'd bet their blondness came from the same brand name. Not that I'm criticizing. I change my own hair color about as often as my mood varies.

They talked softly, which was fine with me. I didn't care what they said, and I much prefer the quiet ones to those who wail and scream in grief. They have that right, but it's my responsibility to comfort them, and I always worry someone will have a stroke or heart attack. Not so in this situation. These two were much younger than many of our mourners, both appeared in great physical condition, and neither seemed very distraught. Of course, exteriors can be deceiving. Some people don't show their emotions as much as others.

Dalmation! I was thinking about all this when I looked up and got such a shock that I almost fainted.

He was kissing her.

Not a brotherly kiss.

As long as I've worked at Middleton's I'd never before seen anyone slip the tongue to a widow while standing beside a man's casket.

Did they not know I was standing in the back of the room? Or was I so insignificant to them that they didn't care?

After what seemed like forever, they broke off sucking face and walked over to me.

"It's fine," Mrs. Sparrow said. "Didn't Mr. Middleton say you're the cosmetologist? You did a good job." She opened her expensive purse, pulled out a five dollar bill, and thrust it at me.

"No, thank you," I said, barely managing not to spit out the words.

"Oh, go on and take it," the man said. "They probably don't pay you much."

If I hadn't figured Otis or Odell would find out, I'd have had a sharp answer to that, but I've been working hard at controlling myself since I lost my temper with Frankie at the emergency room. I escorted them to the front door. As "Immortal, Invisible, God Only Wise" began, the man handed me a business card.

I couldn't keep from laughing before I had the door closed behind them. Mr. Tongue's card offered tennis lessons at the St. Mary Country Club.

• • •

Jane and I have been friends so long that I think of her as the sister I didn't have. I swear, there are times that our minds work together just like they say happens with twins, though I don't know too much about that. Otis and Odell are different, and I don't know how alike Miss Nina and Miss Nila were. Anyway, right when I was thinking of calling Jane, she called me.

"Have you heard? Frankie's going home today. Your dad called and invited me to ride with him and Mike to pick him up. They asked if I wanted to stay over at their house for a few days with him." She sniffled. "Why do you think that is? Do they want me to take care of him while he gets better because I made him get hurt?"

"Don't be ridiculous." Honest, I almost screamed at her. "First off, you didn't hurt Frankie. He acted like an idiot."

"It wasn't his fault. He was drunk."

"Good grief! Your hormones must still be out of whack for you to think that. He wasn't drunk when he started drinking, and Frankie knows he doesn't have any sense when he drinks. So far as taking care of him, Mike and Daddy can do that." I giggled. I felt a little guilty to laugh about it, but it wasn't like my brother had a broken leg.

I stopped with the giggle. "They're trying to be nice to you if you want to be with him. You can't expect them to ask you if they can bring him to your place, can you?"

"No, I guess not. I think I'm going to take them up on it and spend a few days there. Maybe I can help Mike with your dad, too." My brothers and I wouldn't admit it, but since Daddy's heart attack, he's begun acting older and needs more help around the place.

"Just wanted to let you know where I'll be, but I'll have my cell phone if you need me."

"Okay. I'm glad you let me know Frankie's going home from the hospital, and I'll talk to you later." I was ready to say, "Goodbye," when Jane interrupted.

"Have you been listening to the radio?"

"No, why?"

"The sheriff is having a press conference this afternoon. They've identified the dead man you made me sit by at the fair."

"I didn't *make* you sit by a dead man. He was behind you, not beside you, and I didn't know the body was there when we sat down."

"Yes, and because you sat me by a corpse, you got to date that cool Mr. Patel."

"Well, he's left town now, and I'm all by myself again."

"I may be by myself if Frankie blames me about the baby and for shooting himself."

"Do you really want to be with Frankie? He's my brother, but you must love him a lot to want to marry him."

"That's part of the problem. I'm not sure I want to marry Frankie. I'm not sure I want to marry anyone, but then, sometimes I'm afraid I'll be all alone when I get old."

"Been there. Done that. We'll talk about it later. Did they say if the body from the fair was someone local or was it really a midway worker?"

"I don't know. Just listen to the radio or watch television at one o'clock."

Chapter Twenty-Three

Sheriff Harmon didn't do a whole lot of public relations, so when Odell told me the press conference was being held in front of the sheriff's office and I could go over there if I wanted, I went.

Wayne stood on a podium in full uniform with a dozen microphones fanned out in front of him and a group of fourteen deputies at parade rest behind him. All of them, including the sheriff, with tasers and semiautomatic pistols visible in holsters at their sides. For just a moment, I wondered if I should get a taser. I did seem to be in the way of trouble more than my share of the time.

The mayor introduced Wayne. This was big stuff.

"We've been blessed to live in St. Mary, a town without known gang activity," Wayne began, "but we have seen a recent increase in vandalism, theft, and other evidence of possible gang involvement. The Jade County Sheriff's Department is implementing a four-point plan to address these concerns.

"First, increased control of access in and out of the county and especially the town of St. Mary. This is because I feel that a lot of the problem is coming from outside our county. Second, stepped up crackdowns on drugs and DUIs. Third, greater focus on any gangs that might be roaming Jade County and soliciting our youth. Fourth, we will shut down any businesses that are selling alcohol to underage drinkers.

"My purpose today is to encourage our citizens to be alert to what goes on around them and to urge you to help us. If you see something that's suspicious, we need you to call—not videotape the event on your cell phone or stand around rubbernecking.

"We are also looking into adding more surveillance cameras and taking whatever steps are needed to prevent crime."

"What about that kid shot at the fairgrounds? We heard he's been ID'ed." A voice called from the crowd.

"Yeah, was that gang warfare?" A different voice.

"The victim at the fairgrounds has been identified as twenty-three-year-old Leon Pearson from out-of-state. His death is still under investigation. After the inquiry is completed, the full results will be made public."

"What about the doctor?" Yet another voice from the group.

"That remains under investigation, also. When it's completed, we'll release a full report. Until then, we can't discuss it."

"Are the two murders related?"

"That's one of the possibilities, but I can't confirm that at this point."

"Can you tell us how Pearson was identified?"

"A citizen came forward and gave us enough information that we were able to locate his family and identify him through fingerprints."

"Then his prints were on file? He'd been in trouble before?"

"That information will be released when the investigation is completed."

Wayne looked at his watch with a relieved expression. "That's all for today. I'll schedule another press conference when we have more information to release."

He ignored the reporters shouting additional questions and walked off the dais resolutely. I knew he was disappointed not to be able to announce more, but progress of the cases was not where he wanted it to be, and Wayne firmly believes that releasing info before its time impedes investigation and makes prosecution more difficult.

I was ahead of Wayne getting inside the sheriff's department. His clerk is used to me showing up and waiting for him if he's not in. She let me go on into the office, and I was waiting for him when he came in. He sat down behind his desk. Disappointment all over him.

"Callie, how bad did it sound? We really haven't made much progress in either case, but my purpose in calling the press in wasn't related to the two murders. I want people to know what's going on. I don't like what I fear is happening in our town."

"What *is* happening?"

"Thefts, signs of increased drug activity, tagging, and two murders. It's not pretty."

"What's tagging?"

"This graffiti we're seeing on signs and walls. That's tagging and it's gang-related. Gangs tag to identify their territories."

"Gangs in St. Mary? That's hard to believe."

"I think it's happening right here, right now."

Right here, right now, in River City, I thought, then wondered where that came from. Sometimes, not frequently, Wayne tells me things about cases. So far, I've managed to never repeat what he tells me unless it's common knowledge. I had the feeling I was about to hear something that hadn't been told at the press conference.

"Callie, ballistics show that the bullets that killed Leon Pearson and Dr. Paul Sparrow came from the same gun."

"What?"

"The same gun. It doesn't make sense unless one of them was accidental. Leon Pearson isn't from around here. He was actively trying to recruit local kids into a gang."

"The reds or blues?"

"Neither. A totally new gang."

"How would he do that?"

"He provided things that they're too young to buy, like beer and liquor. He sold them drugs at prices below street rates.

The idea there is to get them hooked. When they're addicted, the discounts stop, and the kids are cut off unless they join the gang and participate in gang activities to earn enough money to support their habits."

"How do you know this?"

"About gangs? I've been to classes."

"No, about it all being tied together here."

"A local boy told me."

"Anyone I know?" I asked, but I was hoping, praying the answer would be, "No."

"Afraid so. Tyrone Profit came to me and spilled his guts after Leon Pearson's right-hand-man ice picked your Mustang. Tyrone was scared they were going to hurt you or Rizzie because he'd refused to join them. They'd been taking his lunch money and made him give them the school issued iPad. He gave me Leon's name and where he's from. I checked it out, and Leon had a rap sheet a mile long."

"Do you think they'll try to hurt Tyrone?"

"I don't see how they'd know who ratted them out or even that my men didn't learn it without anyone telling us. I didn't even name Tyrone in my report. I've already picked up Leon's partner. It seems they're the ringleaders. What doesn't make sense are the murders. I understand about the church break-ins, vandalism, graffiti, drugs and alcohol. That's all typical gang activity, but the killings don't fit. So far as I know, there's only one gang attempting to operate here. Ride-by shootings are usually gang activity, but these two murders don't fit."

I looked out the window.

"What are you looking for?" Wayne asked.

"Hoping it doesn't rain," I answered. "I'm praying it doesn't rain anymore until my new ragtop comes in at the Ford dealership. I patched the holes, but they still leak." I bounced back to our other subject. "What do you know about Leon Pearson besides his gang involvement and where he's from? Could there be some other reason someone killed him?"

"Naming Leon's killer would be easier to answer if we

knew *how* it was done. There's no stippling to show the weapon was fired at close range, but there's no evidence that the body was moved from another crime scene into Mother Hubbard's tent either. I know the noise is loud at the fair, but Patel said business had been good that day. Someone in the kitchen or dining area should have heard a shot fired that close."

"Or seen them go into the storage area," I added, thinking of my tour of the beer garden tent. "Are you going to warn Rizzie that she and Tyrone could be targets if someone else comes to town to groom our kids?"

"I plan to, but there's still a chance that Tyrone's involved in the shootings. He never came up with a weapon for us to compare to the ballistics of the killings, and he can't name anyone who can verify where he was the night the doctor was shot. Tyrone's the only connection I can see between the two victims. Leon Pearson was harassing him, and he hated Dr. Sparrow."

"But he came to you and gave you information. That doesn't sound like he's a killer to me."

"Callie, you wouldn't believe Tyrone was guilty if you'd seen him shoot them."

"Well, he's got a pretty good alibi for the time that Leon Pearson was shot. He was running Gastric Gullah with his grandmother and then at the hospital. After he left the hospital the first time, he was with Rizzie until after they went back. Then he was with me."

"Yes, and that's the only reason I don't have him in a holding cell now."

"You don't really believe that kid killed anyone, do you?"

"These people weren't playing around. Don't forget that they attacked your car, and they fire-bombed the Profits's van. The paint at Mother Hubbard's and Middleton's was done by Leon Pearson's side man and two local kids he'd already enlisted. I believe that was meant to tell Tyrone that he'd better come around to the gang's demands. After all, he was seen with you and Patel at the fair."

"You know for sure that Rizzie's van was set on fire intentionally?"

"Positively."

"I think I've seen someone smoking a cigarette out by the oak tree in front yard a few times."

"Why didn't you tell me about that?"

"I never thought too much about it until you told me all this."

"You do realize that you're not to tell anyone about what we've talked about, don't you?"

"Do I have 'stupid' written all over my face?"

"No, but women talk a lot."

"Watch it. You're starting to sound like my daddy."

Chapter Twenty-Four

The instrumental "God's Other World" that announced the opening of the front door at Middleton's should have been "Here Comes the Bride." Miss Nila Gorman and Arthur Richards met me in the front hall. She wore a stunning white wedding gown that had to be from the Atlanta *Say Yes to the Dress* television show. It's hard to believe they make mermaid styles to fit short, round, little old ladies, but they do because Miss Nila wore one. It had beading and sequins all the way down to a flouncy, tiered chiffon bottom, and sequins accented the sheer fingertip veil she wore. I might have expected Mr. Richards to have on the tuxedo he'd worn to Miss Nina's funeral, but instead he wore white tails.

Oh, no, was my first thought, *she's going to want us to exhume her sister and change her clothes again.*

Miss Nila held her left hand out to me. No, actually, she thrust it into my face, somewhere in the vicinity of my nose. On it were a gigantic diamond solitaire and a band encrusted with at least two karats of sparkle.

"We're married! I'm Mrs. Arthur Richards," Miss Nila announced—as proud as if she'd married a crown prince.

Mr. Richards beamed.

"I wanted you to see the dress before Artie and I leave for our honeymoon." Miss Nila twirled around so I could see every angle.

"Congratulations! When was the wedding?" I asked.

"This morning. We had an early ceremony followed by a

champagne breakfast. We're leaving now for Florida to go on our honeymoon cruise." She giggled like a thirteen-year-old. "I apologize for not inviting you. It was just so fast that I hardly had time to arrange everything, and I forgot some people." Her apologetic smile didn't last long. She grinned again. "Miss Parrish, I'm so happy I can't even think, but I insisted we stop by here. I've changed my mind. When we get back from our trip, I'll send you my bridal clothes and I want to be buried in them when the time comes. You do have somewhere safe to store them, don't you?"

"Yes, ma'am. I'll take care of it. You just send them to me." My assurances were off the top of my head. I don't know a whole lot about proper storage of extravagant wedding gowns. My own hadn't been anywhere near as elegant as hers, and it wasn't in storage anyway. I was so mad when I divorced Donnie that I built a bonfire and burned my dress and all the wedding pictures except the big wall-sized portrait of me in my gown and veil that hangs in the living room at Daddy's. I've tried and tried to get him to take it down or at least move it to his room, but he says, "As much as I paid for that picture, I like to look at it. I don't see why it bothers you. You look real pretty, and Donnie's not in it."

"Would you like some coffee?" I asked. Otis and Odell have taught me to always offer refreshments, and I thought that at their ages, coffee might be a good follow-up to a champagne breakfast.

"No, we're on the way. Thanks for everything." Miss Nila kissed me on the cheek, one of those air kisses that barely touch skin. Mr. Richards planted a loud smack on the other side.

They left, and I hoped they lived happily ever after.

Back at my desk, I wasn't too surprised when the fax machine sounded. I turned around and picked up the printed paper.

Stunned silence. That was my reaction to the correspond-dence I held in my hand. Otis had told me about something similar to this happening before I came to work at the funeral home, but it was a first for me. My official title at Middleton's is cosmetician, which is Funeraleze for a person who's not a mortician but does hair and makeup for deceased people. In South Carolina, anyone with a state cosmetology license can work at a funeral home so long as they're not involved in embalming. I'm not hankering to do that no matter how many times Otis and Odell offer to send me to mortuary college.

If all I did was hair and makeup, I wouldn't be worth what they pay me. Not that I make a fortune, but my pay is decent, comparable to what I'd make if I went back to teaching or working in a beauty parlor. Besides cosmetizing, I write and submit obituaries to newspapers and post them on our website. I also do some paper work. Not book-keeping, but checking over records, ordering death certificates, filing, and confirming intake information.

I hadn't expected any trouble when I organized the paper work for Dr. Sparrow. We had his autopsy report from Charleston. Cause of death was gunshot wound. Manner of death was homicide. Our copies were for filing and to send when I ordered death certificates. The sheriff's department would have received their own.

Another part of my job is verification of facts. This isn't usually much trouble. Most survivors bring in copies of the insurance policies. Mrs. Sparrow had assured us that the doctor was insured and filled in the name of the insurance carrier and an amount more than sufficient to pay for services. She'd signed the forms so that Middleton's payment would be sent in a separate check, directly to the funeral home, but she hadn't shown Otis or Odell the actual policy nor a document from the insurance company. I'd faxed a copy of the signed papers to the carrier and considered it done.

Now I had before me a faxed reply stating that Robin Sparrow wasn't the beneficiary on the policy and was, therefore, not allowed to authorize assignment of payments. Certainly not my personal problem, but I felt like I'd been slapped in the face. The insurance company advised me to contact Dr. Sparrow's attorney, Adam Randolph, Esq., to obtain information about the estate and to make arrangements for disbursement of funds.

I knew what to do about that. Give it to Otis to handle. I went looking for him. He wasn't in his office, and we didn't have anyone scheduled for prep, but I'd bet a month's pay that he was in the prep room. I stood outside the closed door and knocked. That door is kept shut at all times. "Otis, Otis!"

I pounded harder and louder.

"Hold your horses." Not that I have any horses. Daddy has a few on the farm, and Tyrone had a pony named Sugar when I first met the Profits a few years ago, but horses never interested me, not even as a little girl. "Hold your horses" is a Southern expression meaning "Wait a minute." It's not exactly courteous, but it's a whole lot better than, "Don't get your panties in a knot," another colloquialism, which Otis would never say to me no matter how unhappy my interruption made him.

"Come in." When I heard Otis's voice, I opened the door. He stood in front of me clutching a towel around his waist with both hands and glowing with the pink complexion he has right after tanning. I held the letter out to give it to him. He looked down and said, "Hold on. I'll be right back."

He was back in a few minutes, dressed and grumpy. He held out his hand, and I placed the letter in it, hoping he'd say, "I'll take care of this."

Not so. "Handle it," was his response.

What next? I'd hoped this was just a matter of filing. I don't want to hurt anyone's feelings, but lawyers aren't my favorite people. I guess that's because every time I've ever needed one, it's been an unpleasant experience—especially my divorce proceedings back in Columbia when I dumped my husband for what he did, and, no, I didn't catch Donnie on the dining room table with another woman like Stephanie Plum caught her ex.

A telephone call to Mr. Randolph's office got me nowhere.

Mr. Randolph was in court, and I would need to see him to handle this matter.

"Can any of his partners help me with this?" I asked.

"No." The voice was young and male, slightly flirty. "Mr. Randolph handles Dr. Sparrow's affairs. We'd prefer you speak to him."

"Are you one of his paralegals?"

"Nope, I'm a male receptionist."

"When will Mr. Randolph be back?"

"I'm not sure, and our fax machine isn't functioning properly. We've called the repairman, but he hasn't come yet. I know that Mr. Randolph will want to see these papers you say Mrs. Sparrow signed. Can you bring them over?"

"Are you telling me to bring copies of the forms to Mr. Randolph's office?"

"I'm sure that would help. I'd volunteer to pick them up, but we're short-handed today. Do you know where our office is?"

As a matter of fact, I did. I told him I'd be right over.

For no particular reason, I'd worn another blowup bra that morning, after vowing to never wear one again after falling into the corner of the hearse door. Not that it would explode. I'm using "blowup" in its meaning of "inflatable," and buh-leeve me, I'd pumped The Girls up so that I matched Rizzie and Jane in that department. The black dress I wore was buttoned up the front all the way to my neck. Now, I could say, "Don't ask me why, but I unbuttoned the top buttons on my dress." That, however, would be a lie. The clerk had sounded secretive, but young and masculine. I knew exactly what I was doing. I wasn't proud of it, but I wasn't dumb about it either. I wanted information, and I didn't want to wait for the lawyer to get it, but I also hadn't had a date in weeks and, who knows, that male receptionist could be looking for a girlfriend.

Adam Randolph's office was only a few blocks from the

funeral home, so I walked over. Well into fall, the weather was more spring-like. Not too warm, not cold. Bright sunshine. I was almost glad I had to be out. I'd never been inside Mr. Randolph's building before, but the exterior delighted—a well-kept old colonial home with two-story columns in front. Lots of businesses around here occupy antebellum houses. It makes sense. Most families can't afford the upkeep on those big buildings, but businesses can. It would be a shame to tear the buildings down or let them deteriorate.

The spacious office was furnished with couches and chairs with red leather upholstery studded with nailheads. The hunter green walls were set off by wide cream-colored chair railings and deep molding around the ceiling. A lot of offices in St. Mary have historical pictures hanging on the walls. Mr. Randolph's office had a theme—magnolias. Displayed on each wall were gigantic paintings of creamy white magnolias with deep green leaves framed in heavy gold frames.

A slim young man with dark eyes and hair sat behind a highly polished, oversized mahogany desk.

"Welcome to Randolph Law Firm. My name is Furman. What can I do to help you?"

"I'm Callie Parrish from Middleton's Mortuary. I spoke to you by telephone."

"Aw, yes. Did you bring the papers Dr. Sparrow's wife signed?"

I offered him the folder. Of course, it didn't contain any of the originals, only copies I'd made for the lawyer.

"I'll be sure Mr. Randolph receives these," he said and placed the folder on the basket labeled "in."

"Can you give me any information about who will be paying for our services?" I questioned. "Dr. Sparrow has been embalmed and is already casketed in the extremely expensive unit selected by his wife. His obituary with funeral plans is on our website and has been forwarded to the newspaper. Mrs. Sparrow requested several papers be notified at an additional charge. I'd really appreciate any information you can give me about the insurance policy."

I said all that and felt pretty good about sounding so professional. Didn't think Otis or Odell could have done better.

"You know I can't do that." The smile turned to a grin. "I could lose my job for that, and you know how the economy is these days."

"Buh-leeve me, I do. That's why I need the information. I don't want to lose my job either."

I've seen girls and women do it all my life, but until I discovered my inflatable bras, I never had enough in the boob department for it to make any difference. With my wonderful bras, I still don't have much in the way of cleavage, but The Girls do stick out well and will bunch together when I lean forward while holding my arms tightly on the sides with my elbows pressing my ta tas together. I know because I've practiced it in front of the mirror at home, but I've never tried that move outside the privacy of my bedroom.

I did it. I leaned over Furman's desk and gave him a full view, hoping he saw the skin above the bra and not just lace. But then, some men love to see fancy underwear. It couldn't hurt.

What did he do? Ignored me and The Girls.

"Can't you tell me what's so secret about Dr. Sparrow's insurance?" I asked in my best imitation of Roxanne.

Did no good. The man ignored my extra efforts and looked down at his watch.

"I'll see that Mr. Randolph receives these papers, and he will probably be calling Middleton's this afternoon to schedule an appointment to discuss this." His tone was dismissive as he glanced toward the door and then back at his watch.

"Couldn't you just give me a hint about the insurance?" I didn't sound like Roxanne anymore. This echoed in my ears more like begging.

"It's the will." Furman couldn't keep his eyes off his watch. "Please excuse me a moment."

He stood behind his desk, obviously waiting for me to

leave. He'd paid no attention to me, so I gave none to him.

"I'll be right back." The man virtually ran out of the office, but he was true to his word and returned in only a few minutes. His hair had obviously been combed, and it glistened with water or some kind of styling gel. He smelled slightly of mouth wash. With my job, noticing little things about appearance are important.

Before I had time to process the need for this grooming, the door opened and in walked a real hunk, a hottie for sure.

"Ready?" Hot Stuff asked in a low, melodious voice.

"Miss Parrish, I hate to do this, but when Mr. Randolph isn't here, I lock up while I go to lunch. I'm afraid you'll have to leave now."

I took one more shot. "I know you could tell me what's in Dr. Sparrow's will. It would certainly make my life easier when I get back to work." I flashed my sweetest girly smile.

"I've told you I would be violating client confidentiality to tell you." Furman shot a pleading look at his friend as though the man might rescue him from this insistent female who was preventing them from going to lunch.

"Does she mean that doctor's will? The one you told me about?" The lunch date may have been just talking or showing off that he knew what I wanted to know, but I used it.

"What's Mr. Randolph going to think when I tell him you wouldn't give me, a representative of someone with a legal interest, any information, but you told your friend here about it?" I made sure to use an accusing tone but switched immediately to assurance. "If you tell me, I promise to never let anyone know about it. What's in that last will and testament might help us at Middleton's, and I'm sure Mr. Randolph will tell us when he hears about the problem anyway."

"Oh, tell her, Furman." Now the friend looked at *his* watch. "You know it's our anniversary. I've made reservations."

"I don't know." Furman seemed torn. What to do? What to do?

"I'll solve this," his friend offered. He smiled at me. "Now, you promise this is in strictest confidentiality?"

"I do."

"Oh, don't say that. I never want to hear a girl say that to me." He and Furman laughed like that was the biggest joke either of them had ever heard.

"Furman told me about the will this doctor made. He left *nothing* to his wife, absolutely nothing. The insurance is made to his estate and everything he owns is to be sold and all that money put into a trust fund. His wife is the heir to the trust fund, but it's all tied up. She'll only receive a small allowance each month, and if she remarries, she loses that, too."

"What about funeral arrangements? Anything in the will concerning that?"

"Furman didn't tell me that." He frowned at his watch again. "Now can we go?"

"Oh, what the hell." Furman was ready for his lunch date. "The will states there will be no funeral. He wanted a direct cremation without even a memorial service." A direct cremation means no embalming, no cosmetizing, nothing. The body is picked up and cremated with no fanfare.

"We've got to go now. I've attached a message to the folder you brought asking Mr. Randolph to call you, but he'll probably just tell me to call and schedule an appointment. Now, please go."

I left.

Otis turned a whiter shade of pale beneath his tan when I told him what I'd learned, but the only thing he said was, "I'll talk to Odell about it."

"If they won't pay for the casket, can we use it again?" I knew the answer, but I asked anyway.

"Callie, you know perfectly well that caskets are never reused. The rentals that we use for visitations and viewing of people who will be cremated are made special for that purpose with removable linings which are replaced between clients. That casket has no value at all once a decedent has been in it."

"Am I going to have to deal with the attorney?"

"No, but you did a good job getting information for us. Odell and I'll take it from here."

Chapter Twenty-Five

"I know how it was done." Wayne burst into my office as excited as I've ever heard him. Personally, I was still a bit sleepy and wondered about all this enthusiasm so early in the morning.

"How what was done?" Chalk up another duh for me.

"How Leon Pearson got himself shot in that pantry."

"Who killed him?"

"I don't know that yet, but I know that no one was in there with him."

"How could someone who wasn't there shoot him?"

"The bullet came through the roof of the tent."

"Through the top?"

"Yes, we examined the side walls, but we didn't check the ceiling of the tent. I guess if Pearson had been shot in the top of his head, I'd have thought about it. Being shot in the back made us think the bullet came from the side of the space. It came from *above* Leon Pearson."

"Are you telling me he was killed by a 'falling' bullet?"

I'd read about that phenomenon, but never had any experience with it. My family might not be the brightest lights on the Christmas tree, but we've all got better sense than to fire guns into the sky. Besides, if Daddy ever heard we'd fired into the air, he would have made sure we didn't forget again. He used to tell us, "What goes up, must come down, and it could come down on your head."

Then he'd say, "Bullets go a long way up when they're fired, but no one knows where they'll land. If you drop a bullet from an airplane or helicopter, it could reach a terminal velocity at about one hundred miles an hour, which probably won't do fatal damage, but a rifled bullet will have a much higher terminal velocity and could kill or injure someone." Funny how Daddy always sounded so much smarter talking about guns, cars, and fishing than at any other times.

I grew up around guns, but I don't understand all that terminal velocity business. I only knew that if my daddy told me never to fire a gun into the sky where it could go astray or directly into the ground where it could ricochet, then I wouldn't do that. I had an even greater respect for the possibility of a bullet ricocheting since Frankie pulled his stupid stunt.

My mind moved back to the present. "I know about that. Jim told me stories about people who fired guns in the air to celebrate weddings and important events in some of the countries he's been to since he joined the Navy. He said it's more common in other countries, but a lot of idiots in America do it, too, especially on New Year's Eve. Certainly not every time, but he said that sometimes, people are hit by these 'stray' bullets and on more rare occasions, 'falling' bullets."

"That's what I'm talking about. Leon Pearson was hit by a falling bullet. That's how it happened. I know it's freaky, but it makes sense, and when I contacted Patel and had him check the tent, there's a perfect bullet hole in the canvas that would have been directly over Leon Pearson when he was shot."

I confess. My mind wandered again when Wayne mentioned J. T. Patel. There are just too many incidents of "another time, another place" in my life. I really liked Patel, and I respected his honesty about his attraction to me being related to his deceased wife, but when will it be my turn to live happily ever after? I'd thought Dr. Donald and I were headed toward that until he dropped me so hard I bounced.

"Do you know what kind of bullet it was?" I spoke to take my mind off Patel.

"Yep, a .308 Winchester. Used to be considered military, but some people hunt with them now."

"If Pearson was killed with a falling bullet, could the doctor have been hit by a stray bullet?"

"Not likely. He was hit square in the middle of his forehead as he came down the steps leaving the ER, a half an inch lower and it would have been smack between his eyes. That was an aimed bullet fired by a skilled marksman. I don't believe in coincidence, and two freakish accidental gun deaths are too much to even consider. I haven't totally eliminated his wife as a suspect either. She doesn't have an alibi, but I don't have a real reason to suspect her except that we always start at the people closest to the victim and work outward. I'd sure be happy to learn she won marksmanship prizes in high school or something to directly tie her to her husband's death."

"I don't believe Mrs. Sparrow killed her husband." Wayne gave me a surprised look. "I know she's a cheating liar, and I don't like her, but I can't see her as the killer."

My mind went back to Tyrone shooting stars out of targets at the fair, but, once again, I kept my mouth shut, which made me feel guilty since I don't usually keep information from Wayne. The teenager was with Rizzie and me the night Maum died. At least, he was until I went home and left Rizzie cleaning while he told us he was going off to see his friends, which turned out to be a lie. The most recent tale was that he'd gone looking for a root doctor. Would the next version be that he'd taken his rifle and gone looking for a bone doctor with a bad bedside manner?

"I just wanted to let you know what's going on since you're usually so curious." Wayne gave me a quizzical look. "You seem awfully distracted this morning."

"A lot on my mind." That was true. A tall Indian man was on my mind as well as a teenaged boy I'd grown to love like a brother.

Thank heavens Wayne got a call from his office and left then. I didn't want to go into detail about all I was thinking.

The rest of the morning was slow, and I was happy when Jane called and asked if I wanted to come over for a sandwich and coffee for lunch. She didn't mention Frankie, so I didn't know if he was there or not. I kind of hoped not. I wanted to tell her more about Patel and the feelings he'd stirred up in me. Jane had always declared that the key to anyone's heart is how the other person makes them feel, not necessarily how they feel. Patel made me feel marvelous. Being with him was exciting, yet comfortable at the same time. The chemistry was right, too, but I wouldn't be seeing him again.

At home, I dashed into my apartment. I saw the message light blinking on my answering machine, but Otis had cautioned me to take a "reasonable" lunch time today. I took Big Boy out for a bathroom break, then went to Jane's, Big Boy by my side. He likes to visit Jane because she always gives him a treat and sometimes feeds him table food. I don't give Big Boy any people food except MoonPies.

Frankie's truck wasn't there, so I assumed we'd be able to talk privately at least until he showed up. Jane opened the door the minute I knocked.

"Your brother's furious. He moved out. Took everything of his and went back to your dad's. He says it's for good." She spoke so fast that her words tumbled over each other.

I couldn't understand it. Jane wasn't crying. She'd just calmly told me her engagement to my brother had ended without a tear or much emotion. "Come on in. Let me get Big Boy a doggy bone, and we'll have coffee while I put the sandwiches together. I made that special chicken salad you like with the sliced grapes and walnuts, but I didn't make the sandwiches ahead because I don't want the bread to get soggy."

Jane loves coffee—all kinds. Today she'd prepared a special blend flavored with cinnamon. It smelled almost as delicious as I knew it would taste. Years ago, when Jane and I decided to "learn" to drink coffee so men would think we acted grown up, I'd been scared she'd burn herself pouring it. Foolish me. Jane's method is to hold the cup so that the tip of her finger is slightly over the rim. She can sense when the liquid is getting near by the heat. She fixed my coffee and handed it to me—exactly right as always.

"Do you mean it?" I asked Jane in disbelief as I took the first sip. "Frankie's gone?"

"Yes, I mean it. I thought I was going to do something to make him happy." Jane dropped four pieces of whole wheat bread into her toaster. She opened her cabinet and took out two brightly colored lunch plates.

"What did you do?"

"I checked into another occupation instead of being Roxanne, the fantasy actress."

"What occupation?"

"He hates my job. He hates Roxanne, and you know, Callie, a little bit of Roxanne is *me,* but I thought changing professions would make him happy. I called the College of Professional Masseuse and found out I could get a scholarship because of my vision. They would even provide transportation. What does your brother do when I told him the good news?"

The bread popped out of the toaster, and Jane put two slices on each plate.

"I can guess, but what did he say?"

"I can't tell you exactly because he used a lot of cuss words that aren't kindergarten cussing."

"Just leave those out. He doesn't want you to go back to school?"

"He *forbid* me."

Now I knew that Jane had put up with a lot more crappola from Frankie than she ever would from anyone else, but she wasn't exactly the kind of girl—no, woman—who would react well to her man forbidding her to do anything.

"Your brother threw a fit. Went charging around gathering up his belongings and left." She piled chicken salad into sandwiches, slapped them closed, and handed a plate to me.

I noticed that Frankie had become "your brother" now that their relationship had hit what could be the final skids.

"Why?"

"Because being a masseuse means I'd touch other men."

Jane and I both began eating the best chicken salad sandwiches I'd ever tasted.

"Somehow, his reaction isn't surprising. My brothers all have a jealous streak." I spoke while I chewed. I know better, but I did it anyway.

"Well, I hope it doesn't interfere with you and me and our friendship, but I'm finished with him. You have no idea how much better I feel. My stomach's not hurting, and I haven't thrown up since all this happened."

"Good. Maybe the time isn't right for you to consider marriage."

"I'm going to work Roxanne every night and save up enough money to go to Florida. Do you want to go with me?"

"Do you mean *move* to Florida?"

"No, for a vacation. Just a trip for fun."

The thought of going to Florida, where Patel lived, made me a little sad since I didn't expect to see him again, but the idea of a vacation with Jane sounded good. "You know, I think I'll save up for that, too."

"What's going on at work?"

She'd changed the subject, so I told her all about Dr. Sparrow's wife and the insurance sham. I ended with, "The sheriff hasn't eliminated her as a suspect. After all, we know she's dishonest because of the lies she told the Middletons, and she was cheating on him before he was killed." I didn't tell her that Leon Pearson was killed with the same gun that shot the bird.

"Oh, no, you need to reconsider," Jane said. "The doctor's wife doesn't sound like a murderer to me if she wasn't going to get rich from it, and she's certainly not someone who would kill for love. Matter of fact, I'll bet the only person she's capable of loving is herself."

"You may be right, but what about her acting like she did with the tennis pro?"

"As Roxanne, I deal with people who'd kiss a stranger without a second thought, and they don't really know me nor feel any love for me or who I pretend to be. A kiss doesn't mean much to a lot of people."

"Standing beside her husband's casket?"

"Just shows a lack of good taste and good manners toward her husband, not necessarily love for the man she's kissing.

We had a great time, just like before my BFF began dating my brother. I hadn't realized how different our friendship had been while she and Frankie were together.

"I've gotta go," I finally said. "Odell told me to be back by one o'clock." I stood and started toward the door.

"Don't leave that big animal here," Jane said and pointed toward Big Boy lying asleep on the floor by the refrigerator.

I didn't bother to ask. She'd probably heard him breathing or snoring though I hadn't. I clipped Big Boy's leash to his collar and took him next door to my place. As I started to leave, I noticed the message light still blinking and decided it could be important business, so I hit "play" for my messages.

"Callie? J. T. Patel here. I'll be tied up all day in business meetings today, but please call me tonight. I know what I told you, but I'm having second thoughts. The things about you that make me think of Shea are the characteristics that a woman must have for me to be truly attracted to her. I've thought and thought about you, and I don't want to throw away what we might have. Seeing you wouldn't be 'replacing' Shea. It would be moving on with my life, and that's not only what she would want me to do, it's what I want to do. Please think about it and call me."

I squealed with joy, then I noticed the message light still flashed. I pressed "play message" another time.

"This is J. T. again. I wanted to let you know that if you're willing to see where our friendship leads, it won't be just by telephone and Internet. I'm willing to travel back and forth between Florida and St. Mary to see you." He coughed self-consciously. "Have a good day."

Have a good day. My day had just turned to great!

Chapter Twenty-Six

Otis and Odell stuck me with finishing up with Robin Sparrow. Guess I should have been grateful that they'd dealt with the lawyer themselves. The cremation was complete, and I was sent to the Sparrow home that afternoon to deliver Dr. Sparrow's cremains (Funeraleze for the ashes after a cremation) in the bronze urn Mr. Randolph had given to Odell. While there, I was to pick up the folding chairs, register stand, and wreath of white silk roses Odell had delivered before we learned that Robin Sparrow wouldn't be responsible for the bill.

My mental picture was of a renovated old Southern mansion, but Dr. Sparrow's house was far different. The building extended longer than the length of a large ranch style home, but it was three stories high. A separate four-car garage stood slightly behind and to the right of the circular driveway. The silk floral arrangement had been taken off the door and lay on the inlaid tile porch floor. When I rang the bell, I heard music inside. Not a hymn like when the door opens at Middleton's and certainly not like the James Brown song my cell phone plays—just soft jazz.

I expected a uniformed maid to answer the door, but Robin Sparrow herself invited me in, though she didn't seem especially happy to see me. She grimaced when she saw the bronze and stainless steel urn I held, and she didn't reach for it. She wore some kind of black robe that might have been part of a negligee ensemble or could have been a hostess gown. Made of satin, it flowed to her slippered feet and was embellished with dark gray pearls and fluffy black feathers at the wrists and hem. I thought the choice of black was more because the outfit was stunning than because she was in mourning. I have to say that black generally looks great on blondes, and Robin Sparrow was no exception.

"Come on in." She repeated and led me down the long entrance hall. We wound up in a gigantic great room. The focal points were a tremendous multi-tiered crystal chandelier and a beautiful winding staircase from the second floor where a balcony circled the downstairs room. If this had been a historical home, I would have pictured children in their nightgowns and pajamas peeking through the balcony railings watching adults in old fashioned evening gowns and tuxedos dancing and socializing. This wasn't a historical house. It had obviously been built new, probably for Dr. Sparrow. I wondered if Robin had shared in planning it or if the house came with the doctor when they wed.

Across the room, Mr. Tongue sat on an expensive upholstered couch. He didn't look especially happy either.

"Just put the doctor on that table." Robin motioned toward a Chinese carved table with an inlaid marble top. I set the urn on it.

"I saw the floral piece on the porch, and I'll get it on my way out." I looked around the room. No folding chairs. "Didn't Odell bring you some chairs?"

"He delivered them, but we've put them in the walk-in pantry near the kitchen. With no funeral or memorial service, none of his friends have come to the house." Her voice was so sad that I almost felt sorry for her. "That wooden stand with the guest register is in there, too."

The tennis pro stood and walked over to her. He put his arms around her waist and nuzzled his face against her neck. "You'll be fine." His mumbled words barely reached me. "I love you."

She pulled away, but gently, not in an angry way. "We have company." She nodded toward me. I remembered their kissing at the funeral home while standing beside her husband's body. She hadn't been worried about who saw them back then.

"Have you heard anything more from the sheriff?" That wasn't a very thoughtful thing to say, but I spoke without thinking. I really wanted to know if she'd heard about the bullets that killed Leon Pearson and Dr. Sparrow coming from the same gun.

"No, nothing." Her pained expression looked real.

"At least the way the will and pre-nup turned out, nobody can accuse you of killing your husband." Good grief! My mouth rambled on in overdrive while my brain was in neutral.

"What do you mean?" Robin Sparrow frowned. "Are you suggesting anyone thought I killed Paul? Why, I hate guns. Tell her, Mickey, tell her how I froze when you took me target shooting with that rifle. Besides, everyone knows that teenaged boy killed Paul. It's all over town that he threatened my husband. The sheriff's just too much of a wimp to arrest him."

"Tyrone didn't kill your husband!"

"How *dare* you defend that kid! He killed Paul, and you know it." The frown rapidly morphed into anger. "I haven't been the perfect wife, but I'd never kill anyone, not even a bitch like you. I told you. I can't even shoot a gun for fun without having a meltdown. I hate guns. When Mickey and I went target shooting that afternoon when the fair was in town, I couldn't even force myself to fire at a target. I shot straight up in the air."

She sniffled and snuffled some more while I did some math—put two and two together and came up with who fired the bullet that killed Leon Pearson. She coughed, then continued, "I heard about your going behind my back to talk to my husband's lawyer. If it hadn't been for you, we would have had that beautiful funeral before the lawyer got involved. Now I'll never know which of Paul's rich friends might have been there and offered to comfort his widow. How do the Middletons put up with you sticking your nose in everyone's business?" Her tone was hateful, spiteful, and sent spit flying out of her mouth as she sputtered at me. If she'd bobbed her finger in my face, I would have bitten it. Nobody gets away with shaking their finger at me, and I could tell she wanted to do just that.

"I didn't say you killed him. I said the opposite. You'd be a fool to murder him, and I didn't stick my nose in your business. You lied about insurance to pay for your husband's funeral. Part of my job is to verify insurance information for Middleton's. I had every right to consult your husband's lawyer about funds to pay the bill. I'll bet the doctor's office won't hesitate to chase money from his patients—at least the ones who survived."

That last crack was hitting below the belt, but I wasn't over Maum's death. Maybe she would have died anyway, but I couldn't help thinking that Dr. Sparrow didn't do a lot to ease her pain. Thank heaven for Hospice!

"What do you mean lied about . . ." Mickey Thompson tried to ask, but Robin Sparrow wasn't listening.

"That attorney violated my privacy telling you the terms of Paul's will before it was officially read."

"What about . . ." Thompson tried again, but this time I talked over him.

"Don't tell me you didn't know what it said." I didn't bother to tell her that I got my info from the lawyer's receptionist, not the attorney, nor even a paralegal.

"I knew about the pre-nup." She cleared her throat. "I admit that, but—"

"What about the insurance?" This time Mickey Thompson screamed his interruption.

"All assets, including insurance, are to be liquidated and put into a trust fund." I admit it made me happy to tell him.

"No problem." He looked relieved. "I'm sure Dr. Sparrow has made generous provisions for Robin."

"Yes, she'll have an allowance that's about what I earn per year." I took even more pleasure in telling him that.

The look of shock on his face was priceless. Wish I'd had a camera.

Thompson turned toward Robin Sparrow. "What about this beautiful house? You'll stay here, won't you?"

"It will be sold." I took enormous gratification in butting in with that news.

"You never told me any of this." He growled at Mrs. Sparrow.

"I didn't see where it was any of your business." She turned toward me. "And, yes, I knew about the provisions of the pre-nup. I signed it, didn't I?"

"What about *us?*" he demanded.

"*Us!* What do you mean *us?* Paul wasn't that old. I didn't expect him to die. I figured I'd stay married to him until I met someone else. He wasn't very pleasant, and I planned to divorce him sooner or later, but not for *you*. You were a fling, someone to hang out with until a man richer than Paul came along, but surely you didn't think I'd *marry* you!"

He slapped her. The sound resonated all over that big room. Robin Sparrow's face collapsed in tears as his handprint blossomed bright red on her cheek. Her shocked expression was genuine.

That's when it hit me. Mickey Thompson had figured that Robin would be a wealthy widow with Paul out of the way. He'd planned to be by her side and live off her money.

"You! You shot him." I didn't think at all. The accusation just popped out of my mouth.

He didn't slap me—he slugged me. Hard. On the chin. I stumbled backwards and fell against the Chinese table and then to the floor. Robin jumped on his back, wrapping her arms around him—not in love, but in rage.

"You fool!" she screamed. "I've got nothing now, and it's all because of *you*. Paul and I would have been fine. He only wanted me dressed up and looking good when we went to medical conventions and places where he wanted to show me off as his wife. So long as I looked good, I was free most of the time to do whatever I wanted. You ruined it all! Now I'm trapped by his will and that damned trust fund."

"You told me you love me. You tricked me. I'll kill you like I did him." His words cut through the room like a knife or one of Dr. Sparrow's scalpels. He wrapped his hands around her neck and squeezed. Robin raised her arms and tried to press her fingers beneath Thompson's hands on her throat. Tried to loosen his hold. No dice. He pressed harder and harder, squeezing the life out of her.

I've shot a man and killed him. He was a bad man, a horrible man, but that memory haunts me. I vowed never to kill again, not that it mattered. I didn't have a gun with me anyway.

Robin's face turned blue, and her tongue bulged out between her lips grotesquely. *Do something or watch the woman die right here, and when she's dead, he'll grab me.* I confess that for a moment I thought about running—just dashing out of the house.

I couldn't do that. I pulled myself up on the carved table and grabbed the heaviest thing within reach—the bronze and stainless steel urn with Dr. Sparrow's ashes in it. I raised it as high as I could and smashed it down on Mr. Tongue Mickey Thompson's head. *What if he lets Robin go and grabs me?* No need to worry about that. Thompson released Robin's neck and crumpled to the floor. Robin coughed, sputtered, and opened her eyes. I thought I should get her a glass or water or something, but I didn't know where the kitchen was. I pulled the phone from my bosom and hit 911.

Chapter Twenty-Seven

"I still don't understand some of what happened. I'm confused," Jane said as I handed the sheriff his plate and sat down beside her across from him in the booth. Oops! I was supposed to set the plate on the table, not give it to the customer, especially one who was handicapped by casts on five fingers.

Since Rizzie'd reopened Gastric Gullah, she'd been slammed with customers. Tyrone assisted, but without Maum in the kitchen, Rizzie had to spend most of her time cooking. She'd been interviewing additional staff, but until she decided on someone, I'd been helping her out waiting tables when I wasn't at Middleton's. After only a day and a half, I'd decided I'd rather work in the mortuary than in food service. Buh-leeve me. I *will* tip better from now on when I go out.

"Don't understand what?" Wayne questioned Jane while using his left hand to lift a spoonful of shrimp and grits. I'd be glad when those casts came off his right hand. Sometimes he winced in pain, and I knew his shattered fingers hurt him as well as being inconvenient on the job when filling out reports even though most of them were on the computer. He'd been practicing shooting with his left hand because his surgeon said he'd need a lot of physical therapy to rebuild the right hand's strength when the casts came off. Shooting would be impossible with that hand for a long time, not that Wayne has shot that many people anyway.

Jane and I had eaten before Wayne arrived at the restaurant. We both sipped sweet ice tea while he ate.

"I don't understand. If the bullet that killed Leon Pearson was falling from the sky, how was he shot in the back?" Jane continued.

"Because he was bent over when he was hit, leaning forward. Otherwise, the bullet would have hit him in the head. It would probably still have been fatal, but his skull would have given some resistance. With Leon bowed forward, the bullet went into his back, missed a rib, which might have slowed it down, and was a direct hit into the rear of his heart.

"Wonder why he was bending?" I mean, get real, the kid wasn't hiding in a storage closet to exercise. "For that matter, what was he doing in the beer garden anyway?"

"We found a quarter on the ground beneath Leon Pearson's body. Once we identified him, the kids were willing to talk about him. They said he was a tightwad. Actually, they said he'd steal a penny if given a chance. He had a hole in the pocket of his jeans. The quarter must have fallen through, and he leaned over to pick it up. So far as why he was in the storage area, he was under age to buy alcoholic beverages. Plus, he liked stealing anyway. He'd stolen the Middletons Midway jacket so people would think he was working there when he carted out a few cases of beer."

"That makes sense." Jane turned toward me. "Callie, I think I'm hungry after all. Can you ask Rizzie for a plate of what the sheriff's eating? It smells scrumptious."

"Sure." I went to the kitchen and waited while Rizzie served up a plate for Jane. Andouille sausage is an important ingredient in Rizzie's shrimp and grits; and the sausage, onions, and bacon give the dish a mouthwatering aroma.

When I got back to the table, Wayne and Rizzie were discussing theft and shoplifting.

"You know that I don't do any of that stuff anymore, don't you?" Jane asked.

"Yes, you've come a long way in staying on the right side of the law," Sheriff Harmon smiled. He turned toward me. "You do realize that you're the reason I had the top of that tent examined, don't you?"

"No, what did I do?"

"When you were worried about the Mustang's ragtop leaking after the ice pick attack on your car, it made me think about holes in canvas rooftops even though the top of a convertible and a tent aren't exactly the same," he explained. "We'd checked the walls of Mother Hubbard's but not the overhead fabric."

"This is a little morbid for me," Jane said, "but did the doctor's ashes spill out when you hit that tennis pro with them?"

I had to laugh, definitely inappropriately. "That just happens in the movies and on television. Cremains aren't just poured into the container. They're sealed in a very heavy plastic bag that's put into the urn." I looked at Wayne hopefully. "Mickey Thompson is going to be okay, isn't he?"

"He'll be fine for his trial, but you gave him one helluva headache."

"What about all those boys in the gang?" I asked.

"Really, there aren't that many, and my department is dealing with them in lots of ways. Leon Pearson's side man and the two who painted Patel's tent and the Middletons' caskets will be prosecuted, but most of the local kids didn't get that far. They were being groomed for a gang by Leon Pearson and his followers, but they hadn't broken the law themselves. I'm trying to turn them around by starting after-school programs. I can't force them into joining, but we'll encourage it. Try to involve them in sports and reward them for better grades. I think Leon Pearson's death scared those kids big time even if it turned out not to be gang-related."

He glanced over his shoulder at Tyrone, cleaning off tables across the room. "I'm hoping Rizzie can work it out so that Tyrone will have at least one or two afternoons a week to be involved in athletic activities. We really need to show that young man that we realize how brave he was to stand up to Leon and the others who tried to force him into the gang. It took courage for him to come forward after they vandalized your car."

"I admit I get aggravated with him at times," I admitted, "but bottom line is that he's a decent kid. I hope Daddy and The Boys will be good influences on him, too."

Wayne gave me an uncomfortable look. "I'm sure they will in everything except that some of your brothers don't have very strong work ethics."

"We'll leave that up to Rizzie. I think she'll instill that in him."

Jane frowned, obviously not liking the direction our conversation was going. "I think you can find something else to talk about," she said.

Wayne accommodated her by changing the subject. "What made you think Mickey Thompson killed the doctor instead of Robin Sparrow, Callie?"

"Jane said that Mrs. Sparrow was too vain to love anyone but herself. I still thought she might have done it until I found out she'd signed the pre-nup with the doctor. That woman would have stayed much richer with her husband alive. He pretty much let her have whatever she wanted, but the pre-nup and his will both stipulated that when he died, everything would be sold and the proceeds put into a trust fund. Mrs. Sparrow gets a reasonable, regular monthly allowance, but not a large inheritance and not nearly enough to live the way she has been since their marriage. Even the doctor's insurance money goes to the trust fund."

"I don't know how he was as a doctor, but the man was smart about not leaving his new trophy wife any reason to knock him off." Sheriff Harmon used his biscuit to wipe the remaining shrimp gravy off the edge of his plate.

"The lawyer told Otis and Odell that before Robin, the doctor found insurance policies on his life made out to a previous wife. His signature was forged on them. He made sure that Robin wouldn't be tempted to try that. She won't be able to continue living in the McMansion that Thompson lusted for.

It's to be sold and the proceeds go to the trust fund." My words made me feel sorry for Robin Sparrow, but just a little. Not much.

"So, in reality, Mickey Thompson screwed Robin Sparrow?" Jane said.

Wayne laughed. "In more ways than one."

About the Author

Fran Rizer is the author of the Callie Parrish Mysteries. She lives in Columbia, South Carolina, near her sons and grandson. To learn more or correspond with her, visit her website: www.franrizer.com.

CPSIA information can be obtained at www.ICGtesting.com
Printed in the USA
BVOW07s2105250713

326831BV00001B/233/P